THE Duke IN My Bed

THE Duke IN My Bed

Amelia Grey

St. Martin's Paperbacks

This is a work of fiction. All of the characters, organizations, and events portrayed in this novel are either products of the author's imagination or are used fictitiously.

THE DUKE IN MY BED

For information address St. Martin's Press, 175 Fifth Avenue, New York, NY 10010.

ISBN: 978-1-250-04220-0

Printed in the United States of America

St. Martin's Paperbacks edition / January 2015

St. Martin's Paperbacks are published by St. Martin's Press, 175 Fifth Avenue, New York, NY 10010.

10 9 8 7 6 5 4 3 2 1

Chapter 1

What's done cannot be undone.
—*Macbeth*, act 5, scene 1

Hyde Park, 1815

Bray Drakestone, Marquis of Lockington, heir to the dukedom of Drakestone, sat in the curricle, every inch of him shuddering in pain. Not that anyone would know to look at him. He'd learned from a young age not to show any emotion, much less reveal pain. That this pain came from an overabundance of brandy didn't make it better. In fact, his father would have preferred he experience the searing agony of a bullet or saber wound than a pounding head and blurry eyes from drink.

Bray had never listened to his father, other than to absorb the lesson of never displaying emotion, any emotion. *That* skill had served him well.

"Are you going to take what's left of the night to decide if you are up to the challenge, Lockington?" Viscount Wayebury asked him.

Bray pressed his eyes closed. The challenge. Damn.

After a moment, Bray glanced in the viscount's direction. Whorls of misty fog that drifted across Rotten Row made it nearly impossible to make out the man sitting in the curricle not ten paces from him. Earlier, Bray had noticed an eerie halo surrounding the oil lamps that lit the well-worn road.

His horse stamped and snorted puffs of warm air while jerking its head and rattling the harness of the small sporting carriage. The animal obviously didn't like being out in the damp cold either.

Bray didn't know Wayebury as well as some of his other friends. The two of them hadn't attended the same schools, but they spent a lot of time together whenever the viscount was in London. Wayebury had said that he preferred the quietness of his estate in northern Cornwall, but if that was the case, he seldom went there. He seemed always to be in London, behaving as wild as the next young buck who had nothing but time on his hands. They were both members of the Heirs' Club and they enjoyed their share of bets on gaming, shooting, and horse racing, but never had they made a wager on such a dark and murky night.

Bray heard the viscount's dog bark up at his master. Lord Wayebury looked down at the spaniel and said, "Don't worry, ol' boy, I know what I'm doing." He then shot another glance at Bray and bragged, "It wouldn't be worth the money we're betting if there wasn't a little risk involved, now, would it, Lockington?"

Those were brave words coming from the viscount, so Bray huffed a laugh and released the brake handle. The bleating tosspot possessed stellar gambling fortitude. "Indeed, the dark and the fog make the amount and the win all the sweeter," Bray answered.

The broad but fairly short pathway called Rotten Row

could be hazardous for two carriages careening side by side in the light of day and best of weather, but on such a dreary night, not even the lamps could alleviate the gloom. Quite frankly, Bray couldn't have cared less if they raced or not. Losing a couple of hundred pounds wouldn't lessen his pockets nor would winning it add to their weight. But since his days at Eton, what he didn't like was losing—be it a fortune, a horse, or a shilling. He always played to win.

Like him, Wayebury had been at the Heirs' Club since early evening, and the brandy was now talking and thinking for both of them. Bray had never declined a bet or rejected a dare, no matter how dangerous the challenge or how foxed he was. He wasn't going to start tonight.

He had no idea how good Wayebury was handling the horse and lightweight curricle, but Bray didn't figure he'd lose, even though he'd felt none too steady on his feet when he left the club. He'd been racing curricles as fast as the horses could pull them since he was big enough to climb onto the seat. And the carriage under him now was well sprung and built by a master of the trade.

"Does everyone have their bets placed?" someone called to the gathered crowd of a dozen or so men who had trailed the two young bucks out to the park. Some were afoot, others on horseback, and one or two were in their own carriages. They all would follow Bray and Wayebury down Rotten Row, but at a much slower pace.

Bray heard the grumbling rumble of various voices, which he took for a collective yes.

He wanted to get this over with. He was through with the night and ready for bed. He gave his head a quick shake and tuned his senses to the night and the restless stomp of his horse. He looked over at the man who had agreed to start the race and said, "Step back, pull your weapon, and fire when ready."

The pistol shot cracked the air. Bray slapped the horse's rump with the strips of leather, and the carriage took off with a jerk and a rattle. The road seemed bumpier than usual, at times lifting Bray out of the seat as they sped down the lane. He leaned forward, blinking several times to clear his eyes, but the brisk wind and the overindulgence in the brandy had taken their toll.

Knowing they were near the end of the lane, Bray glanced over at Wayebury. They were staying dead even until Prim's carriage wheel inched dangerously close to Bray's. His hands tightened on the ribbons, but he didn't try to check the gelding. Bray had never been known for his self-restraint.

The viscount grinned excitedly and bore the leather down again on his own horse.

Moments later, Wayebury had inched ahead of Bray. Determination to win rose up in him. He flicked the reins hard, urging his animal faster. Instantly, thick fog engulfed him, completely blinding him. His heart leaped to his throat. Over the roar in his ears and the rumble of wheels and hooves on hard-packed ground, Bray heard a loud thump, the whinny of a horse, and the chilling sound of wood splintering apart.

Alarm shot up his spine.

"Prim!" Bray yelled the viscount's surname and yanked the reins hard and short. The horse nickered in alarm and the curricle shuddered violently, almost throwing him out of his seat. He dropped the ribbons and jumped down before the carriage rolled to a stop.

"Prim!" he called again, hoping to discern which way to go in the fog. He heard shouts of other men calling their names. "I'm fine," Bray answered as he combed the grayness for the fallen lord. "Find Wayebury!"

"Over here!" someone shouted.

Swirls of fog scattered before Bray as he raced in the direction of the voice. Under a pool of flickering lamplight, he saw the wheel of the curricle slowly spinning in the misty air. At the front of the carriage and tangled in its rigging, the horse seemed unharmed and was trying to stand.

Bray pushed a man aside and knelt down where the viscount lay on the ground, his dog licking his face and whimpering. Bray reached down to lift him, but the man cried out.

"No!" His breath halted and his face contorted in pain. "It hurts like hell. Don't move me."

Bray froze when he saw the piece of wood protruding from Wayebury's stomach, the dark stain of blood soaking the white brocade of his waistcoat. The realization of what had happened slammed through Bray and caused a rare shock of panic to rip him. "What happened?"

"I don't know," Wayebury said, his voice ragged as other men slowly gathered around, whispering among themselves. "Something must have caught in the wheel."

"All right, don't worry about that right now," Bray said, trying to process the tragic turn of events. "We'll figure that out later." He looked up at the concerned faces of the other men. "Someone get my carriage over here," he ordered.

"My sisters," Wayebury managed to say before coughing in pain. "I must get back to my sisters."

"You will," Bray answered, wanting to placate the man.

"They'll be expecting me home by week's end."

"We'll get you there," Bray said, though he was certain that would never happen.

"They depend on me, you know."

"Yes, I'm sure."

"God! It hurts like hell! What did I do to myself?" Wayebury struggled to raise his head.

"Don't sit up." Bray tried to hold the viscount still, but the thrashing man managed to lift himself enough with his feet to lower his head and look down at his stomach. A pain-racked laugh that ended in a wounded animal-like groan blew past his lips and he went limp.

Bray's arms tightened under Wayebury's shoulders. "Just hold on until the carriage gets here. You'll be fine."

Wayebury's trembling hand slipped slowly down to his stomach and felt around the wood. He winced. "No," he said on a moan that carried eerily into the darkness. "I'm not blind. You can't save me. I'm going to die."

Bray knew the man's words to be true, but it didn't seem fair that Wayebury knew it, too. Bray looked into the viscount's eyes and saw fear, but he didn't know what to say to him. Bray had never been that scared. "Lie still and don't try to speak."

"I can feel it's deep, Lockington." Wayebury made an effort to laugh again, but it sounded more like an agonizing growl. "I can see it's too late for me."

"Hell no, it's not!" Bray demanded as if saying so would make it true.

"Don't lie to me."

"I'm not. I've not lost a friend yet, and you're not going to be the first. We'll get someone to help you."

"There's no time, Lockington. My—my uncle will inherit the title. He won't—provide for my sisters—as I have. I can't leave them with him."

"Listen to me. You won't."

"You've got to help me," Wayebury whispered, and closed his eyes.

An oppressive quietness settled over the group of gentlemen. The only sounds Bray heard for a few moments were the viscount's loud, heavy breathing; the hum of crickets; and the lonely chirp of a night bird calling in the distance. All he could think was that if the man was quiet, maybe it meant he wasn't in any pain.

"I must ask a favor of you, Lockington," Wayebury said, opening his eyes and breaking the stillness.

"What is it?" Bray said, noticing the man's lips had lost their color, his breaths coming short and shallow.

"Marry my sister Louisa."

Marry? Bray thought the man wanted a nip of brandy to cut the pain. Having just turned twenty-seven, Bray hadn't even thought about the idea of marriage. He wasn't interested in being leg-shackled by anyone.

"I'm not agreeing to anything like that, you blasted blackguard, because you're not going to die."

Prim reached up and closed his bloody fingers around the ends of Bray's neckcloth and pulled his face close. The smell of blood rose up from the viscount's hand.

"Marry Louisa!" Wayebury exclaimed on a deep breath that slowly died away.

"Hellfire," Bray swore as his hands curled into fists. "That's nonsense talk, and I won't hear more of it. Next you'll have me promising to pay your mistress and all your gaming debts, too."

"No, it's my sisters. Help me, Lockington. Say you'll do it—and help me."

"Quiet now," Bray said again, not wanting to hear more of the viscount's preposterous ideas. "Save your strength."

"Help me!" he cried louder.

"Tell him you'll do it," someone in the crowd mumbled.

"Give the man some peace," another added.

Bray looked up at the swarm of troubled faces urging

him to put the man at ease, but Bray made no reply to their pleas. Instead he demanded, "What's taking so long to get the damn carriage here?"

"I hear it coming," a man answered.

The viscount coughed and blood trickled from the side of his mouth. His dog whimpered again, and Prim's bottom lip trembled. "You owe me, Lockington."

"The hell I do," Bray answered without thinking.

Wayebury's eyelids fluttered. He pulled harder on Bray's neckcloth, forcing his face even closer. "For my sisters—I can't help them anymore. Tell me you'll do it for them—so I can rest in peace. Marry—Louisa."

Wayebury's anguish was understandable, but his request was insane. They were friends, Bray supposed, but he couldn't possibly owe the man a vow that would affect his whole life simply because of a foolish wager and an avoidable accident.

Wayebury cried out in pain again. "Help me! My time is done. Marry her," he gurgled.

"Do it," someone in the crowd said.

"Don't make a dying man beg."

"Show mercy!"

Over the escalating murmured anger, and the crowd demanding it, Bray said, "All right, Prim, all right. Should anything happen to you, I'll marry your sister."

The crowd went silent. Wayebury's hand slipped off the ends of Bray's neckcloth. The viscount's eyes closed, and he whispered, "And my dog, Lockington. Take Saint, too."

Chapter 2

Let me embrace thee, sour adversity,
For wise men say it is the wisest course.
—*Henry VI, part 3*, act 3, scene 1

Bray stood still as stone in his Mayfair town house, staring out the front window. It was only a couple of hours after the accident, but early morning sun had chased away the misty fog, making way for a bright blue sky. He had changed his soiled neckcloth, shirt, and waistcoat. He looked better but he still felt wretched.

How could Wayebury be gone? Damnation, he'd never watched a man die, and hoped he never had to again.

While Bray changed his clothing, his good friend Seaton had gone to the Heirs' Club to find someone who knew where to reach Wayebury's uncle.

"Would you like for me to pay a visit to the new viscount and inform him of Lord Wayebury's death?" Seaton asked as Bray reached for his coat.

Hell yes, Bray thought, but said, "It's my duty."

He appreciated Seaton's offer but couldn't accept. John Aldrich Seaton had been his friend and conscience since Bray joined the Heirs' Club. At sixty years of age, with a thinning mane of gray hair and swarthy skin, Seaton was the oldest member of the exclusive establishment who hadn't come into his title. Seaton's father, Viscount Fieldington, was still thriving at the ungodly age of eighty-seven. On the few occasions Seaton had been known to drink too much, he'd joke that his father would outlive him, his many grandsons, and his recently born great-grandson.

"What about Wayebury's sister?" Seaton asked.

Bray rubbed his temples, willing his head to stop pounding. He'd already vowed never to drink so much again. "What about her?"

"You told him you would marry her."

Bray moved his hand to the back of his neck and massaged it, wishing he could ease the raw tension that had settled between his shoulder blades. "Only because the man was dying and the crowd demanded it."

"Precisely."

"You think I am actually going to wed his sister? He wanted to be reassured before he died, and I did that. I'll do whatever I can to help the girl, but I'm certainly not going to marry her."

A frown slowly twisted Seaton's face, and his small, dark eyes narrowed to slits. "You gave your word."

Bray gritted his teeth and looked away. "The last thing I need or want is a wife. And I assure you, I am the last man any innocent miss needs as a husband."

"More than a half dozen gentlemen heard you."

"You can't believe for a second that anyone would hold me to that? Hell's gate, Seaton! Half the men standing around us urged me to show him mercy and I did. How can saying a few words to give a dying man peace be so binding?"

"Because you gave your word. You can't break it."
Seaton paused. "You wouldn't, would you?"

Without a moment's regret, Bray thought, reminded
yet again of how he was his father's son, two men who
did what pleased them, consequences be damned. But
then he saw the look of horror on Seaton's weathered
face and decided against saying what he really felt. He
exhaled heavily, not wanting to deal with any of this.
"If she's of marriageable age, I'll deal with the spirit of
my word and find a man for her to marry."

"The spirit of the word?" Seaton's jaw cemented and
his lips formed an expression of disapproval.

"Look, I hardly knew Wayebury, much less did I
know he had a sister. We never had a reason to talk
about families."

"Sisters," Seaton said, putting emphasis on the ending *s*.

Bray picked up his gloves and slid his hands inside
the buttery soft leather. "As in more than one?"

"I believe he has five sisters," Seaton said.

"The devil take it, what kind of parents have only
one son?"

"Obviously, your kind."

Bray swore and Seaton rolled his eyes. Unlike Bray's
father, who had never put any restraints or condemna-
tion on Bray, Seaton never failed to take him to task if
he thought the occasion or the comment warranted it.
But it wasn't in Bray to let the man have the last word.

"At least my parents had the good sense not to have
five girls to marry off someday."

Ignoring his comment, Seaton said, "Her father was
a vicar before the title became his, so I'm sure she's a
properly brought up young lady and will be a suitable
match for you."

"Her father was a vicar?"

"Well, up until he inherited the title from his older brother's son, which was four or five years ago. Remember that's when Viscount Wayebury became eligible and joined the Heirs' Club? I think he came into the title himself shortly after that."

"No, I don't remember," Bray admitted, realizing he felt a twinge of sorrow in his heart that the sisters had lost their father and their brother in the span of a few years. But Bray shook off the unwanted feeling before it had time to worm its way into his soul. He didn't need to be reminded of his father's favorite saying: *Emotion is a weak man's Achilles' heel, and a woman's daily sport.* But his father also taught him that a man's true worth was counted in how he kept his word.

His Grace would not be happy to hear about his son's latest incident. Bray's father gave him anything he wanted, allowed him to do anything he wanted, and then wondered why he was London's most notorious rogue. There was no pleasing the man when it came to Bray.

He ground his teeth, making his head pound harder. "Perhaps I'll send a letter telling her I'm obligated to offer for her hand and I'll be around to meet her sometime after she's had a year of mourning."

An incredulous gleam lit in Seaton's eyes. "A whole year to mourn? That's outrageous."

"Are you in a hurry to marry me off to a stranger, Seaton?"

"Of course not, but even six months for mourning would be considered overly long to most."

"With any luck, she'll find someone else to marry during the year, or with better luck, hopefully there already is someone and she'll leg-shackle him instead of me. When you were at the club, did you find out anything about the uncle who inherited the title?"

"Nothing other than he is Mr. Willard Prim. He and the viscount's father were brothers."

"I've never heard of him."

"No reason for you to. He decided against joining the Heirs' Club when he became eligible." Seaton handed Bray a piece of paper. "Directions to the man's house?"

Bray stared at the writing without making sense of the words. How the hell had he gotten into this mess? "Damnation, I wish I had never gone near Rotten Row tonight," he said, biting back the real words: He wished Prim hadn't died.

"Where is Lord Wayebury's dog?" Seaton asked.

Bray grunted another oath, grabbed his hat, and opened the door. "In the garden, where he belongs. If only dealing with a man's sister were as easy as dealing with his dog."

Chapter 3

Women may fall, when there's no strength in men.
—*Romeo and Juliet,* act 2, scene 3

Two years later

Though Bray had never met her, Miss Louisa Prim made his life a living hell since he'd first heard her name. It was time he settled with her.

Bray stared out the carriage window as it rolled to a stop in front of the newest Viscount Wayebury's Mayfair town house. A slow, steady rain fell to the already soggy earth. Bray had known this day was coming. He just hadn't wanted it to come so soon.

Soon?

It had been over two years since Nathan Prim's death on Rotten Row. Many would not consider that quick, but Bray did. He'd hoped Prim's sister would find a beau and be the wife of someone else by now, but she was obviously waiting for him to make good on his promise.

Unfortunately for him.

For the past two years, he couldn't go to a party, a

foxhunt, or even to a club without someone asking him
either when or if he was going to marry Miss Prim. Not
even his snarls and swears could keep the ton's hunger
for gossip at bay.

Since his father's death last fall, Bray had been settling in to the duties of being a duke. He'd never cared
a damn about the title, though he always knew it would
be his one day. He'd half-lived in a way that most men
wouldn't have survived. But he did survive, and despite
his reluctance, he'd realized that along with everything
else, his father taught him well how to handle the constant flow of decisions to make and questions to answer
from the managers of all the estates, horses, lands, and
the many companies presently entrusted to his care.

For now, with brooding resignation, Bray had come
to accept the confining responsibility he inherited. And
with the sense of responsibility, he had also come to the
conclusion that because of what he learned were the underhanded actions of a cowardly uncle, it was time to
make good on his pledge to Nathan Prim. It was time
to tell Miss Prim they would be married.

But he would never like it.

Bray's father had been a dashing, hot-blooded man
who loved many women, and made no bones about being honored that his son had followed in his footsteps.
Neither Bray nor his father checked their self-restraint
when it came to something that brought them pleasure,
be it a voluptuous woman or a new racehorse. Bray wasn't
about to let his duty to Miss Prim change that.

"Do you want me to go in with you?"

Bray grunted a laugh. He had been so intent on his
thoughts, he almost forgot Seaton was in the carriage
with him. "Hell no. I don't even know why I agreed you
could ride with me to Miss Prim's house."

"Perhaps because, like me, you feared you might

have a change of heart at the last second and end up telling your driver to keep going right past the house without stopping."

There was more truth to that comment than Bray wanted to admit. Deciding to willingly give up a portion of one's freedom wasn't an easy choice to make. However, those thoughts were best left in his own mind. "Have you no faith in me, Seaton?"

"None," the old man answered with a twinkle in his midnight-colored eyes.

"As much as you would like for it to be so, I am not a boy who needs help from the schoolmaster to get his assignments accomplished. You are my friend, not my keeper."

"Noted and accepted," Seaton offered with an easy smile, "but you are late fulfilling your commitment."

"I need no reminder from you. I had enough of them from my father when he was living. I've finally grown weary of the constant questions from the ton about Miss Prim, and men placing bets all over London about whether I would live up to my promise to marry her. Then, as if all that weren't enough, I received that terse letter and the documents from her uncle last week. If I ever get my hands on that man, he'll know damned well how I feel about his underhanded tactics."

"That was sly of him."

"Dangerous, Seaton. I'll find a way to repay him for his cowardly acts."

"I can't say that I blame you. I can understand his wanting to force you to take on the responsibility of Miss Louisa Prim, but dumping guardianship of the other girls in your care is unforgivable."

"And you can be sure it won't be," Bray said, his anger heating at the thought. "Even though the blasted blackguard gave me no idea which country he'd escaped to, I hired a runner from Bow Street to go after him immediately, find him, and drag him back here by his hair if necessary."

"I agree going after him is the right thing to do."

"I will see to it the blackguard lives up to his obligations to the other Prim girls."

"Do you still plan to let the Court of Chancery appoint a different guardian for them?"

"You know I do."

"No one would blame you if you did, except perhaps Miss Louisa Prim. I'm sure she is quite happy that a duke will be seeing to her sisters' future."

"I have no doubt of that, Seaton. The only allegiance I feel to her about it is to tell her before I do it. I don't have the time, the inclination, or the know-how to oversee the welfare of bevy of females and make arrangements to ensure that they are all properly married."

"It was most impertinent of Lord Wayebury to assume you would take guardianship of all of them, and damned clever of him to arrange to have the letter sent a month after he left the country so it would be difficult for you to find him."

"Clever and calculating is what it is. I promised to marry Miss Louisa Prim, not to take on the task of caring for all her sisters."

"That said, I doubt you would be here today if not for his taking these matters into his own hands."

Bray agreed to Seaton's words by way of a shrug. "I've always known I'd have to marry one day, but my view of marriage hasn't changed. I don't want to engage in it. I have a woman in my bed any night I choose. But now that I am a duke, I see the wisdom of having an heir and accomplishing it before one gets too old. So, since I must marry, I suppose Miss Prim will do as well as any other chit to give me a son. At least in her case, she couldn't possibly expect this to be anything more than a marriage of duty, so I can forgo the wooing, the flattery, and the feigned devotion."

Seaton laughed, causing Bray to remember that Miss Prim's father was a vicar before he inherited the title. Bray didn't relish the thought of marrying a vicar's daughter. She was probably a timid, fragile little prude who would tremble in fear and revulsion every time he came near her. That type of bedmate held no desire for him, but Seaton didn't care a fig about that. The aging heir held to the old school that a man and young lady didn't have to know each other before they married and they didn't have to like each other or live together after they wed. As long as the families agreed it was the best match, that was good enough for him.

Not even Bray's father, on his deathbed, had been able to force Bray to commit to when he would ask Miss Prim to marry him.

"Have you met her?" Bray asked Seaton.

"No, I don't think anyone has. From what I've heard, she arrived in London only a couple of days ago. It appears her uncle must have timed sending you the letter with her arrival."

"No doubt she grew tired of waiting for me to come for her and she put her uncle up to this."

"That could very well be true. I don't know of a young lady who wouldn't want to marry a duke. You mentioned the uncle said one of the younger girls is making her debut at the first ball of the Season. If she is more to your liking, marry her. I'm sure she would satisfy your debt to her brother just as well as the older one. Once you have an heir, you can feel free to never bother Her Grace again."

"There is some rationale to that thought. It seems to have worked for my parents—and quite nicely, from what I could tell. They lived happily apart for many years."

"True. But if your father had mended his wicked ways when he married, been more discreet about his mistresses and orgies, and spent more time at home with his wife than drinking in his clubs and hunting lodges, he might have lived longer."

Bray remained silent. He couldn't remember a time when his parents were ever in the same house at the same time. Separate was just the way they lived, and Bray never had a reason to question them about it.

He shook off the memories along with the emotion that always threatened to surface when he thought about them. "The prospect of marriage might be a bit more palatable if I had been allowed to choose my own bride."

"There is that line from one of Southey's works about 'the chickens,' that 'always come home to roost.' You've lived your life by your own rules long enough. And if truth be told, it is that life that got you into this mess."

Bray clenched his jaw.

"Listen, my friend," Seaton continued. "You are handsome, fit, and now you are a duke before the age of thirty. How many gentlemen have been given so much power, influence, and wealth at such a young age?"

Bray reached and shoved open the door of the coach and jumped down to the soft ground. He lifted the collar of his greatcoat against the rain and looked up at his driver. "Take Mr. Seaton back to the club or wherever he wants to go."

Seaton raised a brow. "I'm not leaving until I see you enter the house."

Bray chuckled and shut the carriage door. He turned and walked up the stepping-stone path to the front stoop. He rapped the lion's head door knocker twice and waited. A few moments later, the door slowly opened, but only enough to allow the head of a blond-haired girl who looked to be around the age of eight or nine to peep from behind it. Her features were small except for bright blue eyes that appeared almost too big for her cherub face.

Bray had no experience talking with a child, so he just stared at her, wondering why she had opened the door. She was much too young to be a servant.

She stared back at him.

Finally he gathered what little patience he had at this point and leaned down toward the girl and said, "Good afternoon, miss. I'm the Duke of Drakestone here to see Miss Prim."

A smile stretched across her narrow, sweet-looking face. She opened the door wider and gave him an acceptable curtsy. "Hello, Your . . . Your Highness?"

"It's Your Grace."

"Yes. Right." She stamped her foot. "I knew that. I am Miss Sybil Prim, Your Grace."

"Are you, now?" he said, knowing full well she was not the Miss Prim he sought. But if her older sister was half as pretty as this girl would be one day, maybe this ill-conceived liaison wouldn't be so dreadful as he was expecting. "I'm looking for Miss Louisa Prim."

She huffed, the smile disappearing. "She's in the book room."

"I see," he said. "Tell me, Miss Prim, do you always open the door?"

A mischievous glow lit her eyes, and her smile returned, wider now. "No," she said quickly. "Sometimes I close it." And with that she slammed the door shut. He heard a girlish giggle from the other side of the door and her footsteps running away.

Bray didn't know whether to be amused by the imp's brazen behavior or suspect of a family that let such be-

havior occur. He could understand a boy pulling a devilish prank like that. Lord knew he'd been a hellion at
that age, but a girl? That surprised him.

He knocked on the door again, louder, in hopes one
of the servants would hear him this time.

The door opened once more, but this time to a different young lady of perhaps fifteen or sixteen years of
age. She was also blond with big blue eyes but obviously
too young to be the Miss Prim he was seeking. Where
was the butler, or the housekeeper? Even a chambermaid
would do at this point.

"Good afternoon, sir," she said politely. "May I help
you?"

Hopefully this girl had a few more manners than the
last, though that was one wager he wouldn't waste good
money on. "I'm the Duke of Drakestone here to see
Miss Prim," he said.

A flush heightened her cheeks and she smiled pret-
tily at him and then curtsied. "I am Miss Lillian Prim,
Your Grace."

Her innocent mistake made him smile, and straight-
away he realized the error was once again his. "Of
course you are, but I am looking for Miss Louisa Prim."

She gave a disappointed sigh. "She's one of my older
sisters."

A door at the back of the house slammed so hard, it
rattled the windowpanes. Bray heard the running of
feet and high-pitched, toe-curling squeals.

Bray swore silently. "What was that sound?" he asked
the girl.

"Another sister, Your Grace."

"What in the name of Hades is wrong with her?"

The young lady blinked curiously. "Nothing, sir."

"There should be something wrong if someone is
going to scream like that."

More shrieks were followed by the appealing laughter of a young lady. It was genuine amusement and happiness. It wasn't the fake feminine delight he'd heard through the years at the hundreds of balls, dinners, and card parties he attended. It was more musical, more irresistible. That sound tightened his stomach.

The noise of merriment came closer. He saw a girl younger than the two he'd already met burst out of a doorway and bound down the corridor. Right behind her he caught a glimpse of a young lady reaching to grab her prey but missing just before the girl darted away.

"Give me that book right now," the young lady called between bouts of laughter.

"No! It's mine. You can't have it!" The younger one screeched again and sprang across the corridor into another room with the lady on her heels. Bray didn't think he had ever witnessed anything like it, girls running about like hoydens, banging doors and screaming in carefree delight. As an only child of two only children, he'd not interacted with females aside from his mother, his paramours, and simpering ladies at Society parties. He couldn't imagine any one of them acting with such wild abandon.

Seconds later, the two ran out of another room and barreled into the vestibule where he and the other Miss Prim stood.

"Oh," the young lady said as she skidded to a halt in front of him. Before she could catch her breath and speak, the younger child, who had kept running, crashed into her from behind, knocking her straight into Bray's arms. He caught her by softly rounded shoulders before steadying her with his hands.

"Oh," she repeated, this time after an intake of breath. A whiff of her fresh-washed hair swept past him and he inhaled deeply the intoxicating scent. His gaze fell briefly on her breasts, and heat filled him.

Her blue eyes rounded in surprise when they met his. "Excuse me, sir," she said, splaying her fingers on his chest while pushing away from him, clearly embarrassed.

Reluctantly, he let go of her.

She turned to the mischievous child behind her. "Bonnie, we owe the gentleman an apology."

"You first."

The older sister sighed and looked back at Bray. "My apologies."

The little girl then turned a beautiful set of big blue eyes on him and said, "I'm sorry that you got in my sister's way and forced me to run into her."

The older sister glared at her. "Bonnie."

Miss Bonnie Prim folded her arms across her chest and shrugged her shoulders in a pouting stance. "Sorry, uh, *sir.*"

The older one groaned.

Bray couldn't be upset with anyone who pushed a beautiful lady into his arms. "No harm done."

He returned his attention to the young lady, who was undeniably fetching in her simple, pale yellow dress. "Do you always race about the house in such a fashion?"

The older Miss Prim's breasts lifted and fell rapidly as she tried to calm her breathing. Her hand went immediately to her long, sunset-colored tresses. She brushed them to the back of her shoulders as if hoping to make herself more presentable. There was something gentle and alluring in the way she tried to recover her composure.

Unexpectedly, he was drawn to her.

"No, of course not. We were in the book room playing

games because of the rain, and, well, I had no idea we had a guest."

How many young ladies would admit to playing with their younger siblings? And if they were in the midst of such frolic when he knocked, it was no wonder they couldn't hear him. It would be impossible to hear a musket explode with the commotion they were making.

However, at last he was sure he'd found Miss Louisa Prim, or rather, she'd found him. Her cheeks were flushed with exertion. Wispy strands of amber blond hair attractively framed her face. He couldn't help but think that she looked as if she'd just had an exhilarating and rather satisfying tussle in bed with an exciting lover.

If he had to marry, she might do rather nicely after all. "Apparently the winner of the game was to receive that coveted book?" He gestured to the bound copy in the youngest girl's hands.

Miss Prim shyly gave him a hint of a smile. Bray's body tightened with the heady prickling of desire. He hadn't expected Miss Louisa Prim to be so appealing.

"My uncle has so many books we haven't seen, I'm afraid we find ourselves sometimes fighting over who will be the first to read them."

He glanced at the child. "I'm impressed a girl so young can read."

The younger Miss Prim beamed at him, showing a gap where her front top teeth should be while the older one lifted fan-shaped brows and said, "That's kind of you to say. How can I help you?"

Bray saw another blue-eyed, blond-haired young lady, perhaps eighteen years old, making her way toward them. And out of the corner of his eye, he saw the young Miss Prim who had shut the door in his face sneak back into the room. He did a quick count. All five Misses Prim were there.

Bray bit back an exasperated sigh and said, "I'm here to see Miss Louisa Prim."

"I am Miss Louisa Prim," the eldest young lady said, giving him a quizzical look.

The youngest girl, who had squealed to the high heavens, pushed in front of her sister and looked up at him and said, "I have a name. Do you want to know my name?" And without giving him time to respond, answered, "It's Bonnie."

The girl who'd closed the door on him piped up and said, "I have a name, too. I'm Sybil, and this is my sister Lillian."

"I can say my own name, thank you very much. I'm Lillian."

"Then I must be Gwen, since I'm the only one left."

Suddenly all the girls were laughing, except the eldest young lady, who frowned and promptly scolded them by saying, "Girls, stop this at once. This gentleman will think you have no manners."

Too late for that, he thought.

As each girl had said her name, she smiled and curtsied, even the mischievous Miss Sybil and Miss Bonnie, proving they had manners after all. Bray couldn't help but think if someone was going to have that many daughters, they should have made it easy on themselves and named them A, B, C, D, and E or One, Two, Three, Four, and Five.

"And who are you?" the smallest one demanded of him.

"Bonnie!" Miss Louisa Prim admonished, clearly exasperated by her little sister's boldness.

Feeling a stab of impatience at their sport, Bray said, "Ladies," and nodded to them before immediately shifting his attention back to Miss Louisa Prim. Bray's mouth lifted slightly. For the third time, he said, "I am the Duke of Drakestone."

The second he said his name, Louisa Prim went still. Then Bray watched her shoulders and chin lift precipitously. She took a step away from him. Her sisters, sensing the sudden change in her demeanor, moved in closer to support or to protect her. He wasn't sure which.

Miss Prim didn't immediately answer him. It was as if he could see her mind working. He had a feeling she wanted to think of a way to tell him to get the hell out of her house, though do it politely. That made him smile, which he could see infuriated her all the more. The other four Misses Prim were looking at him, too, but not with the dire contempt he saw in Miss Louisa Prim's expression. They were curious yet cautious.

"What do you want?" she finally asked in an unfriendly clipped tone that left him no doubt how she was feeling.

Her voice was cold, and that angered him. He was here because of her uncle, not because he wanted to marry her or be responsible for the assortment of girls before him. He didn't have a hell of an idea what to do with this collection of girls. He'd never lived with one sibling, let alone five of them. What right did she have to treat him as if he were bothering her?

"I'd like a few moments of your time."

"If I must," she said grudgingly.

It didn't appear she was prepared to give an inch, but then neither was he. Her four sisters stayed behind her like a wall of blond-haired, blue-eyed sentinels staunchly guarding their beloved captain, none of them making a move to leave. He couldn't very well talk to Miss Prim about marriage with so many sets of eyes looking warily at him, so he added one word: "Alone."

After a brief hesitation, Miss Prim said, "Very well. Gwen, please go to the kitchen and ask Mrs. Trumpington to prepare tea and bring it into the drawing room.

Perhaps you should help her by picking out a lovely china pattern for the duke."

She looked him up and down with those piercing blue eyes, and Bray felt a shiver of awareness rush through him even though there wasn't a hint of seduction in her appraisal.

"His Grace looks to be the type of gentleman who would appreciate a very delicate cup and saucer," she continued. "One with plenty of colorful flowers painted on it."

Bray's brows twitched as she looked from his face to his big hands. He had the feeling that somehow she knew he despised those dainty cups he was forced to use at teas and dinner parties. Too bad she didn't know he never walked away from a challenge.

"The smaller, the better," he shot back with a grin.

He could see that she was restraining a glower.

"Sybil and Bonnie, it's time for you to return to the schoolroom and continue your studies with Miss Kindred. She should have your lessons prepared by now. Playtime is over for the day."

"What am I to do, Sister?" Miss Lillian asked.

Miss Prim seemed to study on that before saying, "Actually, I believe His Grace would like to hear you play the pianoforte. A fine gentleman like him would enjoy listening to a soothing melody from a young lady as talented as you. Perhaps you could entertain him with that score you were practicing yesterday."

"But I don't know it very well, Sister."

Miss Prim gave Bray a humorless smile and said, "He won't mind. Will you, Your Grace?"

Hell yes, Bray started to say. He would sit through a musical or the opera only when there was absolutely no way out of the invitation for him to do so. The mere thought of hearing a child practice her lessons made him want to bolt for the door. And he was tempted to do just that. But he couldn't resist the defiance in Miss Louisa Prim's eyes.

"Not at all, as your sister said, I'd be delighted to hear you *softly* play while we talk."

Miss Lillian scampered off. Bray was impressed at how, when Miss Prim issued the orders, the girls went scurrying to their duties without question or complaint.

"I apologize for leaving you standing in the front of the house so long, Your Grace."

She might have offered an apology, but there wasn't a trace of regret in her tone or countenance. He was beginning to get the feeling Miss Prim hadn't been pining away for him or eagerly awaiting word about impending nuptials.

No matter. She was proving to be quite intriguing.

"Would you like to come into the drawing room?" she asked in an overly cheerful tone.

"Where the pianoforte is, I presume?"

"Of course."

Another sudden surge of desire for her rippled inside him. His lower body tightened, thickened. He had an intense urge to pull her to him and kiss her.

This visit was not turning out as he had expected.

"May I take your hat, gloves, and coat—that is, unless you've changed your mind and need to leave?" She held out her hand to him, palm up. "No doubt a gentleman such as yourself must be quite busy."

Miss Prim was still talking nicely, though he knew there wasn't an ounce of sweetness in it. It was as if she could see his reluctance to stay and was feeling quite sure she was going to win and send him running from the house with his coattails flapping in the rain.

And once again, he was very tempted.

But Bray hesitated. He didn't want to become involved with such a strange household of females. He was
no nanny, and he certainly wasn't a keeper of innocents.

The first sour notes on the pianoforte sounded, sending a shiver up his spine, and for a moment, he thought
Miss Prim had the victory, too. But then the fighting
spirit rose up in him, and—much to her regret, he was
sure—he handed her his damp hat.

That wiped the victory off her face rather quickly
and put one on his. He pulled on the fingers of his gloves
and asked, "Do you not have a servant to attend to the
door?"

"Not at the present," she said defensively.

That was odd.

He thought about asking why but the determined set
of her full, lusty lips and frown told him she didn't care
much for him questioning her. He handed her his gloves
and then removed his sodden coat and gave her that as
well.

She laid them on a side table and said, "This way,
Your Grace."

As he walked behind her, he saw that she kept her
shoulders stiff and her back straight, but that posture
didn't keep her long tresses from sweeping lightly across
her shoulders and making him wonder how the soft
waves of her hair would feel against his bare chest. But
her thoughts clearly were not in the direction of his.
He had the feeling that, just in case he was still unsure
about her, she wanted to make damn sure he knew she
was not happy he was there.

He wondered if he should tell her he wasn't keen on
it either.

The drawing room was a respectable size, and
thankfully the pianoforte was on the far wall in front of

a window. Miss Lillian looked up at him when he walked in and promptly lost her place on the ivories and made a devil of a mess of the tune.

"Please sit down," Miss Prim said coolly.

She could hold a gaze steadier than most men. "Only after you," he said.

"If you insist." She took a seat on the edge of the settee.

Bray made himself comfortable on a green uphol-stered armchair opposite the small wide-striped sofa, looked at Miss Prim, and said, "Your sisters are rather—"

"I don't believe you came here to talk about my sis-ters, Your Grace," she said, interrupting him without a hint of apology. "Why don't you save us both time and get to the reason you're here?"

Miss Prim had cut him off without blinking an eye as if he were behaving like an errant schoolboy. Her demanding tone set his teeth on edge, and the silence between them made it easy for him to hear haltingly played notes that didn't resemble any score he'd ever heard. She had no respect for his title, forcing him to listen to the poorly played melody and not even letting him finish his sentence. It was hard to believe that this rigid young lady before him now was the same one who had been frolicking through the house with such vigor and happiness only a few minutes ago.

But she didn't know that Bray didn't mind ladies with spirit; he welcomed them. A wayward grin lifted the corners of his mouth again. No innocent young lady had ever had the nerve to openly test him, and it appeared Miss Prim was just itching to be the first. Oddly, he felt like laughing, perhaps in relief, perhaps at the thought of this young lady standing up to him. Either way, if he had to marry, the idea of marrying her didn't seem so dreadful.

"You're right," he finally said. "I didn't come to discuss your sisters. I came to talk about you and me."

She shook her head slowly. "That won't happen. 'You and me' would imply there is an *us* and there is no *us* to talk about."

He gave a short laugh. "But there is, Miss Prim. I never heard back from you on my offer of marriage."

Her shoulders relaxed a little for the first time since hearing his name. "I have not received an offer of marriage from you or anyone else."

"Really?" That was odd. "I know it was a long time ago, but I know my messenger said he delivered my letter directly into your hands."

A deliberate fake surprise brightened her features. "Oh, you're referring to the admission-of-guilt letter you had delivered to me a couple of years ago? That was hardly a proposal, Your Grace. And it wasn't even a halfway decent condolence message. It was an insult, and I dealt with it as such by tossing it in the fire."

His mood darkened. "You don't mince words, do you, Miss Prim?"

"I see no reason to." She rose. "I will further not mince words by adding that we have nothing else to say to each other. I'll show you out."

She walked to the doorway without looking back, as if she expected him to obey her orders as quickly as her sisters had. When it was clear to her he hadn't, she turned to him. Bray kept his seat, calmly watching her. He didn't care for the notion that she thought she'd gotten the best of him. He'd prove to her he hadn't by staying a little longer.

"There is plenty to discuss, Miss Prim," he stated. "Your brother asked me to marry you. In front of witnesses. And I promised him I would. Again in front of witnesses."

He watched as a nearly palpable tension rode through her. After more than a moment's hesitation and probably more than a little consternation, she walked back into the room, folded her arms across her chest, and stood looking down at him with anxious blue eyes. She didn't look happy that he'd won that particular battle.

"I release you of that promise, Your Grace," she said tersely.

"But that's the thing. You can't."

"May I speak freely again?"

"Please don't stop now."

"I don't want you in my house, let alone in my bed. I am in London to see that my sister Gwen has a proper Season, in hopes of a suitable match by the end of it. That is my only duty here. Once that is accomplished, I will return to Wayebury happily unmarried, to take care of my sisters until it is time to return to London for Lillian's Season."

There was fire behind her words, and her steady gaze was unrelenting. He had imagined many things before he knocked on the door. That she was painfully shy and unattractive, insistently chatty and loud, or that she was a demented shrew. But it had never crossed his mind that she wouldn't want to marry him. He'd had young ladies lining up to marry him for years. He'd even suspected she put her uncle up to his brash behavior.

He never expected she'd reject him—and a duke, at that.

"It was your brother's desire that we marry," he said again.

"Thanks to you, my brother is dead."

Her short, flat words hit him hard, but he did nothing to show any emotion in his manner or his expression, and she didn't let up on her attack.

"His death, like my mother's and my father's before

him, has assured that my duty is to my sisters. They need me, not you. So if you want to marry, I suggest you find someone who is willing and command her to marry you, because I am not available."

The last vestige of him thinking she might be a fragile slip of a girl intent on making him her husband before summer came faded from his mind. He had a thought that he might have won a battle, but he wasn't sure he could win the war.

That surprised him.

It surprised him even more that the thought of trying intrigued him.

Bray had had no intentions of taking on the responsibility of caring for a flock of females, but that was before he knew Miss Prim didn't want him to. Who did she think she was to dictate anything to him?

The flames in the fireplace had burned low, but he felt a heat to the room that had nothing to do with the embers glowing in the ashes or Miss Prim's attitude, for she was cold as stone toward him. Yet there was a feminine softness about her that he found comfortable, appealing, and warm.

Bray rose to tower over her.

He leaned in close to her and softly said, "I hope that is not a challenge for me to persuade you differently, Miss Prim, because if it is, I'll have to accept."

Chapter 4

When he is best he is a little worse than a man, and when
he is worst he is a little better than a beast.
—*The Merchant of Venice,* act 1, scene 2

A challenge?

Louisa Prim forced her knees to stay steady as the Duke of Drakestone rose and towered over her with a commanding, primal presence. A weaker woman would have dropped to her knees. That, or fainted. But she had never been a wilting flower. She hadn't had that luxury since her mother died, shortly after Bonnie was born. Louisa had been both mother and sister to the girls.

Despite her determined control, a slight flush crept into her cheeks as the man stepped closer to her, much closer than a gentleman should stand to a young lady he'd just met. Her heartbeat pounded. Instinct told her to flee, but from somewhere deep inside herself she summoned the nerve to look him directly in the eye.

Her courage hadn't failed her.

Perhaps it was the fact that she held the duke responsible for her brother's death. Even she had heard the many rumors about how wild the Duke of Drakestone was. She didn't believe her brother, Nathan, was completely innocent concerning what had happened when he died, but she felt sure he wouldn't have been racing that fatal night if he were not encouraged to do so by the notorious heir now standing in front of her.

Once Nathan became an heir to the title of viscount, he'd gone to London and turned into a different person. Not even her nonjudgmental father had been able to calm Nathan down when he was in London. By his own admission, Nathan left his sensible way of life behind and became just as wild and reckless as the other heirs he associated with.

But Louisa had to believe that Nathan, who always took good care of his sisters' welfare, would never have willingly endangered his life. If her brother were still alive, she and her sisters would have his love and generosity and not be at the mercy of a stingy uncle who didn't care a feather about her or them.

"What about it, Miss Prim?" the duke asked softly while Lillian continued playing the pianoforte. "Was that a challenge?"

"Certainly not," she said, refusing to move an inch, lest he realize she was shaking in her soft-soled slippers and trying desperately to hide it. "I'm not foolish enough to take on a gentleman as irresponsible as you."

Louisa let her gaze fall to his wide chest, covered by a starched white shirt and well-fitted pale brown waistcoat and across his strong-looking shoulders encased in a dark, chocolate brown coat. Her attention slid over his casually tied neckcloth before rolling back up his cleanly shaven neck to study his handsome, chiseled features. And then as with a will of their own, her eyes stopped at his lips—which formed such an appealing half grin that she wanted to reach up and kiss him.

The unexpected urge caused a catch in her breath.

He was so cocksure, she feared he might know what she was thinking.

She stepped back and took a quick glance toward Lillian, hoping her sister hadn't seen just how close she was standing to the duke.

"If that was a compliment, Miss Prim," he said, "thank you."

Lillian hit a sequence of wrong notes in the middle of a chord that was going rather well, and Louisa saw His Grace flinch. She smiled. She saw no reason to make his unwanted and unexpected visit enjoyable. Her brother had adored all his sisters, but when it came time for music lessons, he had always found a reason to leave the house. And when her uncle had visited Wayebury and one of the girls was practicing, he immediately told Louisa the playing had to stop. Apparently some gentlemen couldn't block the sound from their ears and continue on with whatever they were doing. Perhaps the duke was like that and would rather leave than be forced to listen to the unpleasant string of sounds, too.

"I'm assuming your sister Gwen is the one who is ready to enter Society?"

"Yes," Louisa said cautiously, remembering that she'd had to send her uncle three letters before he finally made a visit to Wayebury to discuss her petition to move the family to London for the Season so that Gwen could enter the marriage mart.

Louisa had done her best over the past two years to be accommodating to her uncle and not bother him very often, which was what he'd made clear he wanted. After she had repeatedly refused his demands that she force the Duke of Drakestone to make good on his word and marry her, the easiest thing for her to do was acquiesce to her uncle's wishes that she stay at his es-

tate in Wayebury and be responsible for her sisters'
schooling and welfare.

When her uncle finally appeared at Wayebury a few
weeks ago, it had been apparent he didn't want to live
up to what was expected of him and see to it that Gwen
had a Season befitting the daughter of a viscount so she
could make a good match. In fact, he had been greatly
perturbed to hear her explain they would need a place
to live, new clothing, a coach-and-four, and to be introduced to the appropriate ladies so that Gwen could obtain invitations to the best parties and balls. Louisa had
already determined in her mind that she would have to
deal courageously with her uncle, so she had remained
steady and firm. In the end, he'd agreed to her requests
and made arrangements for their journey to London.

But how shabbily her uncle had treated them in the
past was not this man's concern.

"Naturally," the duke said, "you'll want her to be
dressed in the latest fashion."

That seemed an odd comment for the duke to make,
but Louisa said, "Yes."

"She'll also need to be introduced to the patronesses
of Almack's."

"Of course. Gwen is lovely, sociable, and quite intelligent, and—" Suddenly Louisa gasped. "Your Grace,
do you have designs on Gwen?"

His brows drew together quickly. "Romantic designs
on her? No."

"Good, because I would never allow her to marry
you."

The duke's green eyes darkened, and he stared at her
with a hard, defying expression. He stepped dangerously
close to her again and said, "Miss Prim, *if* I wanted to
marry your sister, you could not stop me."

She hesitated, hating the truth of his words and not willing to admit it. "Perhaps, but I would certainly try."

"But that's not the point. What does your sister need to ensure her appearance in Society is a success?"

Louisa smirked. "Well, Your Grace, since gratefully, you are not interested in her, I don't believe her welfare is any of your concern or any of your business, and I'll thank you to keep out of it."

His brow furrowed again. "Your uncle made it my concern and my business."

His cocksure attitude sent a rippling of alarm through her. "Did he? How? What has he done?"

"You don't know."

Her trepidation increased. "I'm not sure what you are talking about. I don't know how Gwen's Season could possibly be any of your concern."

"Before Lord Wayebury left England to go on his grand tour, he signed your inheritance and that of your sisters over to me for management and disbursement as well as legal guardianship."

Louisa felt as if an anvil had fallen on her chest and she had no means to get it off. "He's gone out of the country? And he left us at your mercy?"

The duke nodded.

"I don't believe you."

"Does this really seem like the kind of thing I would make up?"

"No, no, of course not, but." Her heartbeat surged. "It's just that I'm caught completely unaware."

His expression remained suspicious. "I assumed you knew he'd planned an extensive holiday abroad and changed the guardianship."

"No," she said, feeling shaky again, but determined not to sound as if she were about to fall apart. "Did you ask him to do this?" she demanded of him.

His eyes narrowed again. "I assumed you did."

"Me?" She gasped again. "Of course not. Why would I want you to be guardian of me and my sisters?"

"Perhaps you were eager to marry me?"

"You!" she exclaimed, staring at him in disbelief. "I would not marry you if you were dipped in gold and trussed up with rubies, Your Grace. When we arrived here, there was a letter from my uncle stating that he would be gone for the Season, but not that he had left England. Mrs. Trumpington is the only servant he left behind to help us. I'm sure she doesn't know anything about this either. Surely she would have said something to me."

"Did you travel here alone?"

Feeling numb and bewildered, she said. "Of course not. I knew better than to attempt that. Miss Kindred is the younger girls' governess. She has been with our family since before I was Bonnie's age."

"Did Lord Wayebury leave you without securing Gwen a chaperone for the Season?"

Once more, she shook her head. "His letter stated that his wife's sister, Mrs. Ramona Colthrust, would be here to guide us through the Season, but she wasn't here when we arrived and I've heard nothing from her."

His eyes darkened and narrowed yet again. "I have met Mrs. Colthrust. She is not a suitable chaperone for you or anyone else."

"You are not suitable to be in charge of us either," she said indignantly.

Suddenly Lillian's playing was more than Louisa could bear at the moment. Louisa turned to her and, in as quiet a manner as she could muster, said, "Lillian, would you please go ask Mrs. Trumpington to add some apricot tarts to the tea tray?"

"Yes, Sister," she said, and quietly left the room.

Louisa looked back to the duke, furious her uncle had

been so unkind as to force this man upon them. First her father died, then her brother, and now her uncle had abandoned them, too. She knew the responsibility for five girls was a lot for anyone to manage, but to cast them off like unwanted garments to a stranger proved just how little her uncle cared for them.

She sensed the duke was growing weary of their conversation by the deep frown line between his eyes, but she had more to say. "My uncle never wanted the responsibility for us in the first place, so I am not surprised by his unscrupulous actions. But I can't believe you would accept. A true gentleman wouldn't have."

"A true gentleman did—all because I made a promise to a dying friend. It's also true your uncle left me no choice. I couldn't deny that I was the proper person to take care of the woman I said I would marry. More than a dozen men heard me tell your brother I would. And most of them have long wondered why I haven't made good on my word."

"Rubbish! I don't believe for a minute that anyone even remembers my brother, let alone your vow to him."

"On the contrary, Miss Prim—they expect a gentleman to keep his word, so what am I to do? I can assure you the last thing I want is to be in charge of a gaggle of blond-haired, blue-eyed girls who run around the house screaming like banshees thinking the hounds of Hell are after them."

Louisa expelled another harsh sound. She rose tall on her toes and lifted her face toward the duke. "Did you call my sisters banshees?"

His hard gaze bored into hers. "Did you and your sister race around this house making noises that would have woken the dead?"

She blushed despite her indignation. "You're a beast."

"I'll take that as a compliment, too."

"That doesn't surprise me in the least," she countered. "Say what you truly feel about me, but do not speak of my sisters in such a manner."

She heard him curse under his breath and saw the muscles working in his neck. "I said *like* banshees, not that they are."

"Same meaning," she said, pressing harder, unwilling to let him off the hook for his offensive expression or back away from him. "Would you say something so unkind about your brothers or sisters?"

"Yes. If I had any. It so happens I don't."

"Cousins, then."

"I don't have any of those either."

She blinked slowly as she studied on that pronouncement. "It's not natural for anyone not to have at least one or two cousins somewhere in their family."

"I agree, but that's the way it is. I'm afraid that blame will have to be put on my parents' shoulders for being only children as well. And before you ask—yes, I do have a few friends, and they would only laugh at such a remark as I just made."

"No wonder. It's a testament to the kind of friends you have. But no matter about that, I will see a solicitor tomorrow and tell him we must have a day in the Court of Chancery. I have the right to protest what my uncle did, and I will. I won't have you responsible for us, and the court must get you changed for someone else."

He lowered his face closer to hers. "You know I can't allow that."

His words were spoken quietly, but Louisa bristled all the same, meeting him stare for stare. "How can you stop me?"

"Your uncle left you in my care. The courts are not likely to change that as long as I am willing."

"My sisters are not some wild and reckless duke's responsibility. They are my mine to care for. Furthermore, my uncle could not force me to marry you, and neither can you. I will not marry a man whose culpability led him to send me a halfhearted offer of marriage to try to rid himself of his guilt and shame, a man who is so rash as to race a curricle on a foggy night."

His nose edged closer to hers. "Did you call me wild and reckless?"

"From all I've read in the Society pages and the scandal sheets, the shoe fits perfectly, Your Grace."

"So you get your information from the scandal pages and call it truth?"

"That and from what my brother told me before his death about you and his colleagues at the Heirs' Club."

"I assume he told you this after he'd had a pint or two of ale or more than a few sips of brandy."

"Which you probably gave him to drink before he left London. So yes, I know about your midnight races, your card games that go on for days, and the many bedchambers you have slipped in and out of to accept a dare or to win a challenge. You should be called the Heirs' Club of Scoundrels, from what I've heard, because that is exactly what all of you are."

His chest heaved as rapidly as hers. They were locked in a battle of wills. She stared intently at him, and as she looked into the bright green depths of his eyes, she watched the lines around them ease. Slowly she saw his broad shoulders relax. His angry glare wilted. A smile spread his masculine lips.

His gaze dropped to her lips and lingered there. "You know, you are so close to me right now that I could kiss you, Miss Prim."

All the breath seemed to swoosh out of her lungs and she blinked slowly. "Pardon?"

"You are so bent on getting the best of me that you haven't even realized your lips are a mere fraction of an inch from mine. I'm trying to decide if I should kiss you and be the wild rogue you accuse me of being, or if I should step away and be the gentleman you insist I'm not. Tell me, Miss Prim, which should I be?"

Louisa's lips parted, she lifted her head, but then in a moment of sanity she whirled from the duke. She pushed her hair to the back of her shoulders again, shaken by the strange sensations the duke stirred inside her.

He chuckled softly. "I will take care of you and your sisters for now, Miss Prim. You cannot change that. I'll set up accounts for you at the best modiste, millinery, and fabric shops in Town. I'm sure there are other things you will need, so I'll send someone around tomorrow who can help you. I'll see to it that Miss Gwen receives more invitations than she can possibly accept and that the patronesses of Almack's are introduced to her at the first ball. Then it will be up to you to see that she passes their inspection."

"Of course she will," Louisa said, slowly regaining her composure.

He nodded once. "And as for you, Miss Prim, I will not ask you to marry me again."

"Thank heavens," she whispered, stepping back, her knees wobbly once more, though this time with something not so easily explained.

"I will wait for you to propose to me."

Louisa blinked some more, and then blinked again before her mouth slammed shut and she glared. "Then you will die an old bachelor, Your Grace."

"A challenge it is, then. I accept."

He smiled so devilishly that her breasts tingled and a warm fluttering swirled in her lower stomach.

"I'll show myself out," he said.

Louisa watched the duke leave. What a smug man he was to think she would ever propose to him. But for an instant, if she were truthful with herself, she had contemplated receiving the kiss he offered.

Chapter 5

Crabbèd Age and Youth
Cannot live together
—The Passionate Pilgrim

Sweet mercies!

Louisa had never stood so close to such a powerfully built man. Heat flooded her cheeks once again.

Had she really wanted him to kiss her?

Yes!

But why?

She was supposed to be much too sensible to be drawn to an arrogant, insufferable, and infuriating man. No, she was supposed to be too sensible to be drawn to any man, but especially one with such a disregard for what was right and proper. She should be thinking she hoped she never saw him again.

The front door opened and closed, and she knew the duke had gone. Taking time to collect her thoughts, she wondered what she was going to do about him.

Her father had been a loving, levelheaded man who looked after his family even after he became viscount. For most of her life, he was a gentle vicar, well respected in the village. He never expected to inherit the title, and even after he did and they moved into the Wayebury estate, he still stayed home and took good care of his daughters.

Nathan was good to them, but he hadn't exactly followed in their father's footsteps after he became the viscount upon their father's death. He had once told her the lure of all that London offered was much too great to ignore, and he started spending more time there than at home. Not even his fancy for the village's most beautiful young lady could hold him in Wayebury.

She squeezed her eyes shut. May the saints help her. Her lashes lifted. Well, if truth be known, she knew little of men except her father, brother, and uncle. And not one of them had come close to being as overbearing and overconfident as His Grace was.

But she did wonder how anyone became that self-possessed. He remained steady as a rock even when she'd come close to accusing him of being responsible for her brother's death. She could definitely take a few lessons from him on how to keep her emotions under control. His composure was astounding, and he'd more than proved that everything she'd ever read or heard about him was true.

He'd made her hackles rise faster than a bee's wings could flap. The gall of him saying he would wait for her to propose to him was shocking. Hades would freeze first. The suggestion was so outrageous, so inappropriate—not to mention insulting—that she couldn't even think about it without fuming with indignation all over again.

He was indeed a scoundrel of the highest order.

She knew she didn't really hold the duke responsible for her brother's death. Though, who could blame her if she did? From his own words, Louisa knew Nathan became a different man when he was in London. He'd admitted to being as wild and reckless as the other members of the Heirs' Club when he was there. He'd admitted the pleasures of the city beckoned him and he had to go and satisfy that yearning to overindulge in drink, gaming, and ladies of the evening. She realized it might not be fair on her part, but somehow it made her feel better to lay blame somewhere other than on Nathan. And the duke's shoulders and arms were big enough to carry the weight.

No, she could never marry a man such as her brother had become or like the Duke of Drakestone. Men who left their families for a different life in London and had no care as to how many hearts they broke or how much danger they faced would never hold her heart. If she were ever to marry, she would seek a quiet, sensible man like her father was when he was the village vicar. She wanted a man who loved his family and would rather spend time with his wife and children than with scoundrels at fashionable men's clubs.

Louisa sighed. This predicament of being at the undisciplined duke's mercy for now was her uncle's fault. Or maybe it was her fault. If she hadn't pushed her uncle to give Gwen a Season, maybe he wouldn't have left the country without even telling her. He'd made it clear to her on his last trip to Wayebury that his only concern was that his new, and much younger, wife bear him a son to inherit the title.

Titles!

She supposed for now, for Gwen's sake, she had to allow the duke to take care of them, but she didn't have to like it.

Louisa faced the glowing embers in the fireplace. Watching the flames of a low-burning fire was soothing. And she needed comfort right now. She felt a tug at her heart, and her mind drifted back to the time just before her brother died. She'd been looking forward to her Season, only a couple of months away at the time. Her gowns, headpieces, gloves, and everything she would need were being made for her. Her education was complete. She'd been tutored and excelled in French, music, and dancing. She could draw, paint, and write verse as skillfully as any young lady her age. She knew how to manage a household filled with servants. Nathan had told her he was eager to introduce her as his sister at the many parties and balls they would attend.

She'd lain awake at night and dreamed of dancing with handsome gentlemen on candlelit terraces, tasting her first sip of champagne, and receiving her first kiss under a starry sky. But that wasn't to be for her. After Nathan was buried, she'd agreed with her uncle that she should remain at Wayebury for another year and not upset the lives of the younger girls any more than necessary. And she had dutifully agreed to his same request the following year.

But she would not allow her sisters to follow in her lonely footsteps. Louisa was now content with her life. With no guidance or assistance from her uncle, Louisa had become her siblings' parent. Her goal was to see to it that her four sisters were properly brought up and that they made a match with a well-suited gentleman. Her youngest sister, Bonnie, was only six years old. Marriage for her was more than ten years away.

Louisa's shoulders sagged a little as she felt a stab of resentment. By then she would be thirty and much too old to consider love, marriage, and children of her own. But she was determined not to allow her beautiful sisters to become spinsters, too.

A knock sounded on the front door, and Louisa's breath caught sharply in her throat.

The duke has come back!

He must have forgotten his hat or maybe his gloves.

She folded her arms across her chest. That was too bad. She wasn't going to open the door to him. His hands could freeze or his head could get dripping wet, for all she cared.

The knocker sounded again. Louder. Harder.

She smiled, taking perverse pleasure in imagining the tall, strapping man standing hatless in the pouring rain.

But a moment later, her resolve weakened. She relented and ran her hands down the sides of her skirt. She had to go to the door. If she didn't, he would continue to knock until one of the girls heard and let him in.

She strode purposefully to the door and opened it, prepared to do battle again.

"God's teeth! What in heaven's name took you so long to get here?"

A beautiful lady with coal black eyes swept past Louisa in a swirl of dark green skirts and a black cape. An older, stocky-built woman with a dour expression on her round face walked in behind her, carrying a traveling satchel.

"First, I have to endure a rainstorm for hours in a leaking carriage that was stuck up to its axles in mud. Then when the roads finally dried out and we get a new carriage, a wheel breaks, delaying us further. Dash it all, I thought I'd never get here, and when I do, what happens? I'm left standing on the stoop to freeze in the chilling rain." The lady abruptly stopped her tirade and looked at Louisa and asked, "Which room do you have me in?"

Taken aback by the harsh, demanding tone coming from such a lovely lady, Louisa cleared her throat and opened her mouth to speak, but before a sound was uttered the stranger declared, "Never mind. Manny, go look over all the rooms and take the one you think will best suit me. If someone's things are already in there, move them out. If I'm going to be responsible for half a dozen girls, I'm going to very well be comfortable doing it. Then go out and have the driver bring up my trunks."

"Yes, madam."

The lady looked Louisa up and down and promptly said, "Who are you?"

Louisa started to clear her throat again and thought better of it. She had already seen enough to know that she couldn't show this person any hesitation or weakness. "I am Louisa Prim, and who might you be?"

The woman started taking off her woolen gloves. "Mrs. Ramona Colthrust. I take it you are one of the misses I am to chaperone for the Season."

Not if I can help it, Louisa wanted to say but answered instead, "My uncle told me to expect you." Louisa then looked up at the maid who had almost reached the top of the stairs. "Manny," she called, and the woman stopped and looked down at her. "Mrs. Colthrust's bedchamber has already been prepared for her. It's the second door on the right. It's the largest and the only one with two windows. I think she'll be very comfortable there."

Manny cut her eyes around to her mistress. Mrs. Colthrust threw her gloves on the side table and nodded once to the maid before swinging her cape off her shoulders and saying, "Lord Wayebury told me he had turned your financial matters over to the Duke of Drakestone because you haven't the good sense to force the duke to make good on his promise to marry you. I assume that is still the case."

Louisa thought, as if anyone could make that man do something he didn't want to do. "I have no desire to

marry him, and I would think anyone would understand my reasons."

"Well, we don't. Whatever your reasons are, they
are foolish, and I assure you they have no merit. There
could never be a reason good enough to refuse a duke's
offer of marriage. But I'll leave that decision with you,
as I am not getting paid enough to worry with such
unwise behavior. I shall meet with the duke as soon as
possible and advise him what we will need. We must
get started right away. There is much to accomplish to
get three ladies properly gowned for the Season, and
there isn't much time."

"Oh, we don't have to worry about me. I'm not looking to make a match this Season."

"Ha! Of course you are. You don't expect Lord
Wayebury to be responsible for you for the rest of your
life, do you? You need a husband to look after you and
the allowance left to you by your brother. Heavens have
mercy, he has six of you to marry off."

Louisa stiffened. "There are five of us, Mrs.
Colthrust."

"Oh, well, yes. But he expects two of you will be
married by the time he returns to England. We must
get to it."

Louisa didn't want to get into telling Mrs. Colthrust
about her feelings of being abandoned by her father, her
brother, and now her uncle, so she thought it best to just
pretend she was looking for a husband, too. Only Louisa
had to know that she would never accept the attentions
from a man or marry and leave her sisters without the
love and attention she gave them.

"Now, I will talk more about this with you at a later
time. I must get some rest so that I can see the Duke of
Drakestone tomorrow and speak to him about what we
need."

Louisa caught her as she was turning away, saying, "I've already spoken with the duke about the things we need for the Season, and he said he would see that we have everything we ask for."

Mrs. Colthrust whirled back to Louisa. She lifted her bonnet off her head, revealing hair as dark and shiny as a raven's feathered coat. "You spoke to him? When?"

"Today. A few minutes ago. He said he would be setting up accounts for us in Town and that he would send someone around to see what other things we might want." Mrs. Colthrust's eyes darkened. Louisa could see the woman wasn't going to like it if she wasn't in complete control.

"Did he?"

"Yes, but I am glad you are here now to take over and handle anything he might have overlooked."

"Of course," she said, leaving Louisa no doubt she was miffed. "Since I had carriage problems and was delayed, it's good you sought him to find out what was going on."

"Actually, he came here to see us. My sisters and I have been in London almost a week. Perhaps he heard that you were delayed by travel and thought he should stop by."

"Yes, I'm sure that must be what happened. I can't blame him for wanting to keep up with the whereabouts and care of you and your five sisters. Every eye in Town will be looking at him and how he handles this."

"Four," Louisa said tightly. "I have four sisters."

"Yes, well, however many."

"Mrs. Colthrust, were you aware that my uncle not only left the duke in charge over our inheritance but made him our guardian as well?"

Her eyebrows shot up. "No, I didn't know that, but I

must say, now that I think about it, I'm not surprised. That was a very clever thing for him to have done."

"Clever?" Louisa asked. "I thought it inconceivable that he would leave us to the responsibility of a total stranger."

"Why? It's what Lord Wayebury wanted. He wanted the duke to marry you, thereby making you and all your sisters the duke's responsibility. Obviously since the duke failed to do that, Lord Wayebury took matters into his own hands and settled the duke's debt to your brother." Mrs. Colthrust laughed and then stifled a yawn. "I really must wash and rest before dinner. My journey has left me drained. Send the maid up to my room with hot water as soon as you can."

"I'm afraid we don't have a scullery maid."

"Fine. Louisa," she said testily. "At this point, I really don't care what the maid's title is. Just send one up."

"There is no one here but the cook, Mrs. Trumpington. She's older, and I don't think she is capable of carrying water up the stairs."

Mrs. Colthrust harrumphed. "Where are the other servants?"

"Whoever was here, my uncle took them all with him."

"All of them?" she asked, clearly exasperated.

Louisa nodded confidently.

"That's unforgivable!"

Mrs. Colthrust was unbelievable. It was perfectly fine for Lord Wayebury to turn his charges over to a reckless stranger, but she was shocked and offended that he didn't leave any servants to help care for them.

"What about your servants from Wayebury? How many did you bring with you?"

"None. Most of them left within a year of my brother's

death. Other than our governess, we had only an elderly couple there with us. She took care of the cooking, cleaning, and the kitchen garden. Her husband did a wonderful job with the grounds, horses, and the carriage that took us to the village once a week. The only person who traveled on the mail coach with us to London is the younger girls' governess, Miss Kindred."

"Thank God you have someone to handle the younger girls, and I won't have to worry about them. As the old saying goes, 'Children can be seen, but they never should be heard.'"

Louisa bristled. First the duke was unkind about her sisters, and now Mrs. Colthrust's comment set Louisa's teeth on edge. She had never restrained her sisters from speaking or, as the duke could attest, playing in the house if the weather did not permit recreation outside. She wasn't going to start putting restrictions on them now. Maybe His Grace was right when he said Mrs. Colthrust would not be a suitable chaperone. She was not endearing herself to Louisa.

"I will take care of my sisters," Louisa said, knowing she had been the only constant in their lives the past few years.

"Really?" She gave Louisa a curious look. "Have you ever attended a Season, Louisa?"

"No, but I do have a fairly good idea of what to expect."

"I think not. Let me enlighten you: Once the Season starts, you will have precious little time to do anything other than throw your tired body in bed to sleep and then rise again long before you feel rested and prepare yourself for another round of one social occasion after the other." She paused and threw up her hands and said, "But I am much too tired to go into all that with you right now. I have no idea how we will make do without servants! I'll just have to speak to the duke about this tomorrow as well. For now, have the cook get the water heating. I'll tell the driver I will pay him to wait and carry the water upstairs after he brings up my trunks. And I will make sure the duke repays me—double. And you—" Suddenly Mrs. Colthrust stopped and smiled. Her face brightened.

Louisa looked down the corridor to see what had brought about the abrupt change in the ill-tempered chaperone. Gwen was coming toward them slowly carrying a tea tray.

"Well, now, I see I can forgive you for being tardy in answering the door, Louisa. You took time to send someone for tea. That was thoughtful of you, as I'm famished." She pointed to Gwen and ordered, "Follow me upstairs with that tray."

Mrs. Colthrust swirled past Louisa in dramatic fashion and started climbing the stairs. Gwen stopped by Louisa and said, "Who is she, and what happened to His Grace?"

"She is our chaperone, Mrs. Ramona Colthrust."

"She looks severe, Sister."

Louisa started to agree and list all the things she didn't like about the lady, but quickly changed her mind. "No, no, not at all." Louisa lied without compunction, not wanting her sisters to have any fear or hesitation concerning the woman. Louisa had enough misgivings for all of them. She didn't know how anyone so beautiful could have such a disagreeable deportment.

"She's very knowledgeable and will be a fine and dutiful chaperone for us. As to be expected, she's tired after her journey. I'm sure she's ready for a cup of tea. Take it on up to her."

Louisa turned away from the stairs. She realized how many "if only's" she had in her life. *If only* her parents and brother hadn't died. *If only* Mrs. Colthrus weren't such a rough-speaking chaperone. *If only* her uncle hadn't left them in the care of a handsome duke who made her feel things she had never felt before, her life in London would be so much easier to understand and to bear.

Chapter 6

My thoughts are whirled like a potter's wheel.
—Henry VI, part 1, act 1, scene 5

Bray gave his damp hat, coat, and gloves to the attendant at the entrance to the gentlemen's club. He knew Seaton would be waiting for him at the Heirs' Club, so he'd had the hackney drop him off at White's instead. Seaton was as curious as an old dowager looking at the face of a new bride. Bray knew the dapper fellow wanted to hear all the details of his visit with Miss Prim, but Bray wasn't ready to talk to the old gentleman.

He and Seaton had been good friends since the day Bray sauntered through the door of the Heirs' Club in St. James's. He didn't have a godfather, but if he had, Bray would want the man to be much like John Aldrich Seaton. Bray's father had taught him how to be an unemotional, pleasure-seeking man and a caretaker of the dukedom, but it was Seaton who had taught him what little he knew about being a true gentleman.

Bray had never forgotten that Seaton stood up for him when some members of the Heirs' Club hadn't wanted to approve Bray's membership into the very exclusive society. Too many of the older gentlemen had heard explicit details of his debauchery, fights, and challenges. If they allowed Bray into their club, they feared he would bring in his unruly friends Harrison Thornwick and Adam Greyhawke with him, and eventually he did. The old guard of the stiff-necked group hadn't wanted the scandalous threesome in their exclusive club, making mischief.

There was little chance Harrison or Adam would ever be allowed membership in the club. Harrison had an older brother and nephew in line before him for the title, and Adam had an uncle and two cousins ahead of him. But they could come as Bray's guests, and so they did—often.

Bray had no doubt every morsel of gossip concerning every drunken, pistol-shooting ride through Mayfair in the middle of the night and every salacious kiss he'd given his mistresses in broad daylight on London's busy streets and the many challenges he'd made to poor blokes who tried to cheat at cards were true and then some. Still, it had surprised him that several members sought to blackball him, since he was heir to the Duke of Drakestone.

Seaton had been the first one to address the group and remind them that they were not to judge applicants. There were only two requirements for joining: Was he the next heir in line to a title, and was he of the age to join? Bray met both requirements, so there were no further arguments.

He and Seaton had been good friends ever since.

But right now, for some reason, Bray didn't want to talk about Miss Prim to Seaton or to anyone. He wanted to relax with a glass of wine and think about her. He wanted to remember what she'd said and how she'd said it. He wanted to know what she had up her sleeve, too, for surely she had something in mind. Young ladies didn't refuse to marry a duke without damn good reason. So what could hers be? Was it that she truly thought he had caused her brother's accident?

He supposed that could be true of a fickle female.

The taproom was noisy and crowded, so he bypassed it and walked into the reading room. It was warm, and most of the big comfortable chairs were empty. He nodded to a couple of gents on his way to a vacant chair in a corner by a crackling fire and ordered a glass of wine to shake off the chill of the late afternoon. He swiped a copy of *The Times* off a nearby table, opened it, and put it in front of his face. That should discourage anyone brave enough from wanting to talk to him.

He wanted to do some serious thinking and find out what had gone wrong. He'd gone to Miss Prim's house with the purpose of telling her they would be married and that he was going to ask the Court of Chancery to appoint a different guardian for her sisters. It was supposed to be so simple. He came out of her house without accomplishing either of those things. First, she had surprised the hell out of him by saying she didn't want to marry him. Then she had the unabashed nerve to tell him she would go to the court and ask them to remove him as their guardian. He was the first one to admit he had no business being anyone's guardian, but he didn't want Miss Prim telling him he couldn't be.

How could he allow that?

Somehow she had managed to outwit him, all the while making it seem as if it wasn't planned on her part.

Bray smiled to himself and chuckled silently. Had she actually called his club "the Heirs' Club of Scoundrels"? She was probably more right than she knew.

Miss Prim was lovely—all the sisters were fetching

in different ways. At first glance, he thought all the girls looked just alike, but later he saw they each had distinguishing features. Miss Bonnie was missing her front teeth, and Miss Lillian had a light sprinkle of freckles across her nose. Miss Gwen was the only one with almond-shaped eyes, and Miss Sybil was the only one with a button nose. And the lovely Miss Louisa Prim was the one who had an inner fire that challenged as well as intrigued him. She had charm when she chose to show it, and she was overflowing with a damned lot of courage.

But he still didn't want to wed her, so why did it bother him that she'd turned down his offer of marriage? That should have pleased him. And would have, but he wasn't used to anyone telling no or refusing him.

After giving it more thought, he decided there was a chance he could use this to his advantage. If he let it be known to the ton that he'd fulfilled his pledge to Nathan Prim and asked for his sister's hand in marriage, but she declined, it would stand to reason that the gossip, rumors, and wagers would cease. The ton would leave him alone, and he'd be free to go about his daily life, still a carefree bachelor but without the constant questions and intrusions about Miss Prim.

He didn't give a damn if everyone in London knew she'd rejected him. He just didn't like her doing it.

That's what rankled.

And that was what he couldn't allow.

"Hiding, Your Grace?"

Bray recognized the voice as the meddlesome Lord Sanburne. The young earl seemed to pride himself on irritating almost everyone he knew. Bray kept the paper before his face and said, "I'm reading."

"I can see that. Do pardon my interruption, but Sir

Roger said he saw you walking up to Lord Wayebury's house and entering it earlier this afternoon. We know Miss Prim has arrived in Town, and we thought perhaps you might have some news you wanted to share with us."

Hellfire! Bray swore silently but remained quiet and still. Lord Sanburne and Sir Roger were at the park the night Nathan Prim had died, and they never let Bray forget that he had an unpaid debt to the man.

"Have you nothing to say?" Lord Sanburne asked, sounding a bit perturbed by Bray's lack of response.

"Where's my wine?"

Lord Sanburne grunted. "I'm not your server!"

"Could you get him for me?"

Bray heard a snicker of laughter. Obviously Lord Sanburne wasn't alone, and it was probably his minion, Sir Roger, with him.

"Certainly not. If you had the decency to remove the newsprint from in front of your face as any other gentleman would, you'd see that it's me, Lord Sanburne, talking to you."

Bray lowered the paper and saw that not only was the fuming Lord Sanburne standing before him, but the nervous Sir Roger Wainwright and Mr. Porter Mercer were staring down at him, too.

Sanburne's eyes opened wide, and he said, "Well, did you or did you not enter Lord Wayebury's house?"

It was Bray's turn to frown. "Are you having me followed?"

Sir Roger laughed, Mr. Mercer sniffed, and Lord Sanburne gasped.

The pompous earl stiffened his tall, lanky frame and grabbed hold of his coat's lapels as if to give him courage. "Absolutely not. Don't be ridiculous. Sir Roger happens to live on that street."

"Begging your pardon, Your Grace, I'm just a few houses down from Lord Wayebury," Sir Roger added.

"And you just happened to be driving by," Bray said, turning his dark gaze on the shortest of the three men before him.

"No, no, Your Grace. Actually, I was walking past," Sir Roger said without apology.

"You truly can't blame us for being curious," Lord Sanburne remarked.

"I can't?"

"Well, perhaps you shouldn't," Sir Roger added, appearing flustered and taking a step back. "The whole Town is talking about Miss Prim's arrival in London last week."

The servant quietly approached and placed Bray's wine on the table beside him. Bray laid down the news-sheet, picked up his drink, and took a sip. So much for quiet moments with his thoughts.

"This has been going on for over two years now. We all have wagers placed here at White's and at other clubs throughout London," Mr. Mercer said, speaking up for the first time.

Mercer was the oldest of the three brave gentlemen standing before him and should know better than to approach a man about something he so obviously had no desire to talk about.

Lord Sanburne folded his arms across his chest and harrumphed. "If you went inside and offered for Miss Prim's hand and plan to marry, we think we have a right to know. That way we can settle our debts by collecting our winnings or paying our losses."

"Your gambling is not my concern, and you would not be wise to continue to pursue this line of conversation with me, Sanburne."

"Well, it's not just me, Your Grace. It's everyone."

Bray had had enough of people worrying him about his duty to Miss Prim. While he took another sip of his drink and pondered the idea of telling all three men exactly where they could shove their curiosity and their wagers, another gentleman walked up and joined the trio. Bray immediately recognized the tall portly man as Mr. Alfred Hopscotch, one of the Prince's attendants. On the occasions Bray had been in the Prince's company, Mr. Hopscotch was always hovering around, ready to do the heir to the throne's bidding.

Bray rose, thinking he was about to see the Prince make a rare appearance at White's.

"Good afternoon, Your Grace, my lord, and gentlemen," Mr. Hopscotch said, and gave a stiff bow toward Bray.

Everyone issued their greetings to the newcomer. It was clear Lord Sanburne didn't know the man well, because he immediately asked him if he had just arrived and if it was still raining.

Mr. Hopscotch politely answered and then, not giving Sanburne opportunity for more questions, he said, "Excuse me for interrupting your conversation, gentlemen. I'm sure it was most important, but I wonder if it might be possible for me to speak to the duke alone for a few minutes."

After the trio grumbled their good-byes, Mr. Hopscotch looked at Bray and said, "I had a devil of a time finding you today, Your Grace. I waited at your home most of the afternoon for your return. I then went to the Heirs' Club because I was told you prefer it to all the other clubs where you hold membership. Finally I gave up and came here, which was obviously the right thing to do."

It struck Bray as odd that the man had gone to such lengths to find him. "I do change my routine from time to time."

"I'll remember that. May I sit down and join you, Your Grace?"

Bray nodded and looked toward the door as they sat down. The Prince was still nowhere in sight, so he questioned, "Will the Prince be joining us?"

"No, no, not this time, but I am here on his behalf."

Interesting.

"What will you drink?" Bray asked.

"Oh, nothing for me," the man said, brushing a hand down the ends of his neckcloth. "I never take a sip when I'm on official business for the Prince."

Official business?

Bray had to admit he was curious. He had talked with the Prince on several occasions and they had even played a few games of cards together, but he couldn't say he knew the man well. The Regent had also sent a personal note of condolence when Bray's father died, but he had never personally sought Bray out before.

"How is the Prince?" Bray asked.

"Well, quite well, but he will be even better once he knows he can count on you."

Bray knew he hadn't stepped into the political realm that was expected of a duke, but there were other pressing matters that needed to be handled first. It was important that he make visits to all his estates and meet with all his managers and collect information on all that he had taken charge of since his father's passing.

"Surely the Prince doesn't doubt my loyalty to the Crown."

"No, of course not, but before we go further, I have to say that anything we discuss must be kept in the strictest of confidences. You understand, don't you?"

"I think the Prince knows that or you wouldn't be here."

"True. The Prince will be glad to hear that." The man smiled. "But it must be said so there is no doubt or future chance for misunderstandings among us."

Bray's curiosity moved over to suspiciousness. What could the Prince possibly want with him?

"Understood."

"Good." Mr. Hopscotch ran his hand down his perfectly tied neckcloth again. "It seems the Prince has wagered on whether or not you will be wed to Miss Prim by the end of the Season."

Bray eyed the man coldly. "I'm told every gentleman in London has placed his bets."

He knew the Prince was an excellent gambler by instinct and a rabid gambler by choice, but he thought the Prince usually stayed away from the bizarre wagers. And Bray put whether or not he would marry Miss Prim into that category.

"When do you plan to marry her?"

"That hasn't been settled," Bray said lightly.

"We know. That's exactly why I'm here. The Prince would like for it to be." He leaned forward and added, "Soon."

Bray grimaced. He didn't like the way the man had said the last word, as if he were giving an order he expected to be obeyed. Bray had never been any good at obeying.

Mr. Hopscotch relaxed in the chair again and continued. "Most definitely before the end of the Season, he would like to see you not just engaged but married to Miss Prim."

"The Prince thinks he has a say in this," Bray said cautiously, his suspicions growing.

The man smiled. "He believes so, yes."

Bray studied the man's eyes, which stayed steady as a rock. "Why?"

Mr. Hopscotch looked around the room as if to make sure no ears were within hearing distance and then said, "He was recently having dinner with the Duke of Norfolk and the Duke of York as well as some other gentlemen. They managed to get a friendly wager going as to whether you would make good on your promise to Lord Wayebury to marry his sister."

Bray remained passive. He thought this visit was political. He'd heard a lot of rumors about the Prince over the years, but he'd always given them a wide-open window of doubt because Bray was very familiar with how far rumors could stray from the truth.

"The Prince should have better things to do with his time than indulge in such frivolities."

"Smirk if you want, Your Grace, but the gossip behind this story of you and Miss Prim is riveting, is it not?"

"Riveting?" Bray laughed.

Mr. Hopscotch shrugged nonchalantly. "There is always drama in a deathbed vow. It is the most talked-about wager in London—and with good reason, is it not?"

"I have no idea," Bray said tightly.

"Perhaps it doesn't take much to amuse Londoners. But you do know what *they* say." The man paused.

Bray deliberately took the bait and said, "No, what do *they* say?"

"A promise made is a debt unpaid, and some people don't think the duke will pay this debt. The Prince happens to think you will. Naturally, he knew your father well and knows you are as honorable as your father. He has no doubt you will do the right thing and wed Miss Prim."

Just so the Prince can win a wager?

Bray knew the Prince's arrogance had few boundaries, but this was actually off the charts.

"If I don't, I'm sure he will recover from the losses," Bray offered.

"It's a bit more complicated than that."

That's what Bray was afraid of. "How so?"

"That isn't for you to know. The Prince will take care of everything else. All you need to do is what you are honor-bound to do anyway, and that is to marry Miss Prim—and by the end of the Season. Can I have your word on that?"

"No," Bray said without hesitating. "I don't make promises anymore. You can tell that to the Prince."

"That is not the answer he wants me to take back to him."

"I understand. But that's it."

Just hours ago, Bray had told Miss Prim she would have to propose to him, so there was no way he was going back to her and asking her once again to marry him. Not even for the Prince. Miss Prim was a strong-minded young lady and would not be easily swayed from her stance or fooled.

"Why?" Mr. Hopscotch held out his hands. "It is a simple matter to you. You live up to your word as your father before you always lived up to his word."

Bray's jaw tightened. He needed no lectures about honor. He'd received enough of them when he was growing up. Besides, he'd done the honorable thing. He'd told Miss Prim he was willing to marry her. She was the one who had other ideas. And he was happy she did.

"I don't take marriage lightly, and neither does Miss Prim."

"Of course. Take your time so long as you make the Prince happy by the end of the Season." Mr. Hopscotch rose. "He wants you to know he will be forever in your debt and at your service should you ever need him. Now, I hope to see proof of your upcoming nuptials in print in the next few days. Good day, Your Grace."

"The devil take it." Bray swore under his breath as he watched the robust man casually walk away as if they had talked about nothing other than the lousy weather. What the hell was the Prince trying to do in strong-arming him about Miss Prim?

Everyone knew Bray wasn't easily intimidated. Not by Mr. Hopscotch or the Prince. But he shouldn't be surprised that the Prince thought he could easily coerce him into doing his bidding, because most people would jump at the chance to please the Prince. They had both better think again. Not even his father had been successful in making Bray do anything he didn't want to do.

He picked up his wine and downed half of it. The Prince would just have to do what every other gentleman did and pay his own gambling debts or suffer the consequences.

Whatever they may be.

Bray had no doubt he could eventually talk Miss Prim into marrying him, but did he want to? At least he now knew she was more than attractive and would not be an unwelcome bedmate. He smiled as he thought of her sparkling blue eyes, tousled sunset-colored hair, and full desirable lips. No, he'd have no problem at all taking Miss Prim into his bedchamber.

Bray looked around the room for a server so he could order another glass of wine and saw Seaton leaning against the doorframe. His arms were folded across his chest, and one foot lay crossed over the other ankle. He looked quite perturbed.

"Oh, hell," Bray whispered to himself. The next time he wanted a drink and a little peace, he'd have to go home to find them.

Chapter 7

Strong reasons make strong actions.
—*King John,* act 3, scene 4

It was a usual start to her day.

Louisa and her sisters were always early to bed and early to rise. That schedule hadn't changed just because they had moved to London. At a young age, Louisa had realized it was better to sleep when it was dark and be up at first light. There were so many more interesting things to be done during the day that couldn't be done at night. She never wanted to waste a minute of daylight sleeping.

During breakfast with her sisters, there was more discourse of the visit from the duke. Louisa had remained quiet and let her sisters talk. It was clear they were a little intimidated by the tall impressive gentleman, even though Sybil insisted she wasn't. Both Gwen and Lillian thought him handsome, and when they looked to Louisa for her agreement, she merely shrugged at first, hoping that would satisfy her thirsty little sisters, but they would not be content. They were too eager to know her thoughts. Later, as they pressed her, she had to admit the duke was quite pleasant to look at, but much too arrogant to be pleasant to talk to.

There was also a discussion about the arrival of the stern-looking Mrs. Ramona Colthrust, whom only Louisa and Gwen had met before the lady shut herself into her room for the evening. Louisa indulged the girls' chattering for a long time, and well after breakfast was finished. It was Mrs. Trumpington who finally shooed them out of the breakfast room so she could start the cleanup.

It was the first day of warm, beautiful sunshine since arriving in London, so Louisa suggested they spend time in the back garden. She gave her sisters the choice of playing games, reading, or joining her to explore the grounds and try to name all the different types of shrubs, plants, and flowers that were budding and getting ready to bloom. The grounds were much smaller than the Wayebury estate, but each girl found something to do.

After the morning's outside entertainment, Louisa sent Lillian and Gwen abovestairs to their makeshift schoolroom on the second floor with Miss Kindred, who swore she was getting too old to go up and down the stairs several times a day. She preferred to always have the girls come to her. Louisa left it up to the governess to decide the assignments for the day, be they lessons in history, mythology, and arithmetic or painting, music, and poetry.

A bright beam of sunlight streamed through the east window in the drawing room, making it the perfect place for Louisa to help Bonnie and Sybil work on their embroidery samples. Bonnie was patient and diligent with her sewing, wanting to make each stitch perfect. Sybil, even though she was two years older than Bonnie, found it difficult to sit still and do her best. She wanted to hurry through her pattern with little care for accuracy, so she could be done with sewing and on to something she enjoyed better than making pretty drawings with thread.

Once Louisa had Bonnie and Sybil busy, she picked up her teacup and walked to the other side of the room. She pushed the drapery panel aside and looked out. There was nothing to view except a little patch of blue sky, a hedgerow of yew, and the upper floors of the house next door. That was all right with Louisa. She really didn't want to look at anything. She wanted to stare and think.

Last week, she and her sisters were living a quiet life in Wayebury. Now, she had a feeling her life would never be so tranquil again, certainly not with the likes of the commanding Duke of Drakestone and the brash Mrs. Colthrust in it.

Last night, Louisa had tried to convince herself she wasn't going to think about the duke—but every time she tried to put her mind on something else, the powerful-looking man would stride right back into her thoughts, looking so dashing with his shiny knee-high boots, his pristine white shirt, and beautifully tied starched neckcloth. It was no wonder he was considered the most eligible bachelor in England. And it had to be on his looks alone, for he didn't have the temperament or the charm to enchant any young lady with his wit. Louisa smiled after she thought that, knowing there wasn't a bit of truth in it. She didn't understand why, but the duke's arrogance held a certain attraction for her.

The front door opened and closed quickly with a bang. It startled Louisa and the girls, who looked up from their embroidery hoops.

Louisa heard loud mutterings from a female voice.

"Back to work, girls," Louisa told her sisters calmly. "I'll go see what this is about."

"I can't believe it! The man refused to see me," Mrs. Colthrust remarked, swishing into the room in a dark pink carriage dress before Louisa had time to set down her teacup. "I don't care if he is a duke. I am responsible for two of his charges. He should have had the decency to put his other work aside and talk to me."

There was no mistaking that Mrs. Colthrust was unhappy, but Louisa wasn't sure if the woman was talking to her or to the room. It was well past noon, and Louisa hadn't seen or heard a peep out of the chaperone, so she had assumed the woman was still resting from her long and arduous journey.

"You've been out already?" Louisa queried.

"Isn't it obvious?" she answered testily, untying the ribbons under her chin. "Of course I've been out. I wanted to see the duke the first thing this morning before he left his house for the day. He brushed me aside as easily as a fly on his cuff. His portly butler told me he was busy and unavailable to speak with me. Ha!"

"I didn't know you had even left the house," Louisa said.

"I think you were in the garden. I told you last night I would see him today and discuss some things with him."

"Yes, I remember," Louisa said calmly. "The tea is still warm. May I pour you a cup?"

"No, don't bother," she said, pulling off her bonnet and tossing it on the settee. "I had chocolate earlier, and that was quite enough."

"I don't believe you've met Bonnie and Sybil. Girls, come meet Mrs. Colthrust."

The girls dutifully put their sewing aside, walked over, and said, "Good morning."

Mrs. Colthrust looked down at them as if she were inspecting something on the ground that she would just as soon step on as over. Without a hint of a smile, she greeted the girls and turned immediately back to Louisa. "I've just decided I must go to the duke's house again. Only, this time, I'm going to take you with me."

"Me?" Louisa asked, confused by the leap in her breath and tightness in her lower abdomen at the prospect of seeing the commanding man again.

"Of course. I should have thought about it before I went. You are his ward. If you need to see him, he can't refuse you. I am merely a chaperone in his eyes and not worthy of his precious time."

Bonnie looked up at them with eager eyes and said, "I want to go. Can I go, too?"

"What?" Mrs. Colthrust responded sharply. "Certainly not. The duke's house is not a place for children."

"How about me?" Sybil asked, looking just as eager as Bonnie. "Can I go? I'm older. I'm old enough to go. Tell her, Sister."

"No, no, stop it, girls," Mrs. Colthrust said, sounding offended that Sybil had asked. "Neither of you may go anywhere but back to your sewing, or embroidery, or whatever it is that you are doing with that needle and hoop."

Louisa watched the exchange, and it tugged at her heart to see Sybil's and Bonnie's happy faces sag to disappointment.

"Wait," Louisa said, feeling sorry for the girls because of Mrs. Colthrust's coldhearted tone. "Perhaps it is not the thing to do that children show up at a duke's home unannounced, but I don't see why they can't ride with us. They are well behaved and will give us no trouble. They haven't left this house or the grounds since we arrived last week. I know they would enjoy

the outing and be happy to wait for us in the carriage—
right, girls?"

"Yes," Bonnie and Sybil squealed in unison, their
expressions turning hopeful once again.

"Not so loud, girls, please!" Mrs. Colthrust said, re-
buking them. "I'm standing right beside you, so you don't
have to scream at me." She turned to Louisa. "You are
very free with the funds, my dear. Do you know how
much extra it will cost to have a carriage wait for us?"

Louisa didn't care at the moment. "I'll pay it," she
said firmly.

Mrs. Colthrust stared down at Bonnie's and Sybil's
eager-looking faces. Suddenly a smile stretched across
her face and a wicked gleam shone in her coal dark
eyes. Louisa was astounded at how quickly the chaperone's expression changed from scowling to a look of
victory.

"You two have just given me a wonderful idea! Of
course you can go. Fetch your bonnets and capes."

Bonnie and Sybil immediately dashed toward the
door. "Girls," Louisa called to them. "What do you say
before you leave this room?"

"Thank you, Mrs. Colthrust!" they yelled at the
same time, and went racing out the door.

Mrs. Colthrust looked back to Louisa, still smiling. "I
just had another superb idea. We will all go. As you said,
the girls need an outing and I will tell that to the duke.
Get the other three girls. I'll teach His Grace a lesson he
won't soon forget. After I show up at his house with all
of you under my wing, I guarantee you he will see me
next time when I go alone."

Louisa shook her head, exasperated. "There are two
other girls, Mrs. Colthrust. There are five of us total."
And Louisa wasn't at all sure she wanted her sisters

to be used as pawns in whatever Mrs. Colthrust had planned for the duke.

"Yes, well, of course—you know that's what I meant."

Louisa doubted that, but let the matter drop and said, "Why do you want to see the duke? I thought everything was settled yesterday."

"Not by me. I want to make sure he does right by me—us. I mean you and Gwen, of course, mostly. Besides, I will not have him treating me so shabbily as to turn me away from his door without so much as a glimpse of him."

"But he said he'd take care of everything," Louisa reminded her.

"Ha! He is a man, and I'm sure there are things he hasn't thought about. He must know that we will need a coach immediately to take us to the shops. He should have had one delivered and had it waiting here for when you arrived. It's much too far to walk to the shops, and without a maid to carry our packages. I don't even want to consider how we could manage. Servants! We must have servants to do things for us. Hiring a coach as we must do today is simply too much trouble. So go get your bonnet and your sisters, and we will be on our way. He will deal with me like it or not, even if he is a duke."

If His Grace didn't want to see them, he would not. Mrs. Colthrust may not know that but Louisa did. It was obvious that Mrs. Colthrust had never met the Duke of Drakestone. He was no ordinary man. Everything about him spoke of power, privilege, and wealth. He was a pleasing man to look at, for sure, but in the short time she'd spent with him yesterday, Louisa gathered that the duke took orders from no one.

Louisa left the room with Mrs. Colthrust still muttering about His Grace. If only the laws allowed Louisa to be responsible for her sisters so she didn't have to deal with Mrs. Colthrust or the duke, she would be a very happy lady.

Half an hour later, Mrs. Colthrust, Louisa, and her sisters were seated in the Duke of Drakestone's drawing room. Lillian and Gwen flanked their chaperone on one settee, and Louisa was between Sybil and Bonnie on the other. All the girls were quiet as mice, taking in the elaborate grandeur of their surroundings.

The furniture was upholstered in expensive, well-textured fabrics, and the tops to all the tables had a glimmering beeswax gleam. Vaulted ceilings were trimmed in moldings and fretwork that were edged in gilt. Each wall was adorned with paintings, sconces, and baroque framed mirrors. Louisa had never seen so much luxury displayed in one place.

"Mrs. Colthrust, Miss Prim," the duke said as he strode through the doorway.

All the females jumped to their feet and curtsied.

His Grace stopped and hesitated for a moment as he looked at Louisa's sisters standing like little soldiers behind her. Clearly he was taken aback by the girls' presence, and Louisa wondered if he might throw them all out of his house without a backward glance. But as she stared at him, she detected a chink in his steady armor. She realized he was trying hard to remember the girls' names.

She was pleased that he wanted to, but was convinced he wouldn't even get two of them correct. She wouldn't be surprised if he didn't even know what *her* first name was. But just as the smile spread fully across her face and she was feeling quite pleased with herself for figuring out his dilemma, he bowed to her sisters and said, "Miss Gwen, Miss Lillian, Miss Sybil, and Miss Bonnie. All of you are looking lovely today."

Louisa was impressed that he'd somehow managed to get all her sisters' names correct. Her heart started beating a little faster as she looked at the handsome duke. His black, fine wool coat stretched perfectly over his broad shoulders and back. His pale red waistcoat with its leather-coated buttons fit seamlessly over his flat stomach, enhancing his slim hips and his long, powerful-looking legs. Her gaze stopped at his casually tied neckcloth. She didn't know why, but suddenly she had the strong desire to reach up, untie the cloth, and slowly unwind it.

His gaze met Louisa's, and he said, "This is an unexpected visit."

Louisa's cheeks heated and she prayed the duke had no idea what she'd been thinking.

Mrs. Colthrust stepped forward, not giving Louisa time to respond, and said, "How can it be unexpected when I was just here not more than an hour ago, trying to see you?"

"Exactly." He gave the chaperone an indulgent smile. "I thought Mr. Tidmore made it clear I was busy today and couldn't see you, but that I was making the arrangements you needed."

"Thank you for that, Your Grace, but being a gentleman, you can't possibly know what a woman would need to be properly prepared for a Season in London."

"True, however, I knew my mother would be very knowledgeable, so I enlisted her help."

Mrs. Colthrust's demeanor changed in an instant. She smiled pleasantly. "Your mother, Her Grace?" Mrs. Colthrust said softly, obviously surprised and happy about the information. "Oh, my."

"Yes. She is out right now, seeing that accounts are being set up in your name so that all your needs will be met. I'll see that a list is delivered later today."

"That's so very kind of her to help me—I mean us. Yes, yes, I'm sure Her Grace knows the best shops in all of London. We'll be in excellent hands with her help. Thank you, Your Grace, but—" Mrs. Colthrust rubbed her gloved hands together nervously. "—there is also the matter of servants? Miss Prim and her five sisters have been making do with only a cook and a governess ever since they arrived."

"Four, Mrs. Colthrust," Louisa interjected under her breath. "I have four sisters."

"Yes, of course, dear, I'm sure that's what I said. We'll get them all maids, won't we, Your Grace? You see, though I'm ashamed to admit it, my sister's husband saw fit to take every servant but the cook with them."

Louisa looked at the duke and said, "One maid will be sufficient for us. We are used to helping each other."

The duke gave her a slow, easy appraisal with his questioning gaze. She felt her skin being peppered with little goose bumps that sent delicious sensations through her body.

"However many you wish, Miss Prim," he said.

"The cook will need a scullery maid as well," Mrs. Colthrust added. "And I must insist we have our own coach-and-four."

"It's been ordered and will be delivered to Lord Wayebury's address later this afternoon, along with a driver and a groom," he said. "A housekeeper is being interviewed in the kitchen right now. Perhaps you would like to go meet her, Mrs. Colthrust, and give your opinion as to her qualifications?"

Mrs. Colthrust seemed to grow two inches as her shoulders went back and her chin lifted triumphantly. Her voice softened again as she said, "Why, yes, Your Grace, yes. I'd like that very much."

"Good. Come with me." The duke went to the door and called, "Mr. Tidmore, come here."

An older, rotund gentleman with thinning gray hair appeared in the doorway. Louisa couldn't hear what the duke said to the butler, but Mrs. Colthrust followed him out of the room as if she were walking behind the Prince himself.

His Grace strode back to where Louisa stood in front of her sisters and said, "Are you smiling at me, Miss Prim?"

She didn't realize she was until he'd asked, but readily admitted, "Yes, I believe I am."

"To what do I owe the honor?"

"I'm not sure it's an honor, but I think Mrs. Colthrust almost got the best of you."

"Really?"

"Yes."

"No, you don't."

A tempting roguish grin lifted the corners of his mouth, and Louisa's breathing became shallow and fast. Her heart thudded loudly in her ears. When he looked at her like that, for some ridiculous reason it thrilled her. She was aware her sisters were standing not far behind her, so she stepped a little closer to him and, lowering her voice, asked, "Are you saying I'm fibbing?"

"That's putting it a little nicer than I was actually thinking, but, yes."

"I did say Mrs. Colthrust *almost* got the best of you."

"Still a prevarication," he said.

"If so, not by much," she argued.

The duke laughed softly. "I'm glad you came back with your chaperone."

"Really?" She smiled some more. "Me and all *five* of my sisters."

Again, he grinned. "It takes a while to get the names and the number right. But, when I woke this morning, I had wondered if you were really as lovely as I remember you being yesterday. And you are."

His compliment made Louisa feel shy. She lowered her lashes over her eyes. "Now you are prevaricating, Your Grace."

"If so, not by much."

"What are you talking about?" Bonnie asked from behind Louisa.

The duke looked at Bonnie and said, "I was just asking Miss Prim if she thought—"

A loud clatter sounded behind Louisa, startling her. She turned to see Sybil standing by a table, wide-eyed with fear, clasping her hands together under her chin.

"What happened?" Louisa asked.

"I didn't mean to drop it," Sybil said. "I promise I didn't mean to."

Louisa's heart jumped to her throat and she rushed over to where Sybil stood. Louisa looked on the floor for whatever her sister had dropped but didn't see anything.

"Sybil, what did you touch?" she asked.

"Did it break?" Sybil asked, her bottom lip trembling as big tears quickly welled up in her eyes. "I didn't mean to, Sister," she said again, flinging her arms around Louisa's waist. Sybil buried her face against Louisa's chest and started crying loudly.

The duke frowned as he walked up to them. "What's wrong with her?" he asked. "Why is she crying?"

"She's frightened."

"What about?"

"She didn't keep her hands to herself and she broke something but I'm not sure what."

He looked around the floor. "No. Look, it's not broken." He reached down and picked up a brass handle that looked to be about a foot long. "See, there's no need to be crying like that."

"But she's upset," Louisa explained, rubbing Sybil's back while she boo-hooed louder. "She knows she shouldn't have touched whatever it is and she's in trouble for doing so."

The creases in the duke's forehead deepened. "Why would she be in trouble when it's not broken? And I don't understand her crying when she's not in trouble."

Louisa wasn't sure she understood the duke either. "Perhaps that is because it is you who doesn't understand young girls, Your Grace."

"That is a given, Miss Prim, because, good Lord, this is nothing to cry about."

Louisa gasped. "Did you just swear in front of the girls?"

"What?" The duke looked incredulously at her. "What? No. I mean saying 'good Lord' is not swearing."

Louisa placed her hands over the ears of the sniffling Sybil, and Gwen put her hands over Bonnie's ears. "You said it again."

"I did not, I mean—" He stopped and gave Louisa a deep, penetrating stare that let her know in no uncertain terms he thought she was being unquestionably harsh about her stance.

Her back stiffened.

He relented and said testily, "Then pardon me for my language, ladies."

Louisa was sure that was not what the duke first intended to say. "I think we should wait out in the carriage for Mrs. Colthrust to finish," Louisa said.

The duke touched her upper arm. "Wait."

Louisa looked down at his hand on her arm. His grip

was warm, firm, and gentle, and yet strangely posses-
sive. His expression had softened a little, but she still
couldn't believe he'd actually touched her.

He removed his hand and said, "Do you mind staying a little longer? I want to show the girls something."

She hesitated.

"Something appropriate," he added.

She didn't know if she could trust him until the corner of his mouth twitched with a smile. She felt herself
weakening and she knew that couldn't be a good sign.

"I'll watch what I say."

Louisa finally said, "Very well."

"Miss Sybil?" he asked. She lifted her head and looked
at him with a terrified expression. "Everything is all
right," he said softly. "There is no reason to be frightened
or upset, because you are not in any trouble. Can you dry
your tears for me?"

She nodded and wiped her eyes and her cheeks with
the backs of her hands.

"Do you know what this is?" he asked, and held up
the instrument she'd dropped.

She shook her head.

"It is a handle, a crank, and it's made of brass," he
said. "It would be very difficult for anyone to break
brass. Though it makes a lot of noise if it hits wood.
Like this." He knocked the handle on the table a couple
of times to show her.

"I'm glad it's not broken," Louisa whispered. "Sybil,
why would you touch anything in this house? You know
better."

"She has to touch everything," Bonnie said.

"I do not," Sybil complained. "Tell her I don't touch
everything."

"That's enough from both of you," Louisa said. "Now,
Sybil, what do you want to tell the duke?"

Sybil turned to the duke and said, "I'm sorry, Your Grace. I'm glad it's not broken. Does that mean you aren't angry with me?"

He leaned down and gave her a half smile and said, "I wouldn't have been angry even if something had been broken. There's nothing in this house I can't replace. So no more crying, all right?" He held up the crank for her to see. "Do you want to know what this is for?"

"Yes, please."

"I want to know, too," Bonnie said.

The duke looked over to where the other girls had stayed motionless, fearing that Sybil was in big trouble, and he said to them, "Would you young ladies like to see and hear a music box? Come let me show you one that just arrived from India."

"I love music," Lillian said, and took a tentative step toward him.

"Then come on over. Don't be afraid. Come on, all of you. No one is in trouble." He looked at Louisa and said, "And no one is going to get punished, right?"

Louisa looked from the duke to Sybil and said, "Not this time. I think Sybil has learned her lesson. Now, the rest of you go see what he wants to show you."

The girls joined His Grace by a table in the corner that held an intricately carved chest fashioned with inlay of mother-of-pearl on the top and sides. They all watched while he attached the brass handle to the chest and gave it several turns. He then opened the lid. A pleasant tune played as small lifelike figurines rotated around inside the box. The girls were awed by it. They had seen music boxes before, but never ones with movements.

"See? Still works and it's not broken," he said, looking at Sybil and then over to Louisa. He smiled at her.

Sybil gave him a beaming smile and then gave her attention back to the music box.

When the music and mechanism stopped, Louisa was surprised at how patiently the duke showed Gwen how to turn the crank and start it playing again. He didn't seem the least bit annoyed when he had to let Lillian, Sybil, and Bonnie wind the music box and let it play, too.

When it came around to Gwen's turn again to start the music box, the duke looked at Louisa and motioned with his head for her to follow him to the other side of the room.

"That was very kind of you not to be angry at Sybil and to show the girls your music box. I can tell they are fascinated with it."

"Does that mean I'm forgiven for using foul language in front of the girls?"

"I suppose we are all raised with a different set of values as to what is appropriate and what isn't for children."

"Something tells me our childhoods were vastly different, Miss Prim and Proper."

She started to make a retort about his nickname but on second thought decided to let it pass because he'd been so kind to Sybil and shown the girls the music box.

"Yes," she said. "Starting with you being an only child and me coming from a family of six children."

"And you being the daughter of a vicar and me being the son of a duke who encouraged me to have no boundaries."

Louisa heard a dog bark and turned around to see her brother's dog leap into Bonnie's arms. The little girl squealed with delight, and the other girls gathered around them, giggling and screaming with joy, too, as they pushed and shoved to get their hands on the dog.

The duke flinched from the hysterical sounds, and

his face twisted into a frown. "Good Lord . . . night—what's all the commotion about?"

"It's Saint," Louisa whispered, almost not believing her eyes. She looked up at the duke. "It's Nathan's dog."

Chapter 8

Fetter strong madness in a silken thread.
—*Much Ado About Nothing,* act 5, scene 1

Bray had shuddered when Miss Bonnie's shrill scream came out of nowhere and for no reason. When the other girls joined in, it became madness for a few moments.

"I know who the dog is," Bray answered Miss Prim noticing that the spaniel's coat was very much the color of the girls' hair.

The high-pitched squealing and laughter along with the barking rattled his eardrums. How could such sweet-looking females make such ear-piercing, inhuman sounds?

All Bray saw was a blur of blond hair, blue eyes, and sprigged muslin dresses falling to the floor in a tumble of happiness. Saint was tangled among them, barking, jumping from one sister to the other, licking their faces as the girls fought to pet, stroke, and hug him. Clearly the dog knew and loved the sisters, too.

Without warning, Miss Prim rounded on him, a glare blazing in her eyes. "You are a beast!"

Her words were almost a hiss, but Bray remained calm even though there was no denying the gorgeous blonde standing in front of him looked as if she were ready to put a dagger in his heart.

"I suppose I've been called worse," he remarked, wondering what in the hell he could have said this time that offended her so drastically.

She advanced on him. If it was possible for a beautiful lady to look menacing, she did. "Why did you keep him from us?"

Bray gave her a questioning look. "What? The dog? Saint?"

"Yes."

"I didn't keep him from you."

"You did!" she said earnestly. "You knew we wanted our brother's dog."

There was no mistaking the anger in her voice or her expression. He was beginning to get an idea where her fury was coming from, but he didn't understand it.

And he didn't like it.

"How could I have known that, Miss Prim?"

She inched even closer to him, her eyes fixed solidly on his. "After Nathan's death, our uncle tried to find Saint for us. He searched the streets and the parks. He asked everyone, which would have included you and your friends, and no one knew what had happened to Nathan's dog."

So now he understood the full extent and reason behind her anger.

Bray had always been good at hiding his emotion, until he met Miss Prim. She could get under his skin and rile him faster than the most skillful card cheat.

This time he stepped closer to her, placing his body and his face near hers. "Your brother asked me to take care of him."

"For us, until you could get him to us."

"That's not what he said," Bray answered tightly.

"He shouldn't have had to tell you that's what he expected. You should have known he would want his little sisters to have his dog."

"I didn't."

"Then that doesn't make you a beast—it makes you a monster."

It was getting harder for Bray not to show any emotion. She was deliberately accusing him of withholding something from little girls. She might as well have put a knife in his back.

"I might very well be a monster, a beast, or a monstrous beast, Miss Prim, but I don't steal dogs and keep them from children."

"But you did."

"I didn't know I was," he said again, bringing his face even nearer—so close to hers, their noses almost touched. He didn't know how he was managing to keep his voice so low.

"How could you have not known?"

Bray didn't mind being blamed for anything he'd ever done that was wrong. Everyone knew there had been plenty over the years, and he'd readily own up to any of it. But he didn't like being accused of something he didn't do. If Lord Wayebury or anyone had asked him about the dog, he would gladly have turned him over to the sisters.

Miss Prim's sparkling blue eyes searched his with intensity. "You mean you really didn't think we might want Nathan's dog?"

No, I didn't. It never crossed my mind. I would have been happy to send him to you.

Bray watched tears gather in her eyes. Her anger had melted into pain. This had wounded her deeply. He was surprised at how quickly her anger had turned to sorrow. His heart constricted, and he fought to keep his emotions under control.

She was the most infuriating young lady he had ever met, and those girls could screech to the high heavens, but he wouldn't deliberately cause any of them pain.

What could he say? That he wasn't used to thinking about siblings or dogs? Hell, he wasn't used to thinking about anyone but himself. He glanced at the loud merriment as the girls and Saint renewed their friendship. Blast it all, he could see how the girls loved the dog, and Saint was overjoyed at their reunion, too.

"How the hell was I to have known?"

She gasped.

"'Hell' is a biblical word, Miss Prim and Proper," he said quickly, "and I won't apologize for using it in front of you. Lord Wayebury asked me to take care of the spaniel, just as he asked me to marry you."

Her intake of breath was more like a gulp. "So, Saint has been a chore to you. Just as your word to my brother to marry me was a chore that you have ignored all these years."

"Two years." Bray gritted his teeth. This miss didn't know when to stop. "You, I ignored, but I took care of the dog."

"Sister, look, it's Saint," Miss Bonnie said, heading their way, clutching the dog, who was really too heavy and too big for her to carry in her arms.

Miss Prim spun away from him and lovingly rubbed her hand down her sister's warm blond curls. "Yes, I see."

"Can we keep him? Can we take him home?" Miss Bonnie asked hopefully as the other sisters crowded behind her.

"I can help take care of him," Miss Lillian offered.

"I'll walk him in the mornings," Miss Sybil said.

"I guess that means I will take him for a stroll in the afternoons," Miss Gwen added.

Bray's throat felt thick, and damn, but he hated the emotion that had caused it. He wished he'd thought to send them the dog.

"Girls," Miss Prim said, "he now belongs to—"

"You," Bray interrupted her. "Of course he's yours. Take him. He's been waiting for you. It's about time you came to London to get him."

The girls' peals of laughter and screeching split the air again. Saint barked. Bonnie thrust the spaniel into Louisa's hands and then swung around and threw her arms around Bray's waist. He flinched and then cringed inwardly because he knew Miss Prim had seen him flinch. He held his hands and arms out to his side. The little girl's hug was so unexpected, he froze.

Bray had never felt such small, gentle arms around him before. They were squeezing him with earnestness, but he had no idea what to do. Miss Bonnie placed her warm cheek against his midriff. Suddenly he felt as if she were squeezing his heart, too. Warm, compassionate feelings rose up in him, and he didn't know what to do about them. He fought the desire to hug Bonnie close and tell her he'd never meant to hurt them, but years of training kept him from acting on the gut-wrenching feelings, and he didn't touch the child.

If their uncle had truly been looking for the dog, asking about his whereabouts, he would have known Bray had Saint. There were more than a dozen men with them the night of the accident, and it was talked about in all the clubs and written about for months. Hell, it was still talked about. There was no way Lord Wayebury couldn't have found out where Saint was if he'd tried.

The viscount must simply have lied to the Prim sisters.

Bray didn't like that.

Now he had another reason for wanting to find the coward and put the fear of God in him.

Miss Bonnie looked up at Bray with the happiest blue eyes and widest snaggletoothed smile he'd ever seen. She turned him loose and said, "Thank you for finding him for us, Your Grace."

Bray looked over at Louisa. Saint licked her chin and she laughed and smiled lovingly at the dog while she hugged him and brushed her hand softly down his blond coat. Those old feelings of remorse from the night Nathan Prim died rose up in Bray and threatened to choke him. Silently he winced and swallowed them down.

Damn Miss Prim and her sisters for making him experience emotions that had been so easy to bury in the past.

"Mrs. Woolwythe will be a lovely addition to our home, Your Grace," Mrs. Colthrust said as she floated back into the room, smiling broadly. "Mr. Tidmore picked an excellent choice from the agency, and she can start by the end of the week."

Miss Sybil grabbed Saint from Miss Prim, and the girls ran over to show Mrs. Colthrust the dog. The chaperone put her hands up in front of her and backed away. "No, no—please, girls. Get him away from me. I'm not fond of dogs and don't want him near me."

"But His Grace said we could have him," Miss Sybil said.

"He's going to come live with us," Miss Bonnie added.

"Oh, no, my dears, I'm afraid that won't work," Mrs. Colthrust said coldly. "Not in our house, he won't."

"But the duke—"

"Well, then, His Grace can keep you and the dog," Mrs. Colthrust said, interrupting Miss Lillian. "I'm afraid half a dozen girls is all I can take care of in one household. There is no room for pets."

"No, he's ours," Miss Bonnie said, and burst into tears. "Tell him, Sister."

Bray's throat thickened again.

"He's our brother's dog," Miss Sybil cried. "You can't force us to give him up!"

"They keep Saint," Bray said firmly at the same time that Miss Prim said, "We keep Saint."

Mrs. Colthrust threw back her shoulders and lifted her chin high. "Lord Wayebury—"

"Is no longer in charge, Mrs. Colthrust," Bray cut in. "I am. Now, you can remain or you can go. Your choice. But Saint stays with the children."

Bray turned to Louisa. Her look of pain had been replaced with an expression of gratitude.

He felt a small measure of satisfaction for having done something right.

Chapter 9

Young in limbs, in judgment old.
—*The Merchant of Venice,* act 2, scene 7

"And the little boy promised he would never run away again."

Louisa closed the book and looked down at Bonnie's sweet face, over to Sybil's peaceful expression, and then down to the foot of the bed, where Saint lay curled. They were all asleep. After all the excitement of finding Nathan's dog and then playing with him in the back garden until dark, Louisa thought it would take the girls a long time to settle down and fall asleep. She had been wrong. She was less than five pages into the story when she noticed the squirming and sighing had ceased, but she kept reading. It was soothing and peaceful to read aloud into the quietness.

She slowly rose from the bed and reached over to blow out the candle. Saint had raised his head and was looking at her. "Lie back down and go back to sleep," she whispered. He paid her no mind and started to rise.

"Stay," she said in a stronger voice, and held her hand out as if to stop him.

Saint immediately lay back down but kept his head up and his dark, watchful eyes alert to her every movement.

"Stay," she said again. "You must stay with the girls."

He turned to look at the girls at the head of the bed, and then—as if satisfied that he had a job to do—he placed his head on his front paws.

Louisa knew Bonnie and Sybil would be upset if Saint were gone from their room when they woke in the morning. She blew out the candle and quietly left the room, closing the door behind her.

The light was still on in Mrs. Colthrust's and in Gwen and Lillian's bedchambers as she walked by. It was still rather sad to Louisa that the older girls no longer wanted her to come in and say good night to them. Gwen insisted long ago that they were much too old to be read to or tucked in, and Louisa had reluctantly agreed.

It had been dark for quite some time, but she wasn't sleepy. She decided to go belowstairs and read in the sitting room before dressing for bed. She had so much on her mind, and reading might help get her thoughts off the maddening Duke of Drakestone so she could get a peaceful night's slumber.

She took her book from the secretary where she kept it and made herself comfortable in one of the upholstered wing chairs near the fireplace. The coals had been banked over an hour ago, but there was still a little warmth issuing from the bricks. She pulled her feet up under her and opened the book. She stared at the page but didn't read past the first paragraph before the duke filled her thoughts once again.

Louisa knew His Grace was a scoundrel long before she had ever met him. Still, she didn't want to believe him capable of deliberately keeping Saint from them. But what other explanation could there be?

She supposed he might just have been too busy to think that Nathan's sisters would want his pet? The Duke of Drakestone was obviously a powerful and wealthy man. It was safe to assume he always had people demanding his attention, and mountains of work to do to ensure that his managers and overseers took proper care of his estates, properties, horses, and the like. Even Nathan, who had far less lands and fewer companies than the duke, had to give a certain amount of time each month to looking over account books and ledgers, reading correspondence, and meeting with gentlemen about different kinds of businesses.

And perhaps her uncle had to bear part of the blame. He'd sworn to her he looked high and low for Saint, but now she was questioning whether he'd made every possible effort, as he claimed. If her uncle was capable of turning their guardianship over to the duke—and leaving the country without telling her—then no doubt he was capable of stretching the truth about how diligently he had looked for Nathan's dog.

And now that the heat of the moment had passed and she'd had time to get over the shock of finding Saint alive, she was more inclined to forgive the duke for not trying to get the pet to them. She couldn't get it out of her mind that although he'd kept his emotions tightly under control, it bothered him when she'd accused him of deliberately keeping the spaniel from them. When Louisa accused His Grace of ignoring Saint as he had her for the past two years, his eyes had twitched slightly.

"Good," she said out loud. She wanted to know that he felt some guilt or shame or something because Nathan had lost his life.

She couldn't be too upset with the duke. He had kept Saint safe for them. If he'd been left in the park as she once believed, they would never have seen him again.

Earlier, when Sybil and Bonnie climbed into bed, Saint had jumped up and immediately gone to the foot of the bed and lay down as if he'd been doing it all his life. Of course, he'd done that with Nathan. Louisa couldn't help but wonder if the duke had let Saint sleep on the foot of his bed, too.

She remembered him saying, "You, I ignored, but I took care of the dog." And from all appearances, he had. She could see that Saint was well fed and washed often because of his shiny coat.

"So now, Your Grace, I know that you take better care of your dogs than you do young ladies," she mumbled to herself. "This doesn't surprise me in the least, given your scandalous reputation and your obvious dislike of small children."

That was another reason why she couldn't consider marrying him. Though she did smile and chuckle a little at the thought he might be worried that she would one day actually ask him to marry her. If she ever wanted to put a scare in him, she was sure that a marriage proposal would do it. She was convinced he didn't want to marry her any more than she wanted to wed him.

Louisa laughed softly to herself again when she thought of how the duke had flinched when Bonnie squealed with high-pitched happiness. She had to admit, Bonnie's voice seemed to be higher than that of most little girls, and it *was* ear-piercing, but Louisa was used to it.

He had been completely at a loss for what to do when Bonnie hugged him, and he hadn't known what to say when Sybil was crying over the dropped music box handle. Obviously he wasn't used to emotional little girls. He hadn't had a clue how to handle Sybil's tears or receive and appreciate Bonnie's gratitude.

Now that she thought about it, she didn't think he knew anything about girls.

Louisa knew from her brother and father that men didn't handle situations the way a female would. They were more stoic and less inclined to show their happiness or sadness, though the duke seemed to be much stiffer around children than any other man she'd ever seen. Whenever Bonnie or any of the sisters had hugged her father and brother, they knew how to accept the girls' affection and hug them back.

Too, Louisa was having a difficult time sorting out why she felt the way she did whenever the duke was near her. No, he didn't have to be near her; all she had to do was see him, or just think about him as she was doing right now, and she started feeling strange sensations in parts of her body that had never been awakened before. And during the midst of their heated argument, when once again his face had been so close to hers, why did she have a great urge to feel his lips on hers? That was exasperating—shocking, too. She wasn't sure she even liked the man. He was impatient, arrogant, and formidable, not to mention overbearing and infuriating.

And he doesn't like children!

Still, as much as she hated to admit it to herself, there was no denying she was attracted to him. She remembered feeling his breath against her cheek when he'd vehemently denied keeping the dog from them. With a snap, she closed the book and laid it on her lap. She shut her eyes and laid her head against the back of the chair. She wanted to rest, relax, and summon the delicious tingling that swept across her breasts and tightened them whenever he was near.

Oh yes, she wanted to experience that again.

"Sister."

Louisa jumped. Her eyes popped open and her book fell to the floor even though she immediately recognized Gwen's voice. Thank goodness she hadn't been speaking her thoughts out loud. "Gwen, Lillian, I didn't hear you come belowstairs."

"We didn't mean to startle you," Gwen said, brushing her long, golden hair over her shoulders to her back.

"No, you didn't," Louisa said, picking up her book.

"Were you sleeping?"

"Ah, no, I thought you would have been asleep by now. I was just deep in thought about something and not expecting to hear a voice. What are you two doing down here?"

"May we talk with you about something?" Gwen asked.

"Of course." Louisa put her feet on the floor and said, "Come sit by me and tell me what's on your mind."

"I'd rather stand," Gwen said.

"I'll stand, too," Lillian added.

An uneasy feeling washed over Louisa as she stared at her very grown-up-looking sisters in their long white nightrails, their long curls caressing their shoulders. Lillian held her hands behind her back and swung back and forth, fidgeting as was her habit when she was upset about something. Gwen played with the ends of the ribbon that held her gown together, and she sniffed and twitched her nose nervously.

"All right," Louisa said, feeling the need to rise, too, but she forced herself to remain seated and calm. Something had disturbed them, but what? Was it about Saint, the visit to the duke's house, or something else? "What do you want to talk about?"

"Is it true you are going to marry the duke and leave

us with Mrs. Colthrust?" The words tumbled so quickly from Lillian's mouth that Louisa wasn't sure she'd heard her correctly.

"What?" Louisa jumped up.

"You weren't supposed to just blurt it out like that," Gwen said, chastising Lillian.

"Well, I want to know if she's leaving us," Lillian demanded.

"I do, too," Gwen argued with her. "But next time, you'd better stick to our plan or I'll be mad with you."

"Stop this nonsense," Louisa said, looking at her bickering sisters. "The answer is no. No, of course that's not true. Where did you get such an idea as this?"

"When you were reading to Bonnie and Sybil and getting them ready for bed, Mrs. Colthrust came into our room to make sure the dog wasn't in our room."

"And she told us," Lillian said, piping up to finish for Gwen.

"How dare that woman!" Louisa said, wanting to stomp up to Mrs. Colthrust's bedchamber immediately and take her to task for telling the girls that and scaring them. How dare she meddle in something that was none of her business?

"Tell me everything she said," Louisa prompted.

"She said she didn't want Saint sleeping in our room, because her room is right next to ours. She was afraid she'd hear him whimpering and howling during the night."

"He doesn't howl." Louisa seethed with anger as her hands curled into fists. "She will not dictate where Saint sleeps or anything else. I will speak to her about this to-morrow morning, so consider that settled. Now, what did she have to say about me leaving you?"

Gwen and Lillian looked at each other before Gwen said, "She said that before Nathan died that night of the accident, he made the Duke of Drakestone promise he'd marry you, and that you needed to go ahead and marry him so it would be one less girl for her and Lord Wayebury to take care of."

"Oh, I can't believe she said that to you," Louisa said, her fury rising. "And it's not as if she is taking care of me or any of you."

"So it's not true," Gwen said.

"No," Louisa said softly, and then quickly added, "Well, I mean yes. No, only part of it is true."

"So you are leaving us!" Lillian cried out in distress as tears sprang to her eyes.

"No, I'm not leaving you." Louisa wrapped her arms around Lillian and hugged her close. Her thin body shook with sobs. Louisa's heart broke for her sister. First thing tomorrow morning, she and Mrs. Colthrust were going to have a reckoning. Louisa looked over Lillian's head to Gwen. Thankfully, she didn't look so upset as her sister. "Hush now. It's true what Nathan asked of the duke, but I'm not going to marry him."

"Why won't you, if that's what Nathan wanted you to do?" Lillian asked between sobs.

"Yes, Nathan must have had a good reason to do it," Gwen added.

Louisa could see that both the girls were hurting, and she wanted to take their pain away. Sometimes the whole truth was difficult to explain, but she had to try. She understood their fear. They had lost their mother shortly after Bonnie was born. Their father died less than three years later, and then their brother just over two years ago. It was only natural for them to be upset at the thought of losing her, too.

"Raise your head and look at me, Lillian. Stop crying so you can understand what I'm going to say."

Lillian sniffled and raised her head. She raked the

back of her hand across her damp cheeks, and Louisa brushed tangled curls away from her face.

"First, I would never leave any of you." Louisa looked at both girls. "You will each marry one day. Gwen, you might even marry this year and leave me, but I will always be here. So that is settled, right?"

They nodded.

"Now, I don't know everything, as I wasn't there the night Nathan died, but I'll tell you what I know."

The girls sat on one of the settees, but Louisa remained standing. She started at the beginning when she first received the letter from the Duke of Drakestone telling her that he had been with her brother when he was killed in a carriage accident. She left out the duke's insensitive words saying that Nathan had asked him to marry her, and if after a year of mourning, she thought it might be something she'd want to consider, she should feel free to get in touch with him.

"The duke wrote few words of comfort in his correspondence," she replied honestly. "They were terse. He said when it was clear Nathan couldn't recover from his injuries, he had asked that the duke marry me."

Louisa hated thinking about the afternoon she received the letter from the duke. And it was even days after the duke's letter arrived that she received one from her uncle saying he was bringing Nathan home for burial. She vowed that day that her sisters were her responsibility and she would take care of them.

"Does the duke want to take care of all of us?" Lillian asked.

"Does he want to?" Louisa repeated her words and studied over them briefly. Deciding to be completely truthful with them, she answered, "Of course not, Lillian. How could he? He doesn't know us or love us. But he felt honor-bound to offer because Nathan asked him and he agreed. I believe it was unfair of our brother to ask that of him. I'm sure Nathan wanted us to be cared for in the best possible way and he must have felt the duke could do that better than our uncle. But we have been fine and happy without the duke's help, haven't we?"

"Yes," Lillian said, "but if you married him, you would still take care of us, right?"

Louisa smiled, realizing the situation was difficult for her to understand. "I will always take care of you. I am not going to marry the duke, but if I were to marry him or anyone else, it would be under the condition that all my sisters come with me." She stopped. "You know, I am older and more set in my ways than the rest of you. It may take me longer than either of you to find a husband, but all of you will be with me until the time that you marry and move into your house with your very own husband."

"Why aren't you going to marry the duke?" Gwen asked. "He's very handsome, and who wouldn't want to marry a duke?"

"The duke deserves the opportunity to choose his own bride. I want to pick my own husband. Just as when the parties and balls start in a few weeks, Gwen, you will want to pick your husband. You won't let me choose the man you will marry, will you?"

She grinned. "Of course I won't, so don't you even try."

"And you will feel the same way one day, Lillian. And neither did we want Nathan choosing for us whom we should marry. There was a time when a young lady had to wed the person her father or guardian chose for her." Louisa smiled and touched Lillian's cheek affectionately. "Not anymore."

"Why didn't you ever tell us Nathan asked the duke to marry you?" Gwen asked.

"I felt you were both too young to know."

"We're not children anymore, Louisa," Gwen said, looking and sounding very grown up.

"I know that now, but Nathan died over two years ago. You had just turned sixteen—and, Lillian, you weren't even thirteen yet. Besides, it was a halfhearted proposal from the duke that I never took seriously anyway. I knew he was hoping I wouldn't hold him to his promise. And I haven't. Not agreeing to marry him was the right thing to do."

"Why didn't you tell me before I turned eighteen?" Gwen asked. "You think I'm old enough to marry, but I'm not old enough to know any details about my sister's life or my brother's death."

Even Louisa didn't know any more information about Nathan's death. When she'd questioned her uncle about that night, he told her there was no need going into particulars that wouldn't change the outcome of the fact that Nathan was gone. At the time, she was too shocked to argue with him.

"You are being too hard concerning this, Gwen," Louisa said. "I only received that one letter from the duke. When I didn't hear from him again, I thought he had forgotten all about what Nathan asked him to do. I was as shocked as anyone when he came to see me yesterday. I realize now that you both are old enough to know."

"Thank you for realizing that," Gwen said.

"I also should have realized that even if Mrs. Colthrust hadn't told you tonight, someone would have eventually. After all, you are going to be meeting hundreds of people at parties and balls over the course of the Season. From what Mrs. Colthrust has told me, the vow between Nathan and the duke is still talked about all over London. It was only a matter of time until you heard."

"You can't shield us from everything, Louisa, though I know you try."

Gwen was right but it wasn't easy to let go of the control she'd had these seven years. "So tell me, can you forgive me for not telling you?"

"Of course," Lillian said, and hugged Louisa.

Louisa knew that Gwen wasn't ready to forgive her yet, so she added a little more prompting and said, "I should have told you about this when it happened. I'm sorry I didn't."

Gwen smiled and threw herself into Louisa's arms and hugged her tightly. It was amazing what a simple "I'm sorry" could accomplish.

"You know all is forgiven," Gwen said, "but next time someone thinks about marrying you, will you please tell us?"

"I promise I will," she said, feeling much better now that she'd managed to avert a huge crisis. It was also time to change the subject, so she said, "Now, I don't know about you, but I'm getting excited about your first ball."

"Our first ball," Gwen reminded her.

Louisa nodded. She didn't know when Gwen had become such a capable young lady. "Why don't we work on our dancing tomorrow? We haven't danced since we've been here, and it's always so much fun."

"I'd like that," Gwen said.

"I can play the pianoforte for you while you dance like I did when we were at home," Lillian offered.

"That would be lovely," Louisa answered.

"Except for the fact that Mrs. Colthrust doesn't like to hear you play the pianoforte," Gwen said with a smirk.

Lillian smiled. "She doesn't like to hear Saint bark either."

"Or Bonnie squeal," Louisa added.

The three sisters looked at each other and laughed.

A quick flash of relief washed over Louisa, and she felt as if a great weight had flown off her shoulders.

"Now, both of you young ladies give me another hug, and then back up to bed you go."

A few minutes later, the girls were gone and Louisa picked up her book and settled back onto the comfortable chair. Everything was going to be all right between her and her sisters. If only she felt so confident that everything was going to be all right between her and the duke, now that he was their guardian. It was a horrible thing for her uncle to have done to them.

Louisa curled her feet under her once more. She closed her eyes and laid her head back against the front of the chair. The handsome duke paraded into her mind, looking so tall, so handsome, and so appealing. How could she be so attracted to him and so infuriated by him at the same time? What could she do to banish him from her thoughts?

Chapter 10

. . .'Tis much he dares
And, to that dauntless temper of his mind,
He hath a wisdom that doth guide his valor
To act in safety.
—*Macbeth,* act 3, scene 1

Bray had given up the habit of drinking all day and all night, too, the morning Nathan Prim died. Bray promised himself he'd never get that drunk again, and he hadn't, though he still always kept a glass of stout red wine in front of him when he was playing cards well into the wee hours of morning at one of his favorite gaming clubs. He still raced his curricle a few times a year, but never with the same enthusiasm as before the tragic accident. He hadn't even tried to give up card games and dice, his trysts with actresses and willing widows, or wagers that either won or lost him a fortune. What kind of man would he be if he gave up everything wicked?

But he had less time for such indulgent pleasures since he became the duke. He hadn't appreciated the responsibility his father had when he was alive. Now that Bray was the duke, he was more understanding if not forgiving of all the time his father had spent work-

ing on the responsibilities that came with being a powerful titled man. No one enjoyed the pursuit of pleasure
more than his father, but he'd always told Bray that he
must take care of business first.

After Miss Prim and her chattering, screaming siblings had left, he somehow managed to stay at home and
work on the account ledgers he was reviewing when
Mrs. Colthrust had marched the Prim girls into his
home. But it hadn't been easy. Thoughts of Miss Prim's
accusations had him sitting on the edge of his chair all
afternoon. He still couldn't believe she had the nerve to
accuse him of deliberately keeping Saint from her sisters. Especially when he'd never wanted to take the dog
in the first place.

At times, Saint had been a downright nuisance; at
other times, he was a welcoming friend when Bray came
home. The first night Saint was at his town house, Bray
tried to keep him outside in the back garden. As far as
he was concerned, dogs were for hunting, alerting their
owners that strangers were approaching, or for guarding sheep. Not even when he was a young boy were dogs
kept in the house.

But the first night, Saint howled, barked, and growled
at the back door until Bray went belowstairs and let
him in, thinking Saint would find an old rug to curl up
on and go to sleep. But no, the dog followed him up the
stairs. It was as if Saint had a sixth sense and knew
which bedchamber was Bray's. From a running jump,
he landed on the foot of Bray's bed and made himself
comfortable. He'd slept there every night since, even on
the nights Bray didn't come home, according to Mr.
Tidmore.

Now, here Bray was into his fifth hour of playing
cards and rolling dice at one of the less popular gaming
hells on the east side of Bond Street, having had one

bad hell of a hand and die roll after another. He'd
changed from whist to hazard and back again because
he couldn't concentrate. And the reason he couldn't focus
on the cards or dice was because he couldn't keep his
mind off the infuriating Miss Prim and her damning
accusations.

She had more nerve than the Prince, and he was
drowning in it.

He couldn't believe he'd actually gotten all her sisters' names correct. What were the odds? And blast it,
since when was saying "good Lord" swearing? Only a
vicar's daughter would come up with a foolish notion
like that. He didn't like being taken to task about his
language not being proper for small ears. Now he knew
why their name was Prim.

Miss Prim had asked him how he could not know
they would want the dog. He should have asked her
why she didn't know he'd never keep a pet from a child.
He was thanking the hand of fate that she'd refused to
marry him. He would go mad if he had to live with all
those squealing girls! No man should be expected to
endure that sound.

Being raked over hot coals about swearing, or trying
to understand why a little girl would cry over something that wasn't broken wasn't even the worst of it—
though bad enough, to be sure. When he'd seen tears
gathering in Miss Prim's eyes, it made him angry with
himself that he'd caused her pain. And all because of a
dog he hadn't wanted anyway. Damnation, every mistress he'd ever had cried when he gave them a parting
gift. Young ladies of quality had sought him out at balls
and parties, crying because he wouldn't ask for their
hand in marriage. He'd seen many women cry and pretend he'd crushed and mishandled their sweet affections.

Not even Miss Sybil's big tears rolling down her chubby cheeks had bothered him.

Miss Prim's did.

Though she'd never let them spill over onto her cheek. He was impressed with the fortitude she'd shown in accomplishing that, because she was truly heartbroken the girls had missed those two years with Saint. It took every ounce of willpower he had not to pull her into his arms and comfort her with kisses. Not that he thought for a moment she would have let him.

With kisses?

Hell yes, he would have liked to comfort her with soft, sweet kisses. He wanted to start high on her cheekbone just below her eye and let his lips trail all the way down to the corner of her mouth before capturing her voluptuous lips beneath his. He wanted to pull her close and press her womanly body tightly against him.

Miss Louisa Prim was a fiery and fiercely devoted young lady, and he had no doubt she would be just as passionate as a lover.

Lover?

What was he thinking? Yes, he'd sensed passion in her, but he doubted she'd recognize it—and if she ever did, he doubted she'd let it come out. No, she was the last lady he wanted for a lover or for anything else.

Bray scoffed out loud, and the other gentlemen at the table looked at him with surprise. He went still. That was a hell of a thing for him to have done as the other players were sorting the cards they'd just been dealt. He never made a sound, twitched an eye, or changed his expression when he was playing. No doubt, the other gentlemen thought that his hastily issued sigh meant he had yet another losing hand.

And he probably did, but he didn't want the other players to know. And once again, it was the unforget-

table Miss Prim's fault. It would probably thrill her to
know she had gotten under his skin and irritated him
like a burr under a horse's blanket.

Bray picked up his cards and looked at them. His
spirits lifted. For the first time that night, he had a winning hand. Now all he had to do was take advantage of
it, which might very well be difficult, considering his
gaming faux pas.

He tripled his bet. The other players bought in to his
high-stakes maneuver, and each man raised his bet even
higher in turn. Bray didn't back down as they thought
he would, and he upped them again. One by one, the
other three men bowed out of the game. Bray smiled as
he collected his considerable winnings and rose from
the table. He knew he owed that quite hefty bag of winnings to the inspiring Miss Prim.

The night was still young at only a couple of hours
past midnight. He once again considered the possibility of heading over to the Heirs' Club or to White's to
see if he'd have better luck there, but decided against it.
The reason he'd come to this side of Town was because
he knew he wasn't in the mood to be hounded about
Miss Prim by the likes of Lord Sanburne, Mr. Hopscotch, or any other bloke who didn't have the good
sense to leave him alone.

Thinking about the lovely and bold miss was enough.
He didn't need to talk about her, too.

The gambling hell had been hot and crowded. The
chilling night wind felt good when Bray stepped out of
the club, so he left off his cloak and hat. He glanced up
and down the street, looking for his landau. There were
two other carriages waiting down the street for their
owners to emerge, but his wasn't in sight. Carriage
horses were well schooled to stand still for long periods
of time, but most drivers would take a ride around the

block at least once or twice an hour and give the horses a little exercise to keep them from getting restless. Bray expected his own driver to do that if he was ever gone for more than an hour.

In the opposite direction of the carriages, Bray saw what seemed to be a commotion of some kind going on underneath one of the streetlights. His first thought was that some poor fellow must have been caught cheating at cards and was getting the beating he rightly deserved. Looking closer, though, he wasn't so sure.

There were a total of four men in the fight. One was dressed as a gentleman, and the other three appeared to be common footpads out to rob whatever they could from him. The gentleman must either have been a greenhorn, in a drunken fog, or perhaps he'd been looking for a fight, because Bray didn't know anyone who would be out alone on the east side of Bond Street at night unless he was looking for trouble.

The gentleman was doing a fairly good job of holding his own against the three, throwing some jabs any pugilist would envy, but the gentleman soon grew tired. Two of the thugs grabbed him and held his arms behind his back while the other man started laying into his midsection with his fist. Bray wasn't usually one to get mixed up in anyone else's fight, but the gentleman had obviously tired and was no longer a match for the three ruffians.

If he'd heard it one time, he'd heard it a hundred times while growing up that he had to be tougher, stronger, quicker, and smarter than any other man. His father demanded it of him. Bray couldn't just be better than anyone else; he also had to be the best: the best rider, the best marksman, the best swordsman, and the best grades in school. His father never gave him a pass on anything and never accepted weakness or failure, and the old duke had made sure Bray's masters at school knew that, too.

Bray hadn't been in a fight in a long time, and he didn't really want to get in this one. Over the years, he'd had his share of drunken brawls, fisticuffs, and a few pugilists' rounds at the fighting clubs. He'd been thrown out of more than a few taverns and gaming hells for challenging card cheats. So far, he'd managed to keep all his teeth. Now that he was older, he knew he'd like for it to stay that way.

Besides, he no longer had the itch to fight that he'd had when he was younger. But Bray didn't like it that the gentleman was outnumbered one against three. It just wasn't in Bray's nature to walk away without helping the man.

Bray dropped his hat and cloak to the ground. He wanted to be prepared in case he had to join the fight. He felt around his waist and slipped his dagger from its scabbard. He then bent down and pulled his pistol from the top of his right boot. Thankfully, he didn't have to use his fists tonight. Unlike the gentleman getting pounded into the ground, Bray knew better than to come to this side of Town unprepared.

Staying in the shadows, Bray quietly and quickly walked down the street toward the scuffle. By the time he edged up close, the gentleman was on the ground and the three robbers were huddled over him, picking his pockets clean. Bray pointed the pistol at the men and held his dagger in striking position.

"That's enough, boys," he said in a deadly cold voice. "Lift your hands in the air and stand up slow."

The ruffians stilled, looked up at Bray, and then eyed each other. Their hair and beards were long and shaggy, their clothing worn and dirty.

Bray knew they were trying to decide if they wanted

to take their chances and go against a man with a pistol and a knife—they could get lucky and rob two gentlemen in one night—or if they should make their getaway with what they'd been able to glean from the man on the ground.

It made no difference to Bray which avenue they took.

"Step away from the gentleman, or one of you will get the ball I have in this pistol and another will feel my blade."

The men didn't move. Bray pointed the gun at the chest of the ruffian who looked to be the youngest of the trio and pulled back the hammer with his thumb.

"Your choice, men," Bray said. "But make it quick. I'm not going to stand here the rest of the night while you take your time deciding whether you want to be a hero to your fellow footpads or a dead man."

The roughest-looking character inclined his head to the left, and said, "We don't want trouble from a gent with a weapon."

"Wise choice. Now, I suggest you drop the gentleman's coin purse, the buttons you cut off his waistcoat, his hat, and anything else you might have pinched from him and get the hell out of here."

The ruffians looked at one another again, but finally the man who'd spoken rose and the other men joined him, dropping the gentleman's belongings as they stood.

"Get out of here and count yourself lucky if you don't feel a ball or a blade in your back as you run away."

The footpads turned and fled. Bray replaced his weapons and bent down to see how badly the man had been hurt, and immediately recognized him. "Harrison, is that you?"

"Bray?" The man grunted, trying to raise himself up on his elbows. "Give me a hand, will you?"

Bray helped his boyhood friend to stand. He and Harrison Thornwick had met their first term at Eton and remained good friends.

"Damnation, Harrison, you have better sense than to be on this street alone at this time of night."

"Obviously not." He held his side and winced as he tried to bend down to get his coin purse.

"I've got it," Bray said, grabbing the small leather bag and the buttons off the ground. He handed the items to Harrison.

"Hell's teeth," Harrison swore as he wiped blood from the corner of his mouth with the back of his bruised hand. "There was a time I could take three thugs rather handily. Nearing thirty, I guess I'm getting too old."

Bray looked at his friend. He seemed as fit as he was the day he'd left his teens behind and turned twenty. Bray and Harrison were of the same height and build. They were both tall, strong men, and neither of them had ever been intimidated by another man's purse or power. Bray was certain age and ability had nothing to do with Harrison's being overwhelmed by the men. He was simply outnumbered and spent.

"You're just out of practice. How many fights have you had since you left London?"

"Not many," Harrison said, putting his money and buttons in his pocket. "None recently."

"My point." Bray pulled a handkerchief out of his pocket and gave it to the man. "You probably could have taken those footpads if you'd been on your toes and had a weapon with you. I saw you get in more than a few good punches before they took you down."

Harrison frowned and grunted again. "You saw the fight, you bloody blackguard? Just how long did you watch them pound me before you decided to help?"

"Well, I would have stepped in sooner if I'd known it was you." Bray grinned. "When did you get back to London? Last I heard, you were in Turkey or India or some other godforsaken place."

Harrison held his side and grunted some more, laughing as he touched the handkerchief to the corner of his lip. "Stop making me laugh, Bray. I think they cracked a rib. Oh, sorry about that slip. I received the news about your father. I should have said 'Your Grace.'"

"We've known each other too long to start using titles now. I still shudder when I think about you calling me Lord Lockington when we first met at Eton. What were we, nine or ten years old?"

Harrison nodded. "And *I* still remember your father looking down at me and saying, 'Young man, you will address my son by his appropriate title, or I'll have you thrown out of this school and see that you never step foot in another.'"

Bray laughed at Harrison's attempt to sound like the old duke. "He did enjoy intimidating people, no matter their age. I think you had a few stern warnings about the penalties of not using my title from the headmaster as well, didn't you?"

"More than a few, and I knew quite well what the penalty was. I was getting my knuckles rapped at least once or twice a week for failing to address you as Lord Lockington."

"But I told you then I was Bray, and I'll remain Bray to you today."

"As you wish when we're alone, but I'll be respectful of your title when others are around."

"Fair enough."

Harrison's smile faded and his eyes turned somber. "Your letter about Adam's wife caught up with me a month or so ago. How's he doing?"

Bray looked away. Adam's tragedy and Prim's death were two things he tried not to think about. "I haven't heard from him since he left London. He didn't want to stay here, as you can imagine. He owns a cottage somewhere along the northern coast of Yorkshire. He was going there."

"I suppose I'd want to get away, too, if I lost my wife while she was trying to give birth to my son."

"And then to lose his son, too," Bray added, trying not to remember the pain he'd seen on Adam's face when the physician told him she and the child were gone. "It wasn't easy for him to accept."

"Do you think we should travel up that way and try to find him? Just to see how he's doing?"

"It's been three months," Bray said. "I think enough time has passed. He might be ready to see a friendly face. And I wouldn't mind getting out of London for a few days either. Now, where's your driver?"

"I don't have one. I've been gone over two years, remember. I have to rebuild my staff. I hired a hackney to bring me here. I was waiting for one to drive by so I could flag him, when I was jumped from behind."

"Lesson learned."

"You're still a blackguard."

"Always will be." Bray gave him a cocky grin. "There's a reason for that old saying that a leopard can't change his spots. Are you here just to enjoy the Season or have you decided your wandering days are over and you plan to stay in London?"

"I've seen enough of the world."

"Then welcome home, old friend. We'll have a drink to celebrate you coming to your senses and realizing what the poets already knew—there's no place like England."

"We'll have that drink." Harrison grabbed his side

and grunted one last time. "But not tonight. It might be a few days before I'm up to matching you port for port, winning your blunt, or riding up north with you."

Bray looked at Harrison's face and nodded. There was a cut under his eye and at the corner of his lip, which was swelling rapidly. Blood had dripped onto his neck-cloth, and his clothing was dirty and rumpled from the fight. Bray couldn't help but think of Miss Prim calling his club the Heirs' Club of Scoundrels. Looking at Harrison now, he realized she was right.

Damn, he couldn't get Miss Prim off his mind, no matter what he was doing or thinking. Every last thought always came back to her.

The hell of it was that it bothered him less and less.

Chapter 11

I have lost the immortal part of myself, and
what remains is bestial.
—*Othello,* act 2, scene 3.

It was the second day in a row for rare bright sunlight
and azure blue skies. The heat of the sun felt good to
the back of Bray's neck as he walked up the stone path
to Miss Prim's house. He'd been an inconsiderate blackguard more times than he hadn't, and it was unusual
for his past transgressions to haunt him. In fact, other
than Nathan Prim's death, nothing ever did. But for
several days now, he hadn't been able to stomach the fact
that Miss Prim thought he'd been knowingly malicious
to her younger sisters.

That rankled.

He didn't know much about children and nothing
about girls. Except now he knew girls could squeal to
the high heavens and make one want to put a pillow
over one's ears. They could cry for no reason and touch
things they shouldn't. They could be just as impolite,
naughty, and playful as boys, but he would never mis-
treat them. And he didn't even want to think about little

Miss Missing-Teeth Bonnie hugging him. Most unfortunate of all was that he was their guardian until his runner could find that blasted viscount.

Last night while plowing through a bottle of claret and trying once again, but in vain, to play a game of cards without thinking about Miss Prim, he'd decided he must see her again. He wouldn't rest until he'd taken her to task about her accusations. He wasn't going to be able to let this be and get it out of his mind until he was sure Miss Prim and Proper knew he hadn't kept Saint from them on purpose.

Bray reached to pick up the brass door knocker, but his hand closed around air as the door opened in front of him. Miss Sybil seemed shocked to see him standing there, but he was not surprised to see the little girl. Remembering what she did the last time she'd opened the door for him, he immediately flattened his hand against the wood and stuck his booted foot over the threshold so she couldn't shut the door in his face again.

Her eyes widened in fear, and she stepped out on the stoop with him. "Are you here to take Saint from us?" she asked in a soft breathy voice.

Her question illustrated how necessary it was to clear things with her older sister once and for all. He leaned down to her and said, "No. He is yours for now and forever. I wouldn't take him back even if you tried to give him to me."

A wide smile spread across her face and wrinkled her nose. She whispered, "Thank you, but don't talk so loud."

Bray frowned. "Don't talk so loud?" he repeated her words in a whisper.

Miss Sybil put her forefinger to her lips and said, "Shhh," and pointed inside the house behind her.

"Why? Is someone sleeping?" he asked.

She shook her head and rose up on her tiptoes to get closer to him even though he was still bent down to her. "We're playing blindman's buff and Louisa is *it*," she whispered with a mischievous gleam in her big blue eyes. "I'm hiding."

Bray made a quick assessment of the situation. "Does she allow you to hide outside when you are playing the game?" he asked, following her orders and whispering again.

Miss Sybil's gaze held as steady on his as if she were playing a hand of cards with him. She remained silent. He knew she was trying to decide if she should tell the truth or not.

"Well, does she?" he asked again.

Finally, she pouted and shook her head again.

"Back inside," he said softly.

She jerked her hands to her hips, turned around, and stepped back into the vestibule. Bray followed her and quietly closed the door behind them. Miss Sybil pointed to the stairs and gave him a questioning look. Bray could remember playing the game and hiding on different floors when he was a boy. It was never easy for the one wearing the blindfold, but immense fun for others. He could only assume this was not the first time Miss Prim had played the game with her sisters. She probably knew she'd have to search the entire house to find even one of them.

Bray nodded his approval to Miss Sybil and then whispered, "Where is Miss Prim?"

"Book room," she mouthed to him, and pointed down the corridor. "Everyone else is abovestairs, too. Be quiet and don't tell her."

He made the motion as if to put a key to his lips and lock them and then throw the key away. Miss Sybil grinned and headed up the stairs. Bray smiled, too. He hadn't even thought about the game blindman's buff in years. And he was amazed at how quickly the childhood gesture of locking his lips with a key had come back to him. Maybe little girls could be enjoyable after all—if they weren't crying, or screeching, or hugging.

After watching her climb the stairs, he walked down the corridor as quietly as his boots would allow on the squeaky hardwood floors. He paused to peer through each door he passed until he was rewarded at the last room on the left.

Bray felt anticipation simmer in his loins.

Louisa stood in the middle of the room, her back to him, counting. Her hands were gently clasped behind her, and she was swinging back and forth. Her glorious amber blond tresses tumbled past her softly rounded shoulders. The ends of a black scarf, which was tied around her eyes, mingled seductively in the back of her hair. She wore a simple honey-colored dress that flowed and fluttered enticingly around her legs with each movement she made. She looked so incredibly fresh and watching her like this, he was suddenly overwhelmed with desire for her.

"Ninety-eight, ninety-nine, one hundred," Miss Prim called out loud. "Ready or not, here I come."

With her arms and hands extended in front of her, she slowly felt her way over to the far wall, where there was a window. She patted the draperies to make sure no one was hiding behind them.

"All right," she said. "I'm starting at the window, so I know I will have been around the room when I get back here."

Bray quietly stepped farther into the room and leaned against the bookshelves so he could observe her. There was something about her vulnerable, innocent state that immediately had him wanting to cuddle her to his chest and kiss those soft, warm lips.

She was good at the game, moving the chair away from the writing desk and checking underneath it, walking all around the chairs and settees, feeling the cushions as she went. She searched under the end tables and behind the upholstered wing chairs.

Bray was so intent on just watching her that she was very close to where he was standing before he realized it.

He wasn't sure he wanted her to catch him spying on her without her knowledge—but he wasn't sure he didn't, either.

Should he make his presence known?

It was the right thing to do. But how many times had he ever done the right thing?

The closer she came to him, the less he was inclined to move out of her way.

Yes, I want her to find me.

His anticipation kicked up a couple of notches when he saw her hands reaching out toward him. Closer, closer until her fingertips landed midway on his waistcoat, just about the height of the two older girls.

"Aha!" She smiled wickedly. "I've found one of you."

She must have sensed he thought about bolting away, because she quickly added, "You know the rules: You cannot move once you've picked your hiding place."

All right.

That was fine with him. He didn't really want to move.

Her probing hands went lower. His heart rate jumped. Bone-melting pleasure seared through him and suddenly had his breaths coming fast, short, and shallow.

"Is this Lillian?" Miss Prim asked. "What do you have on? How am I to tell who it is when you disguise yourself?"

Her gentle hands slipped lower, pressing, lightly searching for the clue that would tell her whom she'd found. He didn't know if it was a blessing or a curse that she didn't go wide in her search but kept her hands right up the middle.

Bray winced silently, tightening every muscle in his body, trying to force his manhood not to respond to her innocent exploration. But his will was no match for her touch. He was doomed. His lower stomach tightened, and a surge of hardness caught between his legs.

"I don't think this is in the rules of the game," Miss Prim said while one hand fiddled with the buttons on his waistcoat and the other slid open palm down the front of his riding breeches.

Sweet hell! That felt good.

"You are not supposed to masquerade yourself," she added in an exasperated voice. "And what is this? Are you standing on a box to make yourself so tall? I'm not happy about this, but I'll play along for now."

I am.

Bray sucked in a deep silent breath. His senses reeled in delight. He finally knew the meaning of heavenly torture. It was heaven and it was hell to be fondled by a young lady who had no idea she was touching him, let alone where she was touching him.

"But remember, all of you promised to play fair this time," she said. "I can't possibly ever win if you keep changing the rules. And what kind of clothing is this you have on?"

Her hands moved up to his waist again, and she pulled on the ends of his waistcoat, but he felt no reprieve. All but one part of his body remained still, and it was throbbing and growing rapidly. He threw his head back and almost groaned out loud. Only his years of training, hiding every emotion that threatened to emerge from inside him, kept him still.

Though he couldn't see her forehead, he knew when her brow wrinkled into a frown of confusion as her movements took her south again. Bray abandoned himself to the gratifying torment. He came over wanting to give Miss Prim a piece of his mind, and instead she was giving him the kind of finite torture no man should have to endure but all men wanted to.

"This feels odd," she whispered.

Oh no, it feels amazing and so satisfying. Don't stop.

Perhaps he could forgive her for thinking he'd stolen the dog from her sisters after all.

"And such an odd place to have buttons," Miss Prim said, and crossed her arms over her chest as if she were studying her thoughts.

Suddenly her hands quickly sailed up the eight buttons on his waistcoat, to his neckcloth. "And how and why did you make your shoulders so wide?"

"Gwen, Lillian!" she said in a surprised voice, jerking her hands to her hips. "Don't tell me you got into Lord Wayebury's wardrobe and pilfered his clothing? You know better. He'll have our heads!"

Bray clenched his jaw and, from strength he didn't know he possessed at the moment, said, "It's me, Miss Prim, the duke."

She gasped. Her hand flew to her blindfold and she yanked it off. "You!" Her eyes looked as if they could spit fire at him. "How long have you been there?"

"Not long enough," he said truthfully.

"Where did I—I mean—" Her voice faltered and softened in anguish. "Oh no! Did I touch you?"

Oh, yes and, it was exquisite pleasure.

It pained him greatly to do it, but he didn't twitch an eye or let the corner of his mouth quiver in mirth as he nodded.

"I did, didn't I? Merciful heavens!" She closed her eyes and groaned as she squeezed the black scarf in a tight fist. Her eyes popped open and she stared blankly at him. "Just shoot me right now and put me out of my misery."

"I have no pistol," he answered dryly.

"You wouldn't shoot me anyway. You are too much of a devil, and you want me to be in this agony."

He was in agony, too, but he doubted she would believe him, so he remained quiet.

"Tell me, did I do the unthinkable and touch you where—where I shouldn't have? No," she whispered earnestly, clearly confounded by wanting and yet not wanting to know what she had done. "What am I saying? I shouldn't have touched you anywhere."

Bray watched her cringe in mortification again. Her expression went from shock to horror to fury. Should he tell her the truth?

Miss Prim's problem was that she still thought of herself as a vicar's daughter. He wanted to shake that firm foundation out from under her, and he knew exactly how to do it so she wouldn't forget anytime soon.

"Yes, Miss Prim, you touched me exactly where I wanted to be touched."

Chapter 12

Out, damned spot! Out, I say!
—Macbeth, act 5, scene 1

"What? No! Oh no!"

Louisa felt as if the flames of embarrassment started at her toes and raced up her body to her face as fire through dry brush. She would never be able to look him in the eyes again.

"Yes, touched me exactly where I wanted to be touched," he repeated.

"Dear sweet mercies! Don't say it again," she whispered.

Louisa had never fainted in her life, but her legs were so weak, she thought she might crumple to the floor.

"My heart, Miss Prim," the duke added as calmly as if he were talking about the weather. "You touched my heart."

Could she believe him? No, his answer was too glib. He was too self-confident.

"You are lying," she shot back.

"That is a strong accusation from someone reared under the straitlaced hand of a vicar, Miss Prim."

"But accurate, is it not? You have no heart to touch."

"That is probably so." A smile twitched the corner of his mouth. "If I had a heart, you touched me where it would be."

Did that mean maybe she hadn't touched him inappropriately? She couldn't tell by his expression. He was just too good at masking his true feelings and what he was thinking. She wanted to believe him, but should she? Was it best to just let it go?

No—for some reason, she couldn't. She had to know for sure.

"Did I touch you anywhere else? You know what I am asking, Your Grace. I have a right to know."

He hesitated.

She stiffened.

He nodded.

Her cheeks flamed red hot again. "Oh, I always knew you were a vile beast. Why did you stand there and let me—let me fondle you and say absolutely nothing to stop me?"

"Why do you think I did?"

Louisa was so livid, it was impossible for her to speak at first. "You are more than a beast. You are a scoundrel of the highest order and should never be allowed anywhere near a respectable young lady—or children, for that matter."

"Then slap me for my abhorrent behavior."

That brought her up short and snapped the fury right out of her. "What?"

"Slap me, Miss Prim."

"You are teasing me, Your Grace," she whispered.

"No," he said with deadly calm. "You either slap me, or I will kiss you."

"What? I don't believe you."

"Yes, you do."

He was right. She did believe him.

"And," he added, "before you make your choice, remember: Only one of us will enjoy the slap, but I'll make sure we both enjoy the kiss."

She whirled to run away, but his arm snaked around her waist and he swung her to face him. She struggled briefly before he flattened her back against the bookshelves and pressed his body to hers. Somehow he'd managed to capture both her wrists in one of his hands and he held them behind her. He had her tightly pinioned, but she wasn't alarmed.

She was angry.

Their eyes and their bodies were locked in a battle of wills, and she truly had no idea who was going to win.

"Let me go!" she whispered hotly, and squirmed against his pressing weight, knowing it was futile but unable to simply acquiesce to his imprisonment without a fight.

"No, my indignant Miss Prim. If you were so outraged by what happened between us just now, you should have taken your retribution when I offered you the chance."

Her breath trembled in her throat. His tone, the light of intrigue in his green eyes, made her stomach quiver deliciously. Teasing warmth tingled across her breasts. She was baffled that even though she was furious with him, he could make her feel such pleasing sensations.

She ceased struggling. "I've never slapped a man," she admitted.

He lowered his head, bringing his face close to hers. "You've probably never had reason to before now."

"I haven't."

He caressed her cheek with his fingertips, letting

them slowly trace the outline of her lips. The pads of his fingers traveled over her chin and down her neck to rest in the hollow at the base of her throat, where she knew her pulse was beating wildly.

Slow curls of pleasure came alive inside her, and without conscious effort, her chest lifted to feel more of the weight of his arm lying against her breasts. His hand confidently slipped over to her ear, and his fingertips slowly outlined its shape before moving beneath her hair to caress the soft, sensitive skin there. The warmth and tenderness of his touch seemed to seep inside her soul and weaken her will to resist him.

"I would wager you have never been kissed either, being a properly brought-up vicar's daughter. You've probably never even been tempted."

Not until now.

"So tell me, Miss Prim," he asked huskily as his gaze studied hers, his face so close, she felt his breath on her cheek, "do your stillness and your silence mean the kiss wins over the slap?"

Did it?

If there were ever a man who deserved a slap, it was this one, but did she really want to do it?

"You are holding my hands," she whispered.

He smiled and nodded once. "In that case." He let her go and took one step back. "If the lady intends to strike, go ahead."

She was free of his hold, but she didn't feel free of him. She had room to reach back and bring her hand down on his cheek with all her strength, but she didn't move to take advantage of his surrender. Instead of feeling calmer and slowing down, her breathing increased sharply. The seconds ticked by. She was in no danger of him keeping her against her will, yet she remained still except for the rapid rise and fall of her chest.

He waited, giving her plenty of time to slap him and walk away. She couldn't do either, even though she knew she should. She realized she was more horrified by the fact that she wanted the duke to kiss her than by the innocent conduct of her wayward hands.

How did the duke know she'd never been kissed? Was that why he was tempting her beyond her power to resist? Did he somehow know she wouldn't have the strength to walk away from the possibility of her first kiss, even if it was coming from an admitted scoundrel like him?

"I'm not going to strike you, Your Grace," she finally said.

His expression questioned her.

"Though I do believe I have just cause."

"So do I," he admitted. He placed one hand against the shelf near her shoulder and leaned in close once again. "Do you trust me, Miss Prim?"

"Not at all," she answered honestly.

He smiled again. "That's probably best."

"I have no doubt."

"I know the girls are upstairs, hiding from you. Where is Mrs. Colthrust? In the house?"

"At the agency that will be sending maids over to interview."

"Good," he said, and brushed a long curl to the back of her shoulder. "You know, they say that if you lose one of your senses, the others will become more heightened. Do you believe that's true?"

"Perhaps. I don't know. Why?"

"May I?" he asked, and reached down to slide the black scarf from her tight grasp. She let it go. He untied it and stretched it out and then folded it over several times to form a new blindfold.

"What are you going to do?"

"Nothing that you don't want me to do," he answered. "Stop me whenever you wish."

She couldn't stop him. She was mesmerized.

He slowly placed the scarf over her eyes. "I'm not going to force you to do anything."

For reasons Louisa didn't begin to understand, she let the duke place the scarf over her eyes and tie it at the back of her head, completely blocking out her sight and, much to her chagrin, proving she trusted him after all.

She felt him move nearer, though he touched her nowhere once the scarf was in place.

"Can you see?" he asked.

She tried to open her eyes, but the blindfold had been put on too well. "No."

"What do you hear, other than my voice?"

She listened. "Breathing."

"What do you smell?"

"Shaving soap."

She felt him place his face against her temple, and he whispered just above her ear, "I smell soap, too."

He reached down and picked up her hand and laid it on his face. "What do you feel?"

"Beard stubble," she said, and then heard him chuckle low in his throat.

"What do you taste?"

Instinctively, she licked her lips and replied, "Nothing."

"Ah, the most tempting and the most delicious of the five senses. To taste."

He pressed his body against hers once again. She felt his weight and the firmness of his powerful frame. His hand slid around her neck and cupped her nape. "Do you want to taste my kisses, Louisa?"

"Yes," she said expectantly, knowing she was throwing caution to the wind and her sensible self out the window.

She felt his breath on her cheek. Her abdomen quivered in anticipation of her very first kiss, but his warm lips touched high on her cheek just below her eye. His lips stayed on her skin, slowly peppering tender, short kisses down her cheek to the corner of her mouth.

"Was that a kiss?" she asked.

"It was many kisses," he answered.

"I felt them, but I didn't taste them."

"You will," he murmured.

She heard and felt him rest his hands on each side of the bookcase, boxing her inside his arms. He kissed each corner of her mouth again and each cheek before letting his lips travel down her jawline and across her neck to nuzzle the skin behind her ear before moving farther down to kiss the crook of her neck. And then, without letting his lips leave her skin, he moved back up and placed his lips to hers.

At last!

Her first kiss.

He moved his lips seductively over hers. A soft moan wafted from her. She heard another low, tantalizing chuckle deep in his throat as his mouth continued to move agonizingly slow over hers.

"Open your mouth and taste me, Louisa," he whispered.

Unsure what he meant, she stiffened.

"No, don't shy from me now."

His powerful arms slid around her back and pulled her up tightly against his chest. Louisa melted against him. She had never been held in such powerful arms, and the feeling did strange things to her insides.

"Open your mouth, Louisa. I will taste you first and show you how it is done. Then you can taste me."

Louisa opened her mouth, and the duke's tongue slid inside. Suddenly she knew what he meant when he'd said, "Taste me." His tongue explored the depths of her mouth as his lips moved seductively over hers.

She lifted her hands and clasped them together behind his neck, trying to bring him closer to her. His strong hands slipped down to her buttocks and pressed her against his lower body as his mouth ravished hers. Her breasts flattened against his chest. Their kisses became more ardent with each passing second. His tongue drove deep inside her mouth. Their uneven breaths melted together while his strong body pressed hers hard against the shelving.

"Now it's your turn," he whispered. "Taste me, Louisa."

Without hesitation, she thrust her tongue into his mouth, brushing, swiping, and darting from one side to the other.

He moaned and murmured softly, "What do I taste like?"

"Passion," she answered. "This must be what passion tastes like, for I can't think of any other way to describe it."

"I've never heard anyone say it that way before, but I agree. You taste of passion, too, and I need to get my fill."

Moments later, his lips left hers. He swept his tongue down the length of her neck to the swell of her breasts peeking just above the bodice. He dipped his tongue below the fabric of the dress as one hand cupped her breast, as if he were trying to lift it from beneath the confines of her clothing. Shivers of delight exploded inside her, and a strange feeling of wanting stirred deep within her.

Louisa felt as if he were devouring her. And it was the most exquisite feeling she'd ever experienced. With every movement his lips made over hers, her breaths grew shorter. Her breasts, stomach, and between her legs tightened. His kiss lingered, and she responded by instinct and parted her lips again. His tongue slid between her teeth. He explored the roof and the sides of her mouth with slow, sensual movements.

His hand moved up and down the side of her rib cage, past her waist to the plane of her hip, and back up until his palm covered her breast once again. A small involuntary moan slipped past her lips. He pressed his palm to her breast again and lifted and molded it in his hand. She gave herself up to the new and joyous feeling of being touched by this man.

A tremor shook the earl's body, and she realized he was as affected by these wonderful sensations as she was. That thrilled her almost as much as his touch.

Louisa's breaths became tiny gasps, and her arms tightened around him. Her fingers kneaded his back as he continued the easy, unhurried stroking of her breast. Another moan of pleasure escaped past her lips.

The duke gave her several more soft, short kisses and then lifted the blindfold from her eyes and stepped away from her.

Louisa blinked, adjusting her eyes to the light and her body to the shock of the abrupt change.

He put the scarf in her hands and stepped even farther away from her. "We must stop. I heard movement abovestairs. I think your sisters might be wondering why you haven't found them."

"Oh, yes, well." She wiped her lips with the back of her hand. "Of course, you're right." Coming fully to her right senses, she realized just how easy it had been to forget anyone was in the house save for the two of them.

He smiled. "Don't worry. Your secret is safe. You don't look like you've just been seduced."

"Was I? Seduced?"

He nodded.

"Oh," she whispered earnestly, closing her eyes and lowering her chin. "I should have known that's what you were doing, but I couldn't seem to stop you."

She felt the tips of his fingers under her chin. He gently lifted her head, and her lashes fluttered up. She couldn't deny that just the merest touch from him filled her with soul-shattering sensations.

A roguish grin lifted the corner of one side of his mouth. "There was no reason for you to. It's perfectly acceptable for a young lady to have a kiss or two before she marries. You are hardly defiled, Miss Prim—and believe me, you are as chaste right now as you were when I walked into the house a few minutes ago."

"Are you sure?"

"Quite."

She frowned. "That's hardly true, Your Grace. I touched you in unmentionable places. I tasted you. You touched me, and right now I'm feeling wretchedly wicked."

He chuckled once more, this time good-naturedly. "Take me at my word, Miss Prim. I know a few wicked women, and you are not one."

The soft light in his eyes seemed to indicate he was being truthful with her, but it didn't help her feelings at the moment. "Why did you want to kiss me first with the blindfold on?"

"The truth?"

"Always."

"It was a purely selfish act on my part. I wanted to

see if it would be as thrilling to kiss you with it on as I imagined it to be when I watched you searching for your sisters."

She swallowed hard again. "And was it?"

"More than I could have imagined."

"Will a kiss feel different with the blindfold off?"

"I can only assume so. I must admit, I've never worn one."

"Yet you had me wear it," she said, her ire rising once again.

"You were *it*. Not me."

"Oh, you are impossible!"

"I wish I had time to kiss you now without the blindfold, but we will have to save that for another day."

"I wouldn't let you kiss me again," she said, knowing it sounded childish but unable to stop herself from saying it.

"You should know by now the danger of issuing a challenge to me, Miss Prim. I never decline one."

"Someday I will get even with you for this."

"I can only hope that is true, so please make that a promise. And I think the only way for you to get even is for you to put the blindfold on me and kiss me."

Louisa gritted her teeth. "Did you come here today just to give me a kissing lesson?"

"No, but when the opportunity presented itself, I couldn't deny myself the pleasure of your lips."

"Did you come to see if Saint has missed you? For if you did, I can assure you he hasn't."

"Not for that reason either. I came to make sure you knew that I didn't willfully keep Saint from you and your sisters. I readily admit I'm the lowest kind of scoundrel. I think I just proved that, Miss Prim. However, had I known your uncle was searching for the dog, I would gladly have surrendered him to you."

She had no doubt he was telling the truth. "I believe you."

He nodded once. "I hear a small footstep on the top stairs. You might want to put the blindfold back on and pretend you have been looking for your sisters. I'll see myself out the back door."

Louisa fell against the bookcase and slipped the blindfold back over her eyes, hoping it would also hide the flames of heat licking at her cheeks. She was amazed at how easily she'd gotten caught up in the magical feeling of his kisses. She'd completely lost all thought of where she was or what she was doing. All that mattered was the way he was making her feel.

She didn't even know how she could have let him kiss her. Or how she could have enjoyed it so much. Surely it wasn't natural to enjoy kisses from a man such as the duke. It's a good thing he hadn't asked her to propose to him while he was kissing her, because she would probably have been fool enough at the time to do it.

She needed to find a way to get him out of her life, before he found a way to get inside her heart.

If it wasn't already too late for that.

Chapter 13

Short time seems long in sorrow's sharp sustaining.
—The Rape of Lucrece

Bray and Harrison rode in silence as they had for most of their three-day journey. It was damned cold, and a light mist fell across the foggy landscape. Bray had hated swirling fog ever since Prim's death.

Already, Bray was wishing they'd stayed by the dry warm fire in Adam's cottage. Chilling wind blew moisture down the back of his neck, and even with his woolen gloves and socks, his fingers and toes were growing numb. Adam's housekeeper, a gentle old woman, had invited them to wait inside for his return. Bray and Harrison didn't have the patience for that, so they had asked her where she thought Adam might be and went looking for him.

About half an hour away from the cottage, Harrison broke the silence and said, "I've been away from London almost two years, and nothing has changed, my friend. The gossip is still all about you."

"It's a talent I'm not likely to outgrow," Bray answered, seeing faint traces of bruises on his friend's face from his fight a couple of weeks ago. "One of the many good things about being a duke is that people are often afraid to repeat the gossip to me, with the exception of you and Seaton, of course."

"Why didn't you tell me you were all but betrothed to Miss Prim when we talked the other night?"

Hellfire, he should have known it was only a matter of time before Harrison got around to mentioning her to him. He had hoped that getting away with Harrison would help him forget about Miss Prim and the feel of her warm supple body so willingly locked in his arms, but so far it hadn't. It certainly wouldn't help to talk about her.

"Because I'm not," he answered without bothering to look at Harrison.

"So the gossip's not true," Harrison said with surprise lacing his voice.

The corners of Bray's lips lifted in a sly grin. "I don't know what you've heard, but according to the ton, gossip is always true."

"Well, hell—are you engaged or not?" Harrison grumbled.

Harrison usually had the good sense not to ask for answers Bray didn't want to give. He supposed their three-day journey on horseback was wearing on both of them.

"No."

"Everyone I've spoken to seems to think you're a devilish brute and the worst sort of scoundrel for not keeping your word to her dying brother and making her your bride."

"That's right."

"But most feel you'll live up to your oath in the end and do the suitable thing and marry her."

Bray grunted and shifted in his saddle. "You've been back less than two weeks and you were laid up with a cracked rib for most of that time. How many people have you talked to?"

"I've been out to White's a few times."

Bray grunted again ruefully. "You did say something earlier about it looking as if nothing had changed in London while you were away."

They crested a knoll and saw the man they were looking for standing along the edge of a cliff with his horse hobbled nearby. They reined in their mounts and stopped. Adam wasn't hard to recognize even in the commoners' clothing and workers' hat he was wearing. His six-foot-four height and broad-shouldered frame towered over most men. For a split second, Bray had the awful feeling Adam might be thinking about the possibility of ending his pain.

Bray remained silent as Harrison threw him a questioning look. "You don't think he's considering—"

"No," Bray cut in before Harrison could voice what Bray had just thought. "He's looking over the cliff at something below."

"Do you think he'll know why we're here?" Harrison asked.

"Wouldn't you?"

Harrison nodded. "Right now I'm wondering if we should have intruded on his mourning. Maybe we should have given him longer."

"Don't you think it's a little late to have second thoughts about that, now that we've traveled for three days to get here?"

"Blast it, Bray, what are we supposed to say to Adam?"

"We don't have to say anything about why we're here. He'll know. He'll understand we just wanted to check on him and see how he's doing. He won't want to talk about it. In fact, I'm sure he fights like hell every day to forget it."

"That might take a while. I heard she suffered for days."

Bray knew. He'd been there every agonizing hour with him.

Bray stared at the lonely-looking figure standing on the edge of the cliff and wondered how in the hell anyone could blame Adam if he did decide to jump.

"It's been over three months," Bray said. "I think he'll know we're not here to intrude but to remind him we're around whenever he's ready to come back to London."

A cold wind whipped rain against the side of Bray's face. The night Nathan Prim died flashed through Bray's mind, and his hands tightened on the reins. It had been a cold misty night. He would never forget how desperately he'd wanted to help the man and how helpless he'd felt when he realized he couldn't do a damn thing to save Prim. And Bray didn't have to imagine what a man went through when all he could do was stand by and watch his wife die. He'd seen Adam do it.

Bray swallowed the lump in his throat. Lessons learned from childhood came to his aid. The best way to forget about something bad was to think about something that was good.

Miss Prim's lovely face flashed in his mind again. Now, she was something good. Damn, but he wanted to see her again. He wanted to hold her and kiss her as he had that afternoon a couple of weeks ago. No, not as he had then. He wanted to kiss her without the blindfold. He wanted to look into her gorgeous blue eyes and see the wonder, the surprise, and the pleasure on her face when he taught her all about desire.

He'd thought about coming up with an excuse to go to her house just so he could see her, but every time he thought about it, he'd think again. He didn't need to kiss Miss Prim no matter how much he wanted to. She was an innocent, and he stayed away from innocents. He couldn't have her changing that any more than she already had.

But really, how could he not let her touch him?

"What do you think he's doing?" Harrison asked.

"I don't know," Bray answered, shoving Miss Prim to the back of his mind as he did several times a day since he and Harrison had begun their journey. "We might as well ride down and find out. It doesn't look as if this weather is going to get any better."

But thoughts of Miss Prim had made him feel warmer.

Bray and Harrison nudged their horses and headed down the slope. Adam heard them riding up and turned away from the edge of the cliff. Bray saw a flash of disbelief on Adam's face when he first saw them, but he just stood motionless and watched them ride up and stop their horses in front of him.

Adam pushed his wide-brimmed hat up his forehead. "This is Yorkshire, gentlemen, in case you're lost?"

"We know exactly where we are," Bray said, giving a passing glance to the wet, grassy plain on either side of them. "We thought you might have lost your way, so we came looking for you."

"I'm not lost either."

"You're a long way from London," Harrison said.

Adam shrugged. "Last I heard, you were nowhere near London either."

"It was a hell of an adventure," Harrison said, and then cut his eyes over to Bray. "But as I was recently reminded, there's no place like England."

"This valley is home for me now," Adam said.

"I don't mind finding my way up here once or twice a year, do you, Bray?"

"I guess not. It's probably nice country when it's not cold, drizzling, and foggy."

A touch of a grin twitched the corners of Adam's mouth. "It's always raining here. The fog and the rain suit me."

Bray heard something that sounded like a sheep bleating and looked around. "Where's that sound coming from?"

"A ewe fell over the edge," Adam said, pointing behind him. "I was thinking about tying a rope to my horse and scaling down after her."

Bray and Harrison kicked free of their stirrups and dismounted. They walked to the edge and looked over. Bray saw a sheep standing on a small ledge about thirty or forty feet down with at least another fifty-foot drop to the bottom. The ewe looked unharmed. Even with its thick wool coat to cushion the fall, Bray didn't know how the sheep had made it past all the jagged and sharp rocks without getting killed or breaking a leg.

"Are you tending sheep now?" Harrison asked in a teasing tone.

"It keeps me from drinking all day and all night, too," Adam answered with no emotion in his voice.

Bray looked down again, and the sheep looked up at him with big black eyes and bleated. "I think you should count that one as lost," Bray said. "Those rocks look slippery and dangerous."

"When have I ever not done something just because it was dangerous?"

"You probably haven't," Harrison said, "but I agree with Bray. Even if you make it down without breaking your leg or your neck, you'll never get back up with that blasted sheep. She's not a little lamb you can just tuck under the crook of your arm and hold while you climb up the rope. She looks to be a full adult ewe."

"She is, but I can handle her. I'll tie her feet together and then strap her to my neck and shoulders and climb up. I can't leave her down there to starve."

Harrison and Bray looked at each other, and Bray knew they were thinking the same thing. Their childhood friend didn't care if he lived or died.

"How often are you risking your life for sheep?"

Adam shrugged. "I've risked my life for less."

"We all have," Harrison said quietly.

Bray saw a faraway look in Harrison's eyes and couldn't help but think his friend was remembering something specific and not just the many times the trio had thrown caution to the wind and risked their lives in fool stunts over simple dares.

Since their first year at Eton, the three friends had known they all had their strengths and weaknesses. In their younger years, there were times rivalries had surfaced between them, when one would try to best the others in shooting, racing, fencing, or the attention of a young miss, but they never forgot they were friends.

"Where's the damn rope?" Bray said. "I'll do it."

"Then you'll have to fight me for the chance," Harrison said. "If you'll remember, I'm better at climbing on rocks than either one of you."

Adam blew out a rueful breath as rain fell on his dark brown work coat. "Neither one of you is doing it. You're both dressed like dandies. And look at your fancy knee boots. You wouldn't make it down the first rock before you slipped and broke your necks. What the hell are you two devils doing here anyway?"

"We told you. We came to see how you're doing," Harrison said.

"And it sounds as if we didn't get here a minute too

soon," Bray added. "If you are going to try to kill your-self, you're not going to do it without our help."

Harrison clapped Adam on the shoulder and said, "Now, if you've set your mind to getting that ewe off that ledge, let's get it done and go have a drink. It's damn near freezing out here."

Chapter 14

Our remedies oft in ourselves do lie.
—All's Well That Ends Well, act 1, scene 1

He had kissed her. She had kissed him. They had kissed and kissed and kissed again; slow and soft, hard and fast, and over and over.

And she'd liked it all!

He had touched her breasts. And she had touched him, too, though at the time, she didn't know what she was touching. But every time she thought about the intimacy, flaming heat raced to her cheeks.

Louisa squeezed her eyes shut. She didn't know what manner of madness had come over her that afternoon. It had been more than three weeks since passion had erupted between her and the duke, and still it was all she could think about when she was quiet as she was now. Not just thinking about the duke's kisses and caresses, but also feeling, smelling, touching, and tasting them. Her senses were haunted almost to the point of madness!

And worst of all, sensible Louisa Prim wanted to experience all those enticing sensations again.

She'd tried to rationalize her behavior by remembering the duke's words that it was all right for a young lady to have a kiss or two before she married. That sounded reasonable. It was probably even expected that a new bride would know a little about kissing, but perhaps not so much as she now knew. The duke had been most thorough in his lesson.

And she wasn't sure she was supposed to have enjoyed it so much, and dreamed of more. His kisses had stolen her breath, made her legs feel as if she were trying to stand on water, and made her so light-headed, she almost swooned.

Swooned!

Louisa Prim!

How could the simple joining of his lips to hers make her wish the feeling would go on forever?

Maybe because there had been nothing simple about their kisses. They had been eager, demanding, and passionate. And she'd been caught up and held in his powerful embrace. She'd felt the hard frame of his body against hers. She was convinced that alone would make any young lady swoon.

Louisa sighed silently. She now understood how Sybil felt when she was forced to sit still and work on embroidery samples. Standing on a seamstress box while the hem of her gown was being pinned gave Louisa too much time to think. And when she had time to think, it was always about the Duke of Drakestone.

It was exasperating.

And thrilling.

And she must stop thinking about him. He'd admitted that kissing her was a purely selfish act. Surely that was what most men did, but what kind would readily admit it?

A scoundrel!

Lord Wayebury's house had become much busier, now that they had added a housekeeper, two more maids, and a dog. Mrs. Colthrust was getting used to Saint being allowed to freely roam the house. She had stopped trying to shoo him away whenever he came near her. The two of them had fallen into a pattern of avoiding each other. If one walked into a room, the other one usually walked out.

The chaperone retired early in the evenings to her spacious bedchamber and took most of her meals there. However, she spent an hour each morning going over the names and titles of important people for Louisa and Gwen to remember when they met them at the first ball of the Season, which was now only two weeks away.

Even with looking after her four sisters, Louisa still seemed to have far too much time on her hands to think about the duke and his kisses. She found herself not just wondering if he would come back to their house, but even wanting him to.

And that eagerness worried her.

She didn't know how to keep the man out of her thoughts, but she did have an idea about how to get him out of her life. And for that she needed help. Unfortunately, Mrs. Colthrust was the only person available to help her.

This was the fifth day in a row that Louisa, Gwen, and Mrs. Colthrust had boarded their fancy new coach with four matching bays and headed to Mrs. Rivoire's Fabric and Dress Design Shop. The fitting salon of Mrs. Rivoire's boutique looked more like a drawing room in one of Mayfair's most elite houses than a place of business. The draperies were tastefully fashioned from dark green velvet and edged with gold bullion fringe. The feminine furniture was upholstered in a soft shade of pink velvet. The three floor-to-ceiling

mirrors in the room were framed in fancy gilt wood-
work, and the tea service was silver.

No expense had been spared to make the shopkeep-
er's clientele feel as if they were visiting a dear friend
rather than a modiste. It was no wonder the French
dressmaker was a favorite of ladies such as the Dowager
Duchess of Drakestone.

Their first day of shopping had been spent looking
at fabrics, lace, and all manner of sewing trimmings to
make gowns, wraps, and headpieces more stunning
and different from any other gown the French modiste
had designed before. Gwen and Mrs. Colthrust loved
every moment of it, but for Louisa dress shopping had
been torture. She would much rather be walking in the
garden and seeing what buds had sprouted than trying
to decide what shade of green went with what shade of
blue. And while lace was pretty on a dress, it didn't
have the same beauty when it was all wound together.
They had been measured from head to toe and questioned at length about the colors, styles, and cuts of
garments they liked best. Already some of the smaller
clothing items were arriving at their home.

Today the three of them were having fittings for some
of the many gowns Mrs. Colthrust had insisted they
order. The chaperone and Gwen had gone into the changing room to don another gown, and Louisa was left with
one of Mrs. Rivoire's assistants, who chattered constantly
to herself in French.

Mrs. Colthrust walked back into the salon as Louisa
was stepping off the seamstress box. She took one look
at Louisa and exclaimed, "This will never do!"

"What's the matter?" Louisa asked, thinking something horrible must be wrong with the gown.

"This," she said, and pulled down on the neckline of
Louisa's gown. "An aging dowager shows more bosom

than you are showing in this gown. What was Mrs. Rivoire thinking? You are trying to find a husband."

Louisa looked down at her chest. It looked decidedly low to her. Certainly lower than any gown she'd ever worn before. "I don't think the height of my neckline matters."

"Of course it does. You would think with the woman being French, she would know that gentlemen could not care less if we are intelligent or if we have our health, but they do want to know we have a bosom." She looked at the assistant and said, "Go find Mrs. Rivoire and ask her to come at once."

Louisa looked down again. Right now she couldn't care less whether her gown passed Mrs. Colthrust's neckline inspection.

"I'm sure she will take care of it, but before Gwen comes back in here, may I speak to you in private about something."

"All right," Mrs. Colthrust said in a curt tone while putting on an elbow-length white glove. "But make it quick, as we have three more gowns to try on before we go home. You, my dear, have four more."

Louisa wished the woman would sound a little more pleasant when she was speaking. "I would like for you to help me go to the Court of Chancery."

"What for?" Mrs. Colthrust asked without bothering to look at Louisa, and sounding very uninterested in any answer Louisa might have.

"To see about having the duke removed as our guardian."

Mrs. Colthrust's head jerked up, and she looked at Louisa as if her charge had gone mad. She started pulling the glove up her arm. "Absolutely not! Are you daft?"

"Of course not," Louisa said, remaining calm.

"Doesn't surprise me. Most people who are insane don't know they are, but you must be. You do know that most people would kill to have a duke be in charge of them."

"But his reputation—"

"Means nothing," Mrs. Colthrust cut in. "He is a duke, and he is not only willing, he is also taking very good care of us—that is, you and your sisters. Thankfully, since we all went to his house a few weeks ago, he has not bothered us and we are obviously not bothering him."

Oh, but he does bother me. His kisses have haunted me. I fear I am falling victim to his charms.

"I swear, Louisa, I don't know what to think about you. It's just not sane for a young lady to want to be taken away from a duke. I will have no part of helping you with such a foolish errand."

"Will you keep me from going and talking to someone about the possibility of it so that I can know what could be done?"

"Of course not. See anyone you wish, but quite frankly, I'm surprised that you are so ungrateful to Lord Wayebury for doing this for you and your sisters."

"Turning our welfare over to a rogue is not being good to us."

"Of course it is," Mrs. Colthrust said, tugging on her other glove. "The duke owes you."

"I've never felt that way," Louisa said, affronted that anyone would think the duke owed them anything for her brother's death.

"Well, you should. Besides, Lord Wayebury wouldn't thank me when he returns if I did, and my sister would probably never speak to me again. You would do well to drop this ridiculous notion."

"That is not for you to decide but for the courts, and

I will look into the possibility. My father and brother were viscounts, and so now in my uncle. I am not without standing in the community."

"Of course you are. You are young and have never been in Society, Louisa. You don't realize what you would be up against. A viscount might as well be a tradesman when he's up against a duke for anything. And just whom would you suggest to the court as a replacement?"

Louisa hesitated. "I'm not sure," she said. Her knowledge of qualified people was quite nonexistent. "I thought perhaps the court would know of a kindly old gentleman who wouldn't mind taking on the task."

Mrs. Colthrust laughed.

Louisa didn't back down. "I know it won't be an easy endeavor to take the duke to court. Titles give gentlemen privileges that other men and ladies don't have."

"Exactly. Quite frankly, unless you can show mistreatment at the duke's hands, no court will deny him the rights your uncle signed over to him. Especially since he has offered marriage to fulfill an oath to your brother and you have had the poor judgment not to try to force him to make good on his promise."

"Why would anyone want me to marry a man who was racing my brother when he was killed, a man who is noted for his drunken races through Town, gaming, and—and—"

Mrs. Colthrust smiled. "And what?"

"And has liaisons with mistresses, actresses, and all manner of loose women."

"Wait," Mrs. Colthrust said with a mock look of surprise. "I think you might be talking about our dear Prince, or the Lord Mayor, or perhaps the Lord Chancellor himself and any other gentlemen who reside in

London. Please, Louisa, His Grace did most of what you mentioned when he was younger. Besides, none of that is important to anyone."

"It's important to me."

"Well, you are the only one. A duke is easily forgiven for his transgressions, much like our dear Prince is and any other man of means. Now, take my word for this—no one will feel sorry for you about being under the care of a duke. He's doing what is right by you and your sisters, I might add, and that's all that matters right now."

"Then what am I to do?"

"You could accept it graciously and thank your heavenly angels."

Were she and her sisters destined to be under the guardianship of a man whose kisses made her think of starry nights, warm fires, and magical feelings? A man who would never be home, never be faithful, and—worst of all—who obviously had no tolerance for children, either.

"It's not in me to do that," Louisa said.

Mrs. Colthrust sighed. "But if the duke's wild ways offend your sensibilities, the only thing I can think of that might work is if you found a nobleman willing to marry you and take on the responsibility of all your sisters from the duke. But even then, the duke would have to agree. Which, now that I consider it, he probably would, don't you think? I mean, it can't be an easy task to take on the responsibility of caring for half a dozen girls and see to it that they all make a good match."

"There are five us, Mrs. Colthrust."

"Yes, yes, that's what I said."

Mrs. Rivoire's assistant returned and spoke to Mrs. Colthrust in French, giving Louisa time to think on what her chaperone had said. She was a brash and sometimes cold woman, but her advice made sense—even if Louisa didn't want to hear it.

Find a gentleman she wanted to marry? Louisa hadn't thought about that possibility. She wondered how difficult securing a betrothal might be. Louisa had been to only a handful of dances in the village near Wayebury. She'd enjoyed dancing with the young men, but she couldn't say she'd thought about marriage to any of them. She had never thought about kisses very much until she met the duke, until he kissed her—and now kisses and embraces were constantly on her mind.

But what could she do? She would not, could not leave her sisters to become the wife of any man unless he accepted them, too. Wherever she went, they would have to be welcomed and go with her.

"Mrs. Rivoire will be right with us," Mrs. Colthrust said as the assistant left the room again. "She has to finish with someone else first."

"Thank you for your suggestion, Mrs. Colthrust. It has merit."

"I agree. Perhaps you could find an older gentleman who perhaps would be generous to your sisters for the pleasure of having a young and beautiful wife in his bed."

Louisa remembered the feel of the duke's hard body and his strong embrace. "Well, perhaps he wouldn't have to be too terribly old."

"There's the Earl of Bitterhaven. He might do something like that. He's not a young man but not in his dotage either. His wife died last year, and he has three small children of his own. I doubt a young nobleman would want to be burdened with all your sisters."

Louisa flinched. "I will see to it that my sisters are not a burden to anyone, Mrs. Colthrust. I thank you for your help. At least I now have another option to consider."

"Yes, well, I'm not sure I'm happy that I gave you the alternative you are considering. Something tells me that if you are pleased about it, I shouldn't be. But I would think it would be much easier to find a well-suited country gentleman to marry than to take a duke to court. I don't see that ever ending in your favor. However, if you feel you must look into the possibility, don't let me stop you. I am your chaperone, and I can go with you to the court—but I can't help you."

"I understand, Mrs. Colthrust. You have given me much to think about."

The woman was right, Louisa thought as she turned and headed for the changing room. Going against a powerful duke would not be an easy thing to do, but would finding a gentleman willing to take her for his bride as well as be responsible for her younger sisters be any easier? But at least now she had another option than marriage or guardianship under the Duke of Drakestone, and she would consider it carefully, weighing all possible consequences.

Louisa was a practical person, too. As she mulled over the choices before her, she couldn't overlook the benefits of being under the duke's protection, despite her misgivings.

The problem was that she feared she was now under his spell.

Chapter 15

Life's but a walking shadow, a poor player
That struts and frets his hour upon the stage.
—*Macbeth*, act 5, scene 5

Damned rain!

Bray sat in his book room with his booted feet crossed at the ankles and propped on his desk. He listened to the constant patter of rain hitting the windows and rubbed his forehead. Several times he'd considered rising and pouring a drink but refrained. It was more than the weather that had him feeling restless and in an ill humor this dreary late afternoon.

It was Miss Prim. Lately, it was always Miss Prim.

It had been more than a month since he last saw her, held her in his arms, and kissed her, and still she haunted him. After returning from Yorkshire with Harrison, he'd filled some of his endless days with studying account books and meetings with his solicitors and Members of Parliament, and others with fencing, shooting, or gaming at one of his clubs. The hell of it was that nothing had completely distracted him from thinking about Miss Prim.

And for the life of him, he didn't know why.

Perhaps it was those damned senses they had talked about that afternoon when he held her captive behind the blindfold. It was no wonder she thought him a scoundrel. Kissing her, touching her, letting her touch him as he did that day were devilish things for him to have done to her. He knew she'd never before been touched or kissed.

But the lesson for her had backfired on him.

He couldn't get the taste of her, the feel of her out of his mind. He heard her whispered moans of pleasure in the quietness of the night. He remembered the scent of warm, fresh-washed hair. The only bad thing about having done it was that he kept thinking he wanted to do it again.

And that was madness. He'd already decided she and her sisters were too much trouble. Miss Prim was too headstrong for her own good, and she was too innocent for the likes of him. Her sisters cried over nothing and screeched like banshees when they were having fun. What sane man would want to deal with that every day?

"Damn Wayebury for dying and leaving them alone," Bray said aloud, and swung his feet to the floor. "Foolish man for insisting we race that night!"

Bray rose and walked over to the side table that held the fresh decanter of port Tidmore had brought in when he stoked the fire and lit the lamps. It wasn't that Bray had never been foolish. Damned foolish. Often. He couldn't count all the times he'd done dangerous things and taken unnecessary risks.

It was a wonder he was alive today. When he was younger, he had jumped from high rocks into turbulent waters off the coast of Dover. He let Harrison and Adam shoot milk pails off his head one summer long before they became true marksmen, and probably the most outrageous thing he'd ever done was wrestle a bear just to prove to his friends that he wasn't afraid of anything. But Bray never had five sisters depending on him to see they were properly brought up and wed.

Bray had only himself to worry about—until now.

"And damn Miss Prim's uncle for signing their guardianship over to me," he mumbled to himself as he poured a splash of the deep red liquid into a glass.

Miss Prim had refused to marry him, and he was glad of it. He paid the accounts for her and her sisters, and that was all that was expected of him—except, of course, for the damned vow.

And it was frustrating him.

Bray took a sip of the port. But . . . and often there was a "but."

He couldn't forget the fact that he'd had to force himself not to go over to her house and see her again. His eyes closed, and his hand tightened around his glass. Not going to visit her had been difficult. He didn't understand this unusual yearning to see Miss Prim and hold her in his arms again. Always before, there was just the need for a woman to share pleasure with him. It had never really mattered to him who the woman was, so long as he desired her. Now he found himself wanting to see not just any woman, but in fact, Miss Prim.

For some reason, she made him sense that something was missing; an emptiness in his life had been revealed, and he didn't like that unsettling feeling. Whether he was being lectured by his father, berated by a schoolmaster, or dared by a friend, for as long as he could remember, Bray had always found a way to be content with whatever fate sent his way.

Until now.

"Excuse me, Your Grace."

Bray turned to see Mr. Tidmore standing in the doorway. "Yes?"

"There's a Mr. Hopscotch here to see you. Should I show him in?"

"No."

"Yes, Your Grace," Mr. Tidmore said.

Bray replaced the top on the port decanter and walked to the window to look out over the foggy garden. The shrubs had budded and were a lush shade of green. The raindrops pelted the tender new leaves on the bushes, making them look as if they were dancing. His thoughts drifted back to Miss Prim and her sisters. Were they playing in the house today, since it had rained all afternoon? Had they played chase, blindman's buff, or some other childhood game?

"I'm sorry to disturb you again, Your Grace," Mr. Tidmore said. "But Mr. Hopscotch said he is here on official business for the Prince, and it's most urgent he speak with you."

Bray kept staring out the window and considered not responding to his butler. He really didn't care what the Prince or his lackey wanted. But he knew if he didn't see Mr. Hopscotch today, the man would return tomorrow or the next day, so he relented and said, "Show him in."

"Yes, Your Grace."

"And, Tidmore, if the man ever comes back to my door, don't tell him I'm home."

"Yes, Your Grace."

Bray walked over to the fire, poked the embers, and added a piece of wood while he waited for the Prince's man.

"Thank you for seeing me, Your Grace," Mr. Hopscotch said after he walked in and bowed.

"Since you are on official business for the Prince, get to it and tell me what the Prince wants now."

Mr. Hopscotch didn't appear the least bit perturbed by Bray's curt manner. "Of course, I understand you are a busy man. The Prince wants the same thing he wanted the last time I spoke to you. He wants to remind you that it's been more than three weeks since you've last seen Miss Prim, and there have been no announcements of nuptials."

Bray scowled menacingly at Mr. Hopscotch. He knew exactly how long it had been since he last saw Miss Prim, but how in the hell did the Prince know that?

"Are you following me?"

"Me? No, no, not me," he denied quickly. "That is, of course, well, I can't say how the Prince knew this. It's not for me to question him about anything he does but to do what he asks of me. He doubts whether I made myself clear to you the last time we spoke. He wants you to marry Miss Prim as soon as possible."

Bray put his drink down on the edge of his desk and walked closer to Mr. Hopscotch. "You made it clear. Now you can go."

"But I've returned because you haven't done anything about it. No notice, of nuptials, not even a visit to her house in the last several weeks."

Once more, Bray scowled. "I thought I made it clear whom I marry is none of the Prince's affair."

Mr. Hopscotch cleared his throat. "Well, I must repeat it's always important to the Prince whom dukes marry, Your Grace. Political and financial alliances are usually the best kind of marriages. The Prince wants you to know he understands there might be some other lady you prefer, and if so, by all means have her as your mistress, but marry Miss Prim."

Bray stared the man down, wanting to grab his

neckcloth and tell Hopscotch exactly what he thought about the Prince having him followed, but at the last second, he realized there was no use in terrorizing the messenger.

Instead Bray said, "And I repeat to you, the Prince has no say in whom I marry."

"Very well," Mr. Hopscotch said, and pulled on the tail of his coat. "The Prince had hoped to keep this bit of information from you for many reasons, but now he sees that is impossible. The Prince did not wager from his personal fortune but from England's coffers."

If this was supposed to shock Bray, it didn't. Bray wasn't one to pass judgment on a fellow gambler. He'd made some foolish wagers in his lifetime, too. Bray had lost his share of extravagant bets over the years. He'd been known to put up expensive horses and property as well as blunt, but he never played with anyone else's money or property.

"Then let the dukes he wagered with and his subjects deal with him when he loses."

Mr. Hopscotch sighed and folded his arms across his rotund chest. "This is not about the wager with the dukes. He is not concerned about that one. There is another wager that has nothing to do with them. The Prince was hoping this would never be told, but because time is of the essence, he has given me liberty to tell you why you must marry Miss Prim."

"This conversation grows tiresome. I have no interest in the Prince's gambling habits or debts."

"It's imperative that you listen to me, Your Grace."

Bray bristled at the man's high-handed tone, but he remained quiet.

"A few days after the Prince's wager with the dukes, he had an especially grand evening of much food and wine with the Archduke of Austria. He says he doesn't really remember how it happened, but by the time the dinner was over, he had wagered with the archduke that if you were not married by June one, he would hand over to Austria the Elgin Marbles."

The hairs on the back of Bray's neck rose and "Damnation," whistled past his lips.

The Elgin Marbles had been a bone of contention between Greece and England for several years, not to mention causing many explosive private conversations between friends and brothers alike throughout England the past twenty years. There were the purest, who thought the marbles should never have been taken from Greece by Lord Elgin when he greedily looted and vandalized the Parthenon, and there were those who considered Lord Elgin a hero for rescuing the rapidly disintegrating stones from the clutches of the Ottoman Empire.

Bray gritted his teeth, impatient with the conversation. "The Prince is noted for bringing artifacts into England, not wagering them away. He even helped settle the dispute between Parliament and Greece. Why the hell would he have put up the marbles?"

"Obviously, the archduke caught him at a weak moment. Anyone could understand the archduke trying to get them for Austria. The stones would be a rare asset for the country to obtain. But because of this wager, England stands to gain some rather exquisite pieces to add to the phenomenal collection of treasures the Prince has brought to England. Once you and Miss Prim wed—and, of course, keep the marbles, too."

It was no secret to anyone that the Prince spent money like a drunken pirate in a seedy brothel. He was noted for his extravagant purchases in arts and antiquities and for his many indulgences in other areas, too. He had a penchant for eating and drinking too much, spending lavishly on grand homes, overbuying useless inventions that hadn't yet been proved, and spending England's funds on ridiculously unfounded scientific discoveries. The Prince had long since emptied England's coffers with his madness for spending and merely scoffed when criticized for taxing the citizens to compensate.

Why would Bray want to help the Prince out of this predicament?

Bray was not one to cast stones concerning gaming. Most men, from titled noble down to the footpad on the street, wagered something from time to time. But to wager one of England's treasures, something that wasn't the Prince's to lose, could be considered treasonous. And what would Parliament do if they found out what the Prince had wagered?

Now he knew why some called the Prince a gentleman and some called him a blackguard. Still, the Prince's reputation wasn't Bray's concern.

"Every man is responsible for his own wagers," Bray said. "I've told you, the Prince cannot expect me to be responsible for his."

"Normally that would be true, but this time you are. Why or how this happened is not important now. It is done. The Prince was—"

"Sot-headed," Bray said.

"I won't reference that comment."

"You don't have to."

"Be that as it may, the archduke was a very shrewd man and knew exactly how to exploit the Prince's weaknesses and manipulate him to the archduke's advantage."

"You mean the flamboyant Prince was outfoxed."

"I would never admit to anything so offensive as that. Your Grace, you must understand that this would be a huge embarrassment not only to the Prince but to all of England as well, considering the House of Commons voted to give Greece thirty-five thousand pounds for the Elgin Marbles just two years ago."

Bray remained quiet and walked over to his desk and picked up his drink. He really didn't care about the embarrassment to the Prince over this outrageous wager, but he did care about what it said about England. It would be his luck that if the Prince ended up losing the marbles, Londoners were fickle enough to blame Bray for not marrying Miss Prim rather than blame the Prince for making the wager in the first place.

Everyone knew the Prince had expensive habits, but wagering the Elgin Marbles was a hell of a thing to have done. Bray wondered if anyone else knew the Prince had put England's treasures at risk.

"The Prince has always assumed you would keep your honor and marry Miss Prim. And for doing so, the Prince will be in your debt. He's willing to bestow lands, money, horses, or whatever you desire for your cooperation. So, may I tell the Prince you'll take care of this as soon as possible?"

Bray frowned at the man and took a sip of his drink. "You can tell the Prince I don't need anything from him." Bray walked to the doorway of the book room and called, "Tidmore, come show Mr. Hopscotch the door."

"Remember, Your Grace, that it is your duty to keep the Prince safe from harm just as it is his generals and soldiers who lead and fight his wars. If this gets out, it will harm not only the Prince but England, too. You owe it to him and to your countrymen to keep the marbles safe."

Mr. Hopscotch bowed and nodded before turning away and walking out the door. Bray strode to the side table and added more port to his glass before returning to the window. The rain continued, but with the falling darkness it was barely visible.

Bray remembered that his father's last words to him urged him to establish himself as an honorable man, worthy of the title duke, and to fulfill his duty and marry Miss Prim. Mr. Hopscotch said he owed it to the Prince to marry Miss Prim. Even Wayebury had said Bray owed him. But at what point did one man really owe another?

If he did owe them, what could he do about it? Miss Prim had refused him. Bray had told her she would have to ask him to marry her, and he didn't see that happening anytime soon, certainly not without some wooing on his part.

Bray thought about Miss Prim with single-minded intensity. There was much to like about her. He knew how to go after what he wanted, and he always succeeded once he did. He knew he desired Miss Prim more than he wanted any other woman, but he didn't know if he was willing to pursue her.

He chuckled. The Prince was chasing the wrong rabbit. Bray didn't care if the Prince and England lost the marbles, at least not enough to propose to Miss Prim again.

Chapter 16

Pleasure and action make the hours seem short.
—Othello, act 2, scene 3

The Great Hall looked as if it had been sprinkled with gold dust.

Louisa stood at the entranceway to the large, sweeping ballroom with Gwen and Mrs. Colthrust. The brass and crystal chandeliers glittered and glimmered. Huge mirrors hung on the high walls, reflecting and scattering soft candlelight all over the ballroom.

The ceiling had been washed in a shade of sky blue, a scene of flowers, ferns, and waterfalls painted around the outer edges. Cherubs holding harps, hearts, and bows and arrows looked as if they were dancing across the heavenly tableau. At a quick glance, Louisa counted sixteen massive fluted Corinthian columns draped in pale blue tulle, ivy, and beads that looked like strings of pearls. Large urns overflowing with colorful flowers and statues of Greek gods and goddesses were standing in various places around the room. The décor of the spacious room lived up to its name. It was indeed a great hall.

There were two steps down from the entrance level to the ballroom, which must have held at least five hundred people. To the far side, Louisa saw a vast dance floor where fashionably gowned ladies and dapperly dressed gentlemen twirled, swayed, and hopped as the orchestra played a lively quadrille.

Mrs. Colthrust had chosen an ivory gown with pale pink ribbon fashioned into bows at the high waist and capped sleeves for Gwen, and an alabaster-colored gown with long sheer sleeves and pale green cuffs for Louisa. Both she and Gwen had their hair pinned up with ribbons woven through their golden curls. Mrs. Colthrust wore a low-cut puce-colored gown with strands of beige lace adorning the bodice and skirt. Her headpiece resembled a crown of gold with feathers shooting out of it.

"I've never seen so many candles," Gwen said.

The three ladies stood in the entryway and took in the opulence and frenzied movement of the ballroom below.

"Don't look so awestruck, Gwen," Mrs. Colthrust said in her usual tart tone. "You must see to it that every gentleman you meet thinks you are accustomed to this kind of grandeur, and to be surrounded by it is what you will expect once you marry him."

Louisa smiled at that outrageous comment. She didn't know anyone who would want to or could afford to live amid such grandeur, except perhaps the King, the Prince, and maybe an arrogant duke or two.

"How will I ever get to know anyone in this crowd?" Gwen asked Mrs. Colthrust. "I've never seen so many people in one place."

"Yes, dear, you have. You've been to market day in your village square. I will seek out the people I know well and introduce you. And if the duke keeps his word, he promised to make sure you meet the patronesses of Almack's, which could be crucial to your making a match this Season. But if he doesn't show, I know what to do. I'll find his mother, the dowager duchess, and ask her to fill in for her son. I need to speak to her anyway and thank her for all the help she gave with the merchants. You two need to do the same."

"We will," Louisa said.

"Will all the parties be this big?" Gwen asked.

"Don't be silly, dear girl," Mrs. Colthrust said. "Can't you remember anything I have told you these past weeks? Must I go over all the invitations and the names again?"

"Of course not," Louisa said, speaking up for her sister. "I'm sure it's not uncommon to be a little nervous and a tiny bit intimidated by seeing your first ballroom. I know I am."

"I suppose I was, back in the day, too," Mrs. Colthrust said. "However, Gwen, there will be many parties held in homes. Some will even be intimate dinner parties of less than fifty people. Those are the ones we want you to be invited to as the Season progresses. Gentlemen want to know that the young lady they choose for their bride is sought after by many. It makes the hunt for the right match more exciting. Don't you think so, Louisa?"

"Yes," Louisa agreed, though she wasn't so sure. She had no knowledge of what Mrs. Colthrust was referring to. She took Gwen's hand and said, "You are beautiful, and you will woo every gentleman you meet tonight."

Gwen smiled, too. "I need only woo one."

Mrs. Colthrust continued her explanation to Gwen,

and Louisa listened as she looked at the people in the room below. She was awestruck by the many rich colors of fabrics and the elaborately styled gowns. Some of the ladies wore headpieces that were tall, feathered, and beaded while others, like Louisa and Gwen, wore simple ribbons, strands of pearls, or fresh-cut flowers woven throughout their hair. The gentlemen were handsome, too. All of them wore black coats with tails, but their waistcoats were in a variety of bold colors and adorned with either brass or silk-covered buttons.

Louisa realized she was looking at the faces of the gentlemen in the room, hoping to catch sight of the Duke of Drakestone. It was maddening how easily her thoughts turned to him. She hadn't seen or heard from His Grace since the afternoon he showed up at her house unannounced and tricked her into touching him and kissing him. Her cheeks still heated whenever she thought about that day. She refused to fool herself and say she hadn't enjoyed his touch and his kisses that afternoon—because she had. And though it pained her to admit it even to herself, she wanted to see him and talk to him again.

"Already, I see many handsome gentlemen," Gwen said. "I do hope one of them will ask me to dance."

"Ha! One of them?" Mrs. Colthrust said sharply. "You shall dance with them all. And you, too, of course, Louisa."

"I will do my share of looking over the young men," Louisa assured her chaperone. She had thought she'd be looking only for Gwen, but now she wanted to look for herself as well. She needed a kind and considerate gentleman to sweep her off her feet and banish all thoughts of the duke from her mind—and, of course, accept her sisters, too.

"Look, here comes Mr. Newman. His uncle is a baron

and quite well thought of in Society. Mr. Newman will be the perfect gentleman to start the evening. Both of you stay calm and behave exactly the way I've instructed you, and all will be well.

"Mr. Newman, how are you this evening?" Mrs. Colthrust said in the soft, friendly voice she usually reserved for when she was talking about the Dowager Duchess of Drakestone.

"Quite well, Mrs. Colthrust, and you?"

"Absolutely heavenly. I'm always enchanted by the first ball of the Season. I don't believe you've met my nieces," she said.

"No," he said, taking his time to smile at both Gwen and Louisa.

"They've only recently arrived in London. And they are, of course, Lord Wayebury's nieces, too," she said, and then made the proper introductions.

Mr. Newman bowed. "Ladies, I'm pleased to make your acquaintance. And may I add that all of you are looking lovely tonight."

Mrs. Colthrust laughed softly, flicked open her fan, and fluttered it as she said, "How kind of you to say."

The conversation continued with Mr. Newman asking how they were enjoying the city. Louisa took a step back and let Gwen answer. She wanted to see how Gwen interacted with the young man. And she wanted to look the young man over, too. He was tall, slim, and had a very youthful-looking face. His brown hair was trimmed short. His eyes seemed a little ordinary and without much sparkle, but when he smiled, he was very pleasant to look at.

"Miss Prim," Mr. Newman said, looking at Louisa, "am I correct in understanding that you are spoken for by His Grace, the Duke of Drakestone?"

Louisa opened her mouth to blurt out a strong no

when it dawned on her that perhaps she should leave that bit of information a little vague for the time being. "At this time, there are still many things to be settled between the duke and me."

"I see. Well, perhaps, Miss Prim and Miss Gwen, you'll both save a dance for me later in the evening?"

They both assured him they would, and after he excused himself, Mrs. Colthrust, Gwen, and Louisa moved down into the depths of the noisy ballroom. They met one person after another. Mrs. Colthrust was doing an excellent job of introducing them. It amazed Louisa that the woman could sound so cold when talking to her and her sisters and sound like a sweet and gentle woman when introducing them to the ton.

Louisa was also surprised that almost everyone they met either mentioned the Duke of Drakestone or asked her about him. What was happening between her and the duke was on everyone's mind. She answered them all the same way she had answered Mr. Newman.

Over the course of an hour or so, Mrs. Colthrust was like an out-of-control steamship plowing through stormy waters when they were trying to get from one side of the overpacked ballroom to the other, and like a dainty butterfly flitting from one flower to another when they moved from one group of people to another. After only a few minutes, it was impossible for Louisa to remember half the people she'd met just minutes before. And from the look on Gwen's face, she wasn't doing any better.

Louisa and Miss Kindred were able to teach Gwen many things over the years, but neither of them had the faintest idea how to help her make a good match. Mrs. Colthrust was the most abrasive person Louisa had ever known, but she seemed to know her way around Polite Society. Louisa supposed she had to thank her uncle for asking Mrs. Colthrust to assist them and not leaving them completely on their own.

When Mr. Newman claimed Gwen for her first dance of the evening, Louisa had wanted to watch them, but that was impossible. Mrs. Colthrust took hold of her wrist and dragged her through the crowd to be presented to the Earl of Bitterhaven. As the introductions were made, Louisa was standing almost eye level with the earl. He wasn't a tall, regal, or dashingly handsome gentleman, but he wasn't a poorly looking man either. He was fit for his age, and his brown eyes seemed kind.

"Yes, yes, I knew your father, Miss Prim, and I know your uncle well, though I'm sorry to say I don't remember ever meeting your brother. It was a shame what happened to him, and so young."

"Yes, it was," Louisa said softly, feeling a lump of sadness rise in her throat. Most everyone she'd met mentioned the duke. The earl was the first person to have remembered and mentioned her brother, and for that consideration, she took an instant liking to him. "Thank you for remembering him."

"Where is your uncle these days? I haven't seen the old chap at any of the clubs recently."

"He's on extended holiday," she said, not wanting to tell the gentleman she had no idea where her uncle was.

"He and my sister wanted to get away and explore the world, so we don't know from week to week where they might be," Mrs. Colthrust added.

"I see, yes—well, of course they would enjoy such a journey. And this is your first Season, isn't it, Miss Prim?"

"Yes."

"In that case, if you don't think the Duke of Drakestone will mind, I'd enjoy a dance with you. You don't mind, do you, Mrs. Colthrust?"

"No, not at all."

"Good." He looked at Louisa. "I'm sure they'll be announcing a waltz soon. When they do, I will meet you by the urn on the right side of the floor."

The earl then said his good-byes and walked away.

"Tell me what you thought of him," Mrs. Colthrust said almost as soon as the man's back was turned.

"He seems a very kind man," Louisa said truthfully.

"Is that all you can say?" Mrs. Colthrust complained. "That answer will not land you a husband."

No, she could add that there were no quivers in her stomach, no catch in her breath. Her heart didn't race at the sight of him, and her breasts didn't tingle when he looked at her and spoke to her. And the shame of it was that the only man who made her feel all those wonderful things was a beast. But she couldn't say any of that to Mrs. Colthrust.

Annoyed by Louisa's less-than-satisfactory answer, Mrs. Colthrust excused herself to go to the retiring room. Louisa took the opportunity to unobtrusively make her way over to the long line of dowagers, spinsters, and widows who were sitting against the wall near the dance floor. She stood at one end of a line of about twenty ladies. They were chatting, laughing, and fanning themselves. They seemed to be having a delightful time. Louisa listened to their chatter while she watched Gwen, who was now dancing with a gentleman other than Mr. Newman. It certainly hadn't taken her sister long to lose her shyness. Gwen looked stunning, and she hadn't missed a step since Louisa started watching her dance.

"He's here, ladies, he's here," Louisa heard one of the women sitting in the line say. "Quiet now, quiet."

Louisa looked in the direction they were all staring and saw none other than the handsome Duke of Drakestone. Her stomach tumbled over itself. He stood at the entrance to the ballroom, looking like a magnificent Adonis. She didn't know if her heart skipped a beat, fluttered, or stopped altogether when she saw him. She must have been introduced to more than twenty gentlemen, but so far, none of them came close to making her feel the way the duke made her feel when she looked at him.

There were more murmurings from the ladies lining the wall. She stared at them in disbelief as they moistened their lips, touched their hair, and pinched their cheeks. They all looked at him with adoring expressions. Louisa smiled. She couldn't blame them for mooning over him, but did they really think this arrogant man was going to notice them? Not that they weren't all lovely in their own way, but surely they knew the duke could command the attention of any of the beautiful young ladies in the room, except for Gwen.

He spoke to people as he passed but didn't let any of them deter or stop him for long.

"Do you think he will favor us as he has in years past?" one of the ladies asked.

"I don't see why not," another answered.

"Of course he will," another lady said.

Someone farther down the line said something Louisa couldn't hear, and apparently the other women didn't hear her either, because she said it again only louder, "He's done it every year he's attended a ball, as far, as I know."

"He does it just to make the young ladies jealous that they are not chosen for his first dance."

"He's such a rake."

"Isn't he handsome tonight?"

"And the older he gets, the more handsome he becomes."

"I do believe he's wearing his hair a little longer this year."

"Makes him look even more like a devilish rogue, doesn't it?"

The ladies laughed, and Louisa moved closer to the lady in the chair beside her. The room was so crowded, she didn't think the woman would notice that she was listening to their conversation. She was intrigued by what they said, and amazed she could even hear the ladies with the music and all the other loud chatter going on in the room.

"Hush, now, all of you." Still another lady, farther down the line, said, "Of course he will favor. He always has, and I'm certain he always will."

"At least until he marries."

"If he marries."

"Of course he will. He'll need an heir."

"I heard he wasn't going to marry that Miss Prim. Has anyone heard any more about that?"

Louisa stiffened. The ladies had no way of knowing who she was. She wasn't even sure any of them had noticed her standing there.

"He would have married her long ago if he was going to."

"My brother said the duke is waiting so long because he is hoping she will marry someone else."

Several of the ladies laughed.

"I've heard she's going to be here tonight. Has anyone seen her?"

Louisa remained as straight and stiff as if a rod were in her back. She would have no choice but to admit who she was if the lady she was standing next to turned to her and asked her name.

"Look. He's coming this way. Quiet now, and smile. Here he comes."

"See, I told you he would pay his respects to us before he asks any other lady to dance."

"Which of us do you think he'll pick?"

"I was the first one he danced with last year," said a woman who looked as if she could be the oldest lady sitting in the line.

"It was I who was first the year before that."

"I was picked first one year, too," another lady said.

Louisa marveled that these ladies were bragging about who was the first of the Season to dance with the duke. Obviously, not many gentlemen treated them to a dance, or else the duke's favor wouldn't be so important to them.

Louisa watched as His Grace stopped and bowed before each lady, taking her hand and kissing it, saying a few words before straightening and moving on to the next one and doing exactly the same thing again.

He was getting closer to the end of the line, closer to her. She should hurry away before he looked up and saw her. He'd never know she'd been there, because he didn't let his eyes wander around the room or sneak a peek at the next lady in line while he was talking to whoever was in front of him. He wasn't kissing air or looking as if he'd rather be anywhere else. He gave whomever he was talking to his full attention and, as the lady had said, the respect they deserved for their age and their position be they widow, spinster, or dowager.

She kept thinking she needed to leave before he saw her, but she couldn't make her feet move. When he rose from talking to the last lady, he found himself standing before Louisa. She thought she saw surprise in his eyes—but couldn't be sure because he was too good at hiding all his emotions except annoyance. She's seen that one more than once.

Louisa curtsied, looked into his beautiful green eyes, and whispered, "Your Grace."

He bowed and said, "Miss Prim."

He reached for her gloved hand, and the second his fingers closed around hers, she felt a blanket of warmth as if she were standing in front of a roaring fire. He kissed the back of her hand and then stepped between her and the row of ladies.

His gaze swept up her face, quickly down her body, and back up to her eyes. "You are very lovely tonight. I almost didn't recognize you."

"Well, I—I am all dressed for the ball tonight," she said, thinking she must have looked absolutely wretched the few times he'd seen her at the Mayfair town house. "If you'd had the decency to let me know that you were going to call on me, you wouldn't have caught me in such a state of dishabille while playing with my sisters."

He smiled and—heaven help her—her legs turned to water.

"You looked quite fetching after playing with your sisters, your long sunset-colored tresses dancing across your shoulders, and your cheeks flushed from the exertion. I meant I didn't recognize you without your *four* sisters standing watch behind you."

"Oh, well, of course, you know they are too young to— Thank you," she finally said, wanting to hide her sudden inability to get a sentence out correctly. If she weren't so busy remembering his kisses and embrace, she wouldn't be so tongue-tied.

"How are Miss Sybil, Miss Lillian, and Miss Bonnie?" he asked.

"Doing very well," she answered getting control of her runaway feelings. "They are as loud and noisy as usual, running about the house."

"Just what I would expect from happy girls." He smiled again, this time cunningly. "And how is Saint?"

"The same."

"That's good to hear."

"I hope you haven't missed him too much."

"I haven't missed him at all."

Louisa lifted her chin, and her eyes narrowed a little. "I don't believe you."

"It's true." The duke smiled for a third time. "How could I miss him when I know he is getting all that attention from your sisters?"

"They are happy to have him. Thank you again for giving him to them."

"No more thank-yous needed. Is Miss Gwen enjoying herself tonight?"

"I think she was a little nervous when we first arrived, but once she started meeting people and saw how eager they were to meet her, she relaxed and found her charm."

"And what of you? Are you enjoying yourself?"

"Of course."

"Then why don't you look like you are?"

He could raise the fine hairs on the back of her neck faster than anyone. "I don't know what you mean. I'm having a wonderful time. And if I don't show it right now, it's only because I am talking to you and not some other gentleman who is not only nicer but more handsome, too."

He seemed to be weighing the sincerity of her words. "You look as if you're wondering if I'm going to kiss you again."

"I do not, Your Grace," she said indignantly.

"Am I interrupting anything?"

At the sound of the voice behind her, Louisa turned to see that a tall, regal woman with light brown hair piled high on her head had joined them. Her dark golden gown was lovely, though it was lacking trim, lace, or beads of any kind. After having spent the better part of three weeks looking at fabrics in Mrs. Rivoire's boutique, Louisa knew the dowager duchess's gown had real gold thread woven in it and needed no other adornment. And while her gown and headpiece were plain, her jewelry was expensive and exquisite. The scooped neck of her gown was covered by a spiderweb of intricately woven emeralds and diamonds set in delicate gold filigree. The same pattern was in earrings that dropped almost to the tops of her shoulders.

When Louisa's gaze met the woman's, she thought she could have been looking into the duke's eyes. Her face was much like her son's, unreadable.

Louisa wasn't sure she'd even listened to the introductions so intent was she on the woman herself. The duchess appeared to be a little older than Mrs. Colthrust, perhaps only a few years past the age of fifty.

"Miss Prim," Her Grace said, "I've heard about you for over two years now. I'm glad to finally meet you."

Louisa cast her eyes around to the duke, thinking she could just imagine what the two must have said about her.

"Oh, no need to look at my son," she said with a rather sly smile, and cut her own gaze over to him. "He has never mentioned you to me."

"Really?" Louisa said, finding that statement hard to believe.

"Shocking, I know," she answered. "But he likes to think he's keeping me in the dark concerning his private life, but with the ton and their gossip mills, and the many wagers throughout the city—really, now, how could he?"

"I do try, though, Your Grace," the duke said to his mother.

"As it should be. A mother has no right to know all her son's affairs, does she?"

"Not as far as I'm concerned," he answered.

Louisa liked the easy way in which the duke and his mother talked to each other. Though their tone sounded formal, it was clear from the way they looked at each other that they were very much at ease and enjoying their banter.

Her Grace smiled at the duke before giving her attention back to Louisa. "I've heard your name countless times at dinner parties, card parties, picnics in the park, and private conversations. Wherever there are people, they are always talking about my son, and usually it's about his vow to your brother."

"I'm sorry my brother put him in that position, Your Grace."

"I'm not," she answered. "I've loved every moment of it, though I'm not sure he would say the same, am I right?"

"You are," the duke said, not looking at all uncomfortable that he was the topic of the conversation.

"Why would you love gossip about your son?" Louisa had to ask.

"Well, it's certainly better to be talked about than not even thought about," she said, and then laughed softly.

"You know, Your Grace," the duke said, "I do seem to remember that we spoke once of Miss Prim."

A wrinkle formed on the duchess's brow. "When was that?"

"Shortly after the accident, you asked me what I planned to do about Miss Prim."

The light of surprise danced in her eyes. "Oh, you are right. I did ask once, but that was a long time ago. Forgive me, Miss Prim, my memory's not as good as it used to be."

Louisa didn't believe for a moment that the lady had

a poor memory. She seem exceptionally sharp to Louisa. "What did he answer?" The words tumbled from Louisa's mouth before she could pull them back. She immediately added, "I'm sorry, Your Grace. Forgive me, I shouldn't be asking about a private conversation between you and your son."

The duchess shrugged. "I can't give away his secrets. I don't know any, but I believe his answer to me was something on the order of 'I have no time set that I will.'"

"That doesn't surprise me."

"It didn't surprise me either," the duchess said. "He never does what is expected of him, no matter how rewarding it might be."

"I've noticed."

"And now it's obvious that his tardiness in approaching you didn't upset you either," the duchess said.

"Not in the least," Louisa answered with a smile, appreciating their candid conversation.

"However, Your Grace," the duke said, looking over to his mother again, "you should know that I did tell Miss Prim a few weeks ago that I wanted to marry her."

The duchess's eyes widened as she regarded Louisa. "Well, that is news I hadn't heard. Though there have been many doubters in London that my son would live up to his promise, I knew he would eventually get around to doing the right thing." Giving her attention to the duke she said, "I'm sure your father is now settling comfortably into his grave."

"Not quite yet," he responded. "She declined my offer."

The duchess's expression changed to one of admiration. "You rejected my son? That has to be a first for him."

"I'll not deny or admit that, but I believe Miss Prim's exact words to me were, 'I wouldn't marry you if you were tipped in gold and trussed up with a thousand strings of rubies.' Is that an accurate account of what you said, Miss Prim?"

Louisa felt her cheeks heating and hoped the candles had burned low enough that no one could see her heightened color. She cleared her throat. "You might have missed the count of the rubies by a strand or two, but that's fairly accurate, Your Grace."

"Hmm," the duchess said. "She must have heard about your devilish ways."

"That probably says it a bit nicer than she would have."

His mother laughed a deep, hearty laugh, and Louisa was heartened to know the woman hadn't taken offense at Louisa's disparaging comments about her son.

Louisa wanted to get off the conversation about marriage, so she said, "Thank you for assisting Mrs. Colthrust with getting accounts set up for us at the shops in Town. That was a lovely thing for you to do, and it helped immensely."

"If there is one thing I've learned since becoming a duchess, it's which shops offer the best fabrics. Your gown is lovely, by the way, Miss Prim. Now, if you will excuse me, I promised His Grace—" She paused and looked over at the duke—"that I would find one of the patronesses of Almack's and introduce you and your sister to her. I'll find you and your sister later in the evening and take care of that."

"Thank you, Your Grace," Louisa said.

As soon as the duchess said her good-byes and walked away, Louisa turned to the duke. His face had twisted into a scowl, and he was staring at the dance floor. The dance was a fast quadrille, but Louisa caught sight of Gwen and a dashing young man who definitely knew his way around a dance floor. They were laughing and looked perfectly matched.

"Why do you have such a grimace?" Louisa asked. "Do you think I said something to offend your mother?"

"No. Look whom Miss Gwen is dancing with. Did you or Mrs. Colthrust give her permission to dance with him?"

Louisa studied the man. She knew they had been introduced, but she didn't remember his name. "I'm sure one of us must have. She wouldn't be dancing with him otherwise."

"He is the last person you should want her with."

"We met so many people, I'm afraid I don't remember anything about him. Who is he, and why shouldn't Gwen be dancing with him?"

"He is Mr. Stanly Standish, and she shouldn't be dancing with him, because he's too much like I was a few years ago."

Louisa looked at the duke. "You mean he's—?"

"Yes, Miss Prim. He's a scoundrel of the highest order, too."

Chapter 17

We know what we are, but know not what we may be.
—*Hamlet,* act 4, scene 1

"Are you sure?" Miss Prim asked him.

Annoyed that she'd questioned him, Bray frowned. "Surely this is not an area where you need to doubt me."

"But he seemed such a pleasant and true gentleman when I met him earlier tonight."

"How else would you expect him to conduct himself when meeting a beautiful young lady, her sister, and her chaperone at a ballroom? Even scoundrels know how to behave properly, Miss Prim. They just seldom do."

A twist of worry wrinkled her forehead. "I'm sure you are right about him, Your Grace. I just don't like admitting that you are."

Bray let his gaze feather down her face. He wanted to pull her to his chest and hold her, soothe her brow. At this moment, he didn't necessarily want to kiss her or even make love to her. He'd always loved the feel of a woman in his arms, beneath him, or astride him. He loved the pleasure he gave and received. But he couldn't remember ever wanting to hold a woman just so he could feel her close to him.

Miss Prim aroused things he didn't want to feel, such as caring whether or not Miss Gwen was dancing with a rake. It should mean nothing to him, but for reasons he could not understand, he did care.

"Well, don't just stand there looking at me as if there were other things on your mind," Miss Prim said. "Do something."

There are other things on my mind!

Bray crossed his hands over his chest and shrugged. "What do you suggest I do?"

"I have no idea. What do you usually do when a scoundrel dances with an innocent young lady?"

"Nothing."

"Nothing? That is not a satisfactory answer."

"It's only a dance. They are in full view of everyone, and it's ending now. Just tell her to be careful of him and not to find herself out on a dark terrace with him."

"Is he noted for ruining the reputations of young ladies?"

"If you call breaking their hearts ruining them," Bray said, and noticed that someone had moved into his line of vision just over Miss Prim's shoulder.

It was Mr. Hopscotch. When the Prince's man was certain he had Bray's attention, he nodded in an approving manner, then turned and walked away. Bray checked his impulse to go after the man, jerk him against the wall, and scare the devil out of him.

Bray didn't like being followed. If he decided to pursue Miss Prim, it would be because he wanted to, not because the Prince had unscrupulously wagered the Elgin Marbles in expectation of Bray's nuptials.

"I certainly don't want her heart broken by a rogue,"

Miss Prim said. "I'll be sure to speak to her about him. Thank you for alerting me."

Bray heard the call for the next dance and said, "You'll have to excuse me. The next dance will be a waltz, and I need to collect the lady I've promised the dance to."

"Oh, if it's a waltz, then I must go meet someone, too."

Bray felt a catch in his breath. "Whom are you dancing with?"

She smiled at him and his stomach clenched. "As if you care? Thank you again for alerting me to Mr. Standish. I'll guide Gwen in a different direction should she find favor with him. Excuse me, Your Grace."

In a flash, she turned and was gone. Bray watched her until she was out of sight. She was right. He didn't care whom she was dancing with, but he still wanted to know who the man was.

Bray hadn't kissed a young lady her first Season in Society for more than a few years now. They were too vulnerable and too impressionable. One kiss, and they thought the gentleman would be asking for their hand in marriage the next day.

They fell in love too easily, and the simplest attention had them thinking of their weddings and changing their names. So he'd dance with them, smile at them, and share a glass of champagne with them at balls, but he'd long since stopped asking them out for rides in the park or sought to spend time alone with them. Innocents were just too much trouble. He'd had more than a few young ladies burst into tears in front of him when he refused to offer for their hand. He didn't have to worry about a mistress wanting to leg-shackle him. Discreet affairs had saved him a lot of trouble and the young ladies a lot of heartache.

But Miss Prim wasn't like the usual girl her first

Season out. She was more mature, yet she could seem so young when she was chasing her sisters through the house or playing blindman's buff with them.

Bray claimed the hand of the Dowager Countess of Bloomingville, and they walked toward the dance floor. He had chosen one of the ladies lining the wall for his first dance for as long as he could remember.

The ritual had started just as a ploy to irritate his father. The late duke had flown into a furious rage after three demanding fathers came to him, thinking Bray was going to propose to their daughters. The duke proceeded to give Bray a long and booming lecture about young ladies making their debut Season and how he must never be alone with them.

His father was always fearful that an unworthy chit without proper heritage would catch him in a parson's mousetrap. Bray's father didn't care if he had five mistresses and two widows in his bed at one time, but he'd warned him against taking one innocent miss to his bed or to a dark terrace for a romantic interlude. Since his father did not want him to show favor to the young ladies, Bray had started showing favor to the older ladies in retaliation—and they loved it.

He could still remember the expression on his father's face the first time he walked over to the line of dowagers, spinsters, and widows. Bray had bowed and kissed their hands and then selected one of them to dance with him. For once, the old duke was speechless. The ladies were in no danger from him nor was he in danger from any of them. It was simply an enjoyable dance for all concerned—and a thorn in his father's side.

Bray talked politely with the countess as they danced, but every once in a while, he'd catch a glimpse of Miss Prim dancing with the Earl of Bitterhaven. Bray had nothing against the man, except that he didn't want the earl touching Miss Prim's back or holding her hand while they danced the waltz. Because they were the same height, the earl couldn't get his arm up high enough on the turns, so Miss Prim had to duck when she twirled under his arm. Bray didn't like the fact that she seemed to be having such a grand time either.

The only good thing was that the earl was a harmless man—or he'd better be.

Over the next couple of hours, Bray did his duty as the newest duke in the ton and allowed all the pushy mamas to present to him their daughters who were entering Society for the first time. As was expected of him, he asked some of them to dance, though his thoughts and his eyes were constantly searching the dance floor to see which gentleman had next captured Miss Prim's fancy.

Since her first dance of the evening with Lord Bitterhaven, Miss Prim had turned into the belle of the ball. She was on the arm of a gentleman for dance after dance. Miss Gwen hadn't slowed down either. There were more than two dozen young ladies making their Society debut tonight, and he hadn't seen any one of them dancing as many times as Louisa and her sister. There was nothing like gossip to make Londoners a little curious about a person.

After more than half a dozen dances, Bray decided he'd paid his dues to Society and the ladies and had danced enough. He went in search of a good stiff drink. Unfortunately for him, the Great Hall served only wine and champagne.

"You certainly are making a name for yourself tonight, Your Grace."

Bray accepted a glass from the server and turned to face Seaton. "You mean I hadn't done that already."

Seaton gave him a rueful glare. "Every set of eyes in

the room has been on you and Miss Prim all night, and you've both managed to dance with everyone but each other."

Bray sipped his champagne, and the two moved away from the serving table and over to a corner, where they could talk in private.

"I hadn't noticed."

"You hadn't noticed that you haven't danced with the one lady in the room whom everyone keeps expecting you to dance with?"

"No."

"Well, I don't know what to say to that."

"Sure you do. You always have something to say."

"All right, then, I'll speak truthfully and say I don't believe you."

Bray turned away from the old man and looked around the ballroom. "I wish you didn't know me so well. It's a damn nuisance at times."

Seaton harrumphed. "Don't try to change the subject. You know everyone is waiting for you to dance with Miss Prim, which is precisely the reason you haven't."

Bray shrugged and took another sip of his drink.

"I suppose you're really not hard to figure out. If the majority of people expect you to do something, I can bet money you won't. Everyone is assuming you haven't asked Miss Prim to marry you."

"Are they?"

"It's being whispered."

"But you know I asked her to marry me and that she turned me down."

"No one else seems to know that."

Bray thought on that for a few seconds. "I wonder why Miss Prim hasn't told anyone."

"I doubt anyone has been bold enough to come right out and ask her if you have offered for her hand. By your actions tonight, it's a rational assumption that you haven't."

Bray kept his features passive, but his thoughts went back to the day he told Miss Prim she would have to ask him to marry her. He was thinking now that might not have been his finest hour, but it certainly gave him reason to pursue her if he decided to do so. Pursuit grew more tempting each time he remembered those blindfolded kisses.

"Have you even spoken to her this evening?"

"Yes."

Bray looked up and saw Louisa and Mrs. Colthrust walking toward the champagne table. His stomach clenched again, and he wondered how long he was going to feel affected when he looked at her. She and her chaperone seemed to be deep in conversation and didn't notice him or the other gentleman standing in the corner.

She looked divinely lovely in her dark ivory gown with its provocatively sheer sleeves. And while her hair being swept up on top of her head was quite becoming, he would much rather see Louisa's long silken curls hanging past her shoulders.

"Have you met Miss Prim, Seaton?"

"Not yet."

"Then it's time you did."

Bray and Seaton walked over to the champagne table. Miss Prim's back was to him, and when the server extended a glass to her, Bray reached out and took the glass from the server. "Allow me," he said, and handed her the glass. He then gave one to Mrs. Colthrust and introduced Seaton to them.

After their greetings, Seaton immediately caught Mrs. Colthrust's attention and engaged her in a conversation about a mutual friend. Bray would have to remember to thank him for keeping the chaperone busy while he talked to Miss Prim.

"I don't think you've sat down all evening," Bray said to her.

"I haven't. There's no time between the dances. I'm so glad the musicians finally took a break so I could have something to drink."

"You are very popular."

"So are you."

"So we've been watching each other."

"Your mother was very kind to Gwen tonight."

"Changing the subject, are you, Miss Prim?"

"I think it best, don't you? Your mother introduced us to two of the patronesses of Almack's. They seemed to enjoy talking to Gwen. I'm sure we'll be receiving vouchers sometime during the Season."

"Her Grace wouldn't have helped you if she hadn't wanted to."

"Louisa, there you are!" Gwen said, running up to her and taking hold of both her hands. "I've been look-ing everywhere for you. Your Grace," she said, giving him a hurried glance and half a curtsy before turning back to her sister. "This evening has been absolutely heavenly. I've had the most wonderful time of my life. You'll never guess what has happened!"

"I'm sure I can't possibly guess what has you so thrilled."

"I need your very best wishes because I've met the man I'm going to marry!"

Miss Gwen giggled excitedly. Miss Prim's shocked gaze flew to Bray's. Her sister's pronouncement didn't surprise him. This was what innocent young girls did when they found themselves at their first ball and in the company of a handsome gentleman who was showing them attention, but apparently, Miss Prim didn't know it was to be expected. She was looking as if nothing could have shocked her more.

"You can't have," Miss Prim admonished her sister lightly. "This is only your first ball. You've been here less than four hours."

"And I didn't even need all four hours to find him," Miss Gwen declared. "I only had to look into his eyes once, and I knew he was the husband for me. And he dances so divinely."

"Gwen, you can't be serious."

"But I am," she said again, and gave Bray another quick glance. "I swear I knew it the moment I saw him."

Miss Prim looked at Bray, too, as if to suggest he could do something about her silly sister's proclamation. Bray was staying out of this fray.

"Did I meet him tonight? What is his name?"

"Yes, you met him." Miss Gwen's eyes turned dreamy. "Mr. Stanly Standish. Wait until you see him smile, Louisa—you will fall in love with him, too."

I hope not, Bray thought.

Miss Prim looked to Bray again. And again, he remained noncommittal. Helping an innocent deal with her first blush of love was beyond him. Besides, he was usually the cause of the infatuation.

"He's the most handsome gentleman I've ever seen. I'm in love, Louisa. Be happy for me, I'm in love."

"But you can't be in love—surely you know how outrageous that sounds," her sister argued.

Miss Gwen gaped at Miss Prim as if she were daft. "But I am. Remember you told me you would not try to tell me whom I could and couldn't marry."

"I told you that, but I didn't think you were going to fall for the first gentleman you met."

"Oh, you can be so picky sometimes. He wasn't the first gentleman I met, but I knew the moment I saw him that he was the one for me. And he must be in love with me, too, because he asked me to go for a ride in the park tomorrow afternoon. I told him I'd go."

"Well, you can't go," Miss Prim countered defiantly.

"Of course she can," Mrs. Colthrust said, stepping away from Seaton to add to the discussion. "This is just the sort of thing we want for her. She needs to be sought after by acceptable young men like Mr. Standish. His uncle is an earl, and he's third in line for the title!"

"I don't care who or what his uncle is," Miss Prim said. "It's much too soon for her to be riding in a carriage alone with a man, especially if she thinks she loves him."

"Where do you get these odd ideas, Louisa?" Mrs. Colthrust said. "It's a good thing I am handling her Season and not you, or she'd never make a match. It's perfectly acceptable for her to ride in the park with Mr. Standish. It will help her gain attention from other gentlemen when they see she has met the favor of a well-sought-after young man so soon."

"It won't help her if she is already declaring herself in love!" Miss Prim looked at Bray again. "Do something, Your Grace."

Bray reached over and picked up a glass of champagne. He handed it to Miss Gwen and said, "Congratulations."

Miss Prim's eyes shot daggers at him.

Chapter 18

Why, this is very midsummer madness.
—*Twelfth Night,* act 3, scene 4

Louisa had never slept so late, but then she'd never been up so late the night before either. Mrs. Colthrust had assured her on the way home that every night would be as late or later during the Season and that after a few evenings, she would get used to the change in her sleeping habits. Louisa could tell she wasn't going to like that.

After much talking last night, she'd finally made Gwen admit that she would have to wait until Mr. Standish offered for her hand before she could start planning her wedding. Though Gwen continued to insist that it was love at first sight for both of them and she had no doubts Mr. Standish would ask her to marry him. Louisa thought the conversation would have gone much better had Mrs. Colthrust not agreed with everything Gwen said.

Louisa had spent most of the morning wringing her hands behind her back while helping Gwen get ready for her very first ride in the park. Louisa thought it ridiculous that she wanted to try on every dress in her wardrobe when she'd just had them all made in the last four weeks. But in order to prove she wasn't the hovering nanny Gwen had accused her of being, she indulged her sister and watched while she tried on every dress and some more than once.

Louisa still thought it much too soon to allow Gwen to go for a ride with a gentleman, especially one who was a known heartbreaker, but Mrs. Colthrust had insisted it was perfectly fine. Because of the duke's warning, Louisa had reservations about Mr. Standish that brought her to the point of pacing in the drawing room while she waited for Gwen's suitor to arrive.

Gwen was nervous, too, but for a different reason, of course. Why couldn't her sister have been attracted to Mr. Newman? He was handsome and seemed like a kind and sensible young man.

Louisa heard footsteps rushing down the stairs, and moments later, Gwen flew into the drawing room. "Am I late? He's not here, is he?"

"No, no, don't fret so. You are dressed in plenty of time," Louisa said.

"How do I look? Do I need to change anything?"

Gwen twirled, and Louisa had to laugh. She'd never seen such enthusiasm from her sister.

"You look beautiful, and you know you do." Her pale green dress was sprigged with a darker green thread. She held a matching bonnet, parasol, and pelisse in her hand.

"Thank you, Louisa." She ran over to the window to wait and watch. "He's getting out of his carriage." She spun back toward Louisa. "Are my cheeks rosy and my lips pink?"

"Calm down, my dear. You look perfect. I have Mrs. Trumpington making tea to go with the apple tarts she made this morning. I think he will enjoy them, don't you?"

Gwen clasped her hands together and said, "Oh, do we have to stay here for tea? Please can't we just go out and enjoy a lovely afternoon in the park? Please."

"It's the polite thing to do. You don't want him thinking we don't have proper manners. Besides, it will give both of us more time to get to know him before you go."

"You shall have plenty of time for that, Sister, but not today. Let me get to know him first, please?"

Louisa opened her mouth to deny her sister's request when the door knocker sounded. Gwen kissed her cheek and started to rush out of the room but stopped short when she saw Mrs. Colthrust standing in the middle of the doorway.

"Turn around, young lady. Mrs. Woolwythe is going to answer the door. She will show Mr. Standish in here."

Gwen looked at Louisa for help, but Louisa ignored her request. Gwen stomped her foot, then turned her back to both of them.

A couple of minutes later, Mr. Standish was shown into the drawing room and seated on the settee beside Gwen with a respectable amount of distance between them. Mr. Standish was tall, a handsome man perhaps just a couple of years younger than the duke but not nearly so arrogant. His dark brown hair was a conservative length, but his brown eyes had a mischievous twinkle in them that caused Louisa a little worry. While they waited for the tea to be served, Louisa thought he seemed a little too comfortable and at ease with himself. She would have much rather he be a little bit intimidated or at least nervous to sit across from Gwen's older sister and chaperone, but he was relaxed and handling himself very well.

"How often do you visit the earl's estate in Dover, Mr. Standish?" Mrs. Colthrust asked.

"We just came from spending a couple of weeks there," he said, and took the teacup. "My uncle is generous to my parents, and all his family. He seems to enjoy it when we go for a visit."

"That's lovely to hear. I went to Dover once, and it was peaceful to walk along the rocky cliffs and look down at the water. Do you find it peaceful, Mr. Standish?"

"There's no other place like it, though it can be quite windy there, especially through the winter months." He looked at Gwen. "Have you been there?"

"No," she said, looking at him with dreamy eyes. "I'm afraid my travels have been limited to only short distances from the village where we grew up. In fact, London is the farthest I've been from the Waycbury estate. I would love to go to Dover one day. I'm sure I'd love it."

"Perhaps you shall," Mr. Standish said. "I do believe the moon shines brighter there than any other place in England."

Louisa remained quiet and let Mrs. Colthrust and Gwen do most of the talking to Mr. Standish. Louisa was content simply to watch the beau and see how he spoke and how he looked at Gwen. So far, Louisa hadn't found a thing wrong with his manners or his demeanor, and she saw no reason for concern. She wanted to see if he seemed to be as smitten with Gwen as she was with him. His eyes and voice softened just a little every time he looked at her and talked to her. And was there a reason he'd mentioned the moon when talking about Dover? Was he moonstruck, too?

When the tea had grown cold and the conversation paused, Louisa stood up and said, "You two should get started on your afternoon ride."

Mr. Standish thanked them, and Louisa and Mrs. Colthrust walked to the front door with them. Lillian, Sybil, and Bonnie sat with Saint on the bottom two stairs. Gwen introduced them to Mr. Standish, and he greeted them warmly.

"Can I go for a ride, too?" Bonnie asked him as he took his coat and hat from Mrs. Woolwythe.

"Not this time, Miss Bonnie."

"How about me?" Sybil asked. "I'm older, and I won't be any trouble."

"I'm afraid you'll have to wait for another time, too," he said, and turned to help Gwen don her cape. "I've promised this afternoon to Miss Gwen."

Louisa was impressed that Mr. Standish didn't have to grope for her sisters' names as the duke had had to. Perhaps His Grace could learn a few things from Mr. Standish. Louisa and Mrs. Colthrust waved good-bye to Gwen and Mr. Standish. He had been a perfect gentleman. She was beginning to wonder if the duke had deliberately tried to cause her distress by telling her that Mr. Standish was a scoundrel and as wild as the duke when he was younger.

When he was younger?

Louisa scoffed to herself. What was she thinking? The duke was still a wild scoundrel. In less than five minutes, he'd had her pinned against the bookshelves, enjoying his strong embrace and ardent kisses.

"Now that they're gone, I'll be heading to my room to rest for an hour or so, or I won't be delightful companionship for anyone tonight. Have no fear, Louisa, I'll be belowstairs by the time they return."

"All right," Louisa said, and looked down at the girls on the stairs. "Now it's time for you two to head back to the classroom with Miss Kindred." The girls turned to follow Mrs. Colthrust up the stairs, and so did Saint. "Not so fast for you, Saint." She clapped her hands. "Come. You are staying here."

"Does he have to?" Bonnie whined.

"Yes. He doesn't have lessons, and you do. Now, off you go."

Louisa took Saint outside and walked around in the garden for a few minutes before heading back inside with him. As she made her way down the corridor, she heard a knock on the door. She started toward it, thinking Gwen must have forgotten something. Mrs. Woolwythe came out of the drawing room ahead of her. "I'll get that, Miss Prim. You do something more important than answering a door."

Louisa deferred to the woman, who could at times look almost as stern as Mrs. Colthrust. "Thank you, Mrs. Woolwythe."

It was difficult getting used to allowing so many people to handle things for her. Louisa liked being in charge, be it of her sisters or the door. Giving up control to others didn't sit well with her, but she was allowing it without causing trouble. Louisa heard Saint barking and wondered whether someone he knew was at the door, or if he was causing a ruckus over someone he didn't know.

She had started putting the teacups on the silver tray when Mrs. Woolwythe returned.

"No, don't do that, Miss Prim. I'll do that for you and take it to Mrs. Trumpington." She took the cup out of Louisa's hand.

Louisa was about to tell her she didn't mind putting the cups on the tray when the housekeeper bent close and whispered, "The Duke of Drakestone is here to see you. What should I tell him?"

Louisa had no idea why the woman was speaking so softly but she whispered back to her, "That I'm available to see him, and then show him in here."

The servant's eyes rounded, and she whispered again, "Should I disturb Mrs. Colthrust and ask her to come down if you're going to entertain a gentleman?"

"I'm not going to entertain the duke. I'm going to see what he wants. Don't bother her. She wanted to rest."

The woman nodded and picked up the tray.

It seemed the duke was striding into the room before Mrs. Woolwythe had cleared the doorway. "Get your coat, bonnet, and parasol," he ordered.

Louisa took offense at his demand. "What?"

"Your coat, bonnet, and parasol, Miss Prim. Get them. We're going for a ride in the park."

He was so commanding that she wondered if she should obey him without question, but she quickly came to her senses and said, "How dare you come into my house and start ordering me around, and for of all things, to ride with you in the park! Are you mad?" She grunted a laugh. "I know you find it difficult to believe, but I don't want to go for a ride with you."

"Fine, I'll follow Miss Gwen and Mr. Standish in the park by myself." He turned and walked out, Saint following him.

Louisa gasped. "Wait!" She rushed out of the drawing room behind him and stopped him by grabbing hold of his arm. "Wait, please, Your Grace. Tell me what do you mean 'follow them'?"

"As in staying at a distance behind them in my carriage and keeping an eye on them and making sure they stay in the park in full view of anyone who may be there."

"You think he might—that she might—?"

"I'm not thinking anything in particular, Miss Prim. Do you or do you not want to go with me?"

"Yes, of course I want to go," she said. "Wait right there. Don't move a muscle. I'll get my bonnet and wrap from the back door."

"I want to go."

Louisa whirled and saw Bonnie quietly coming down the stairs. "No—I mean this is not a good time for you to go, Bonnie." Louisa hurried to the back door and grabbed her things. She had made her way to the front of the house just as Bonnie arrived at the bottom of the stairs. The girl's head hung down, resting her chin on her chest.

"I don't see why I can't go." She pouted. "Gwen has gone for a ride in the park, and now you're going for a ride. It's not fair that I don't get to go for one, too."

Louisa's heart squeezed, and Bonnie knew it because she added, "I wouldn't touch anything and break it."

Louisa looked at the duke for help. "She's young and doesn't understand why she can't go."

"All right, Miss Bonnie," he said in an exasperated tone. "Go get your bonnet and coat, but be quick about it. We'll wait for you outside by the carriage."

"Yippee!" She squealed and dashed up the stairs.

"Careful, don't fall," Louisa called to Bonnie's fast-disappearing back. She turned to the duke and said, "Thank you."

"Please," he said in a low voice. "I didn't do it because I wanted to. I was afraid she'd start crying like Miss Sybil if I said no. Besides, what can she hurt in an open carriage?"

The duke helped place the cape on Louisa's shoulders, and they hurried out to the carriage with Louisa putting her bonnet on. He helped her to step onto the floor, and after she'd seated herself, she saw not only Bonnie, but Sybil and Lillian running out of the house, too.

"Oh, no," Louisa said. "This is not good."

"What?" the duke said as he turned and looked behind him. He frowned. "I should have known she would do that, shouldn't I?"

"I didn't think about it either."

"Can I go?" Sybil asked.

"I want to go, too," Lillian added.

"The carriage seat is really only made for two," the duke explained. "We can squeeze in Miss Bonnie because she's so little, but there is nowhere for the rest of you to sit. I'm sorry, girls."

"That's not a problem," Lillian said. "I can sit where Bonnie was going to sit and hold her, and Louisa can hold Sybil, right, Sister?"

"Yes!" Bonnie and Sybil screamed together, and jumped up and down.

"I suppose we could try to make it work," Louisa said, beginning to fear the duke would leave them all at home and follow Gwen by himself as he'd threatened.

"All right, young ladies, you win," the duke said in an annoyed tone. "Go get your bonnets and coats and be quick about it."

Sybil and Bonnie shrieked, and Lillian said, "We already have them with us!" They pulled their bonnets and wraps from where they were holding them behind their backs.

The duke pointed his finger at each one of them. "And one more thing, girls. No more squealing, all right?"

All three of the girls looked up innocently at him as if they had no idea what he was talking about, but they nodded silently.

"Come on, Miss Lillian, you first. Sit on the other side of your sister." He handed her up to the chaise, and she settled between Louisa and the arm of the seat. He then handed Bonnie onto the carriage, and lastly he said, "All right, up you go, Miss Sybil," and handed her to Louisa.

The duke then lifted his leg to climb onto the carriage, and Saint barked and wagged his tail furiously. Louisa hadn't even noticed when the dog followed them out.

"No," he said to Saint. "Stay."

"Why can't he come?" Bonnie said. "I can hold him."

"No," Bray said. "You can't hold him, because Lillian is holding you."

"I can hold him, I'm bigger," Sybil offered.

"You always say you're bigger," Bonnie complained.

"That's because I am," Sybil argued.

"Girls, that's enough," Louisa said, trying to hold on to what little patience she had. "Saint stays. If you are not happy with that, both of you can stay, too."

The girls didn't say anything else. "Look, Your Grace," Louisa said. "Mrs. Woolwythe is standing in the doorway. Take him to her."

Without wasting any time, the duke scooped up Saint, strode to the front door, and deposited him into the housekeeper's arms. He then returned to the chaise, jumped up to the seat, and squeezed in beside Louisa. She immediately felt the warmth of his leg. As he picked up the ribbons, his arm lightly brushed against her breast and sent shooting tendrils of desire rushing throughout her body.

The duke heaved a heavy sigh and asked, "Is everyone seated and holding on to something or someone?"

"Yes!" Sybil shouted a toe-curling screech right into the duke's ear.

Louisa saw him flinch. Suddenly she couldn't see this ride in the park ending on a good note.

Chapter 19

Upon the heat and flame of thy distemper
Sprinkle cool patience.
—*Hamlet,* act 3, scene 4

The girls talked nonstop as the chaise rumbled along the streets. They pointed at horses, other carriages, the occasional mule and cart, and various shops. Bray was beginning to think they'd never been on an open carriage ride before. He had never seen anything like it. Everything they passed excited them, and they wanted to make sure everyone else saw it, too.

There was a comfortable chill to the sunny spring air, and the sky was a fair shade of blue. It was a perfect afternoon for a ride in the park with a beautiful young lady fitted close to his side—and three highly strung youngsters stuffed into a too-small carriage with them as well.

Miss Sybil was like a squirming worm baking in the hot sun on a muddy riverbank. She couldn't sit still on Miss Prim's lap. Miss Sybil was constantly jumping up to point at something, and Miss Prim would pull her back down. If she stepped on the toe of his shiny boot once, she had done it ten times. And he had no idea why she couldn't keep her hands still. She knocked his hat off while pointing to a milk wagon loaded with containers, and twice she'd elbowed him while turning to talk to her sisters. She even placed her hand on his knee a time or two, not that at her age she understood how inappropriate the gesture was.

Miss Lillian was having trouble containing Miss Bonnie's excitement, too. He could never have dreamed that little girls wriggled so much.

The only good thing about the lively jaunt was that Miss Prim fit snugly against him, though there was no chance at conversation between them. He felt the warmth of her inviting body. That helped soothe his impatience concerning the constant chatter and movement of the girls.

The mild weather had brought out an enormous number of people to Hyde Park for the afternoon. Bray maneuvered the horses in line behind a fancy, black-lacquered barouche trimmed in gold that was queuing at the east entrance to the park.

"Is there a princess in that coach, Your Grace?" Miss Bonnie asked.

"Probably not," Bray answered.

"May I hold the ribbons?" Miss Sybil asked him, and immediately reached for the strips of leather.

Bray quickly shifted them to the hand out of her reach before saying, "The horses are much too skittish for a young lady like yourself to handle. I should keep control of them."

"I'm strong. Louisa said I was strong."

Obviously Miss Sybil liked to touch things. "No doubt you are, but you will keep your hands to yourself, and I will keep control of the horses."

"I'm hungry and thirsty," the youngest girl said.

"Now, Bonnie," Miss Prim said. "You can't start complaining. You wanted to come, knowing there was no time to pack a basket."

"What's that for?" Miss Sybil asked, pointing to the horses' riggings.

Frustration caused Bray to grit his teeth, and he inhaled another deep breath, wishing for quiet. "That's what holds the horses to the carriage," he said in a voice much calmer than he was feeling at the moment.

"What's that for?" she asked, pointing to the riggings again.

"That's enough questions, Sybil," Miss Prim said kindly. "And please sit still."

Bray gave Miss Prim a hint of a smile. He didn't know how she stayed so calm when he was going crazy. Somehow she must have known he was near the end of his patience with all the noise, jumping around, and questions. He would much rather shoot himself in the foot than be on a chaise with three excitable girls ever again.

The traffic eased, and they soon rode past the entrance. Bray guided the horses out of the queue of slower carriages and onto the deeply rutted pathway that wound around the perimeter of the grassy openness of the park. Not a fourth of a mile down, Bray looked up and saw Lord Sanburne and Mr. Mercer on horseback and riding straight toward him.

He swore silently.

Much to his consternation, they somehow recognized him among all the bonnets and the two parasols. They moved their mounts to the side and waited. Lord Sanburne would expect him to stop and chat, as it was the polite thing to do, but Bray wasn't in the mood to be polite today. When the carriage approached, the men took off their hats, getting ready to greet Miss

Prim and her sisters, but Bray surprised them. He didn't slow the horses. He gave the stunned gentlemen a brief nod as he passed and kept right on going.

A little farther into the park, he looked at Miss Prim and said, "It's crowded this afternoon. Do you think you will recognize them from a distance if you see them?"

"I'm certain I'll know Gwen's parasol without us having to get too close. I helped her choose what to wear today."

"Are we trying to find Gwen?" Miss Lillian asked.

Bray and Miss Prim looked at each other, realizing at the same time their mistake in mentioning the reason for the ride.

"Well, you never know," Miss Prim said to her sister. "We might see her, since we're both out for a ride today."

"I want to see her, too," Miss Bonnie echoed before Miss Prim once again had to calm the girls.

Sanburne and Mercer weren't the only fellows they passed as they rode the grounds of the park and looked for the curricle with Miss Gwen and Mr. Standish in it. They received waves from other children in the park, a few laughs from three rakes on horseback, and an occasional surprised stare because of the overloaded chaise. Bray could handle the many gawkers. They didn't bother him, but if only the girls would stop talking for a little while and let him have silence.

Bray felt another stab of impatience, and his hands tightened on the reins. He was wishing like hell he'd told the girls an emphatic no when they asked to come—when off to his left, he saw Seaton and his family spreading a blanket for a picnic.

He pulled hard to the left and guided the horses over to where Seaton was standing by his carriage.

"You remember meeting Miss Prim last night?"

Surprise shone in the old man's eyes. "Yes, of course I do," he said, and took off his hat to greet her.

Bray then introduced the other girls, and Seaton spoke to them them warmly in turn before Bray set the brake and said to Miss Prim, "Wait here. I'll be right back."

Bray jumped down, and he and Seaton walked a few feet away from the carriages.

With a twinkle in his eyes, Seaton said, "After knowing you for more than ten years, you still manage to amaze me."

"Sometimes I amaze myself," Bray mumbled. As in why in the hell had he agreed to allow the younger girls to come with them today?

"Last night you danced with almost every young lady at the ball but Miss Prim, and now here you are today with her and all her sisters in the park. In a carriage that's much too small for the group of you, I might add, in case you hadn't noticed."

Oh, I've noticed all right, Bray thought, but said, "Well, not all her sisters."

"What?"

"Never mind."

"Tell me, how did you manage to slight her last night and then end up in the park with her today?"

"I have no idea," Bray grumbled, and realized how true that statement was. "All I know is that I don't have your experience or patience with children, Seaton. You don't seem nearly so tense as I feel right now, and it looks as if you have more children with you than I do."

"I've been blessed with a lot of grandchildren in my old age." Seaton smiled, but to Bray it looked more like a grin that said, *You deserve exactly what you are getting.*

"You do look uncommonly rattled, Your Grace."

"You don't know the half of it," Bray said, and rubbed his temple. "So are you just spending the afternoon in the park?"

"Yes, there's a puppet show that will be starting in about half an hour over there where they are setting up that tent. My wife and I thought the grandchildren would enjoy it."

Bray's breath hitched as an idea came to him. "Do you think she would mind if Miss Prim's sisters watched the puppet show with you and your family?"

Seaton's eyes narrowed, studying over his answer before saying, "No, I don't think she would, and we have plenty of food for them to share our picnic."

"Good," Bray said abruptly, and clapped him on the shoulder before he could change his mind. "Go tell her. I'll bring the girls over. And, Seaton, I owe you."

"I'll collect one day."

"I have no doubt."

Bray waved to his friend, and walked back to the carriage in much brighter spirits than when he'd left.

"How would you young ladies like to see a puppet show?" he asked.

"Yes!" they all screamed at once.

"Well, it just so happens this is your lucky day to be in the park. There's going to be one in about half an hour."

The sisters squealed, clapped, and jumped up and down again.

"Careful, girls, you'll scare the horses," Bray said. "Come, Miss Sybil, you get down first. You can play and have refreshments with the Seatons and their grandchildren and then watch the puppet show with them while Miss Prim and I ride for a little longer."

Bray reached for Miss Bonnie and helped her down,

too, but when he reached for Miss Lillian, she remained sulking in the seat, her arms tightly pressed to her chest.

"I don't want to stay with them," Miss Lillian said. "I don't know them. I want to go with you."

It surprised Bray that she objected.

"I don't care if I don't know them," Miss Sybil said. "I want to see the show."

"Me, too," Miss Bonnie piped in.

"Lillian," Louisa said, but Bray touched her arm, and when she looked at him, he indicated for her to let him handle this.

"You are the oldest, Miss Lillian. The younger girls want to see the puppets. You must stay with them and be responsible much in the same way Miss Prim has always been responsible for you."

Her bottom lip quivered. "I don't want to. There are boys. I've never played with boys before."

"Then this will be a good learning experience for you. You'll manage just fine. Come on and let me help you down. Keep remembering you are the oldest and act like it."

She still didn't move.

Bray struggled to hold on to his temper. Miss Lillian sniffed and looked as if she might start crying at any moment, and Bray felt as if he might start yelling at any moment. But he bit down on his tongue and refrained.

Staying firm, he asked, "How many times do you think your sister has done things for you she'd rather not do?"

Miss Lillian remained quiet, so he said again, "How many?"

"Often, Your Grace," she finally mumbled.

"That's right. Has she ever complained and said she

didn't want to play a children's game with you and your sisters, or sit by your beside when you were sick?"

Miss Lillian raised her head and shook it. Tears collected in her eyes.

Louisa started to speak again, and he gave her a warning look. She returned it.

"That's right, Miss Lillian, and neither should you."

"I don't want to stay," she said, and the first tear rolled down her cheek.

Bray reached into the chaise, took her by the upper arms, gently lifted her out, and stood her on her feet. He heard Louisa gasp, but he didn't even look at her as he continued talking to Miss Lillian.

"Now, as for the young boys, they scream and yell and run around as wildly as you and your sisters do. I have no fear that if they step out of line with any of you, you have the fortitude to snap them right back in their place with a few choice words. Now, come along so we can go meet the Seaton family."

Miss Lillian looked at Louisa and sniffled. "Where are you going?" she asked her sister.

"Nowhere but here in the park," she said, taking her sister's hand and gently squeezing it. "I promise we are not going to leave you here with the Seatons for very long. We will be back for you very shortly."

"Come along," Bray said again. "I'll introduce all of them to you. If you try, you might even enjoy yourself."

Less than ten minutes later, the girls were settled and Bray and Miss Prim were walking back to the carriage.

"Don't you think you were a little harsh on Lillian?" Miss Prim asked as soon as they were a few steps away from the girls.

"No," he said, thinking no more commentary was needed.

"I thought you were," she countered. "You were almost rough with her when you lifted her out of the carriage."

Bray looked behind him at the girls, and then back to Miss Prim. He shrugged. "I don't believe I was rough—in fact, I made sure I handled her gently—but sometimes adults have to be stern with children. That is how they learn."

"You know this from experience, I assume."

"I do," he said a little testily. "Just as no doubt you learned your gentle and loving nature from your father." Bray paused. "He was gentle, wasn't he?"

"Yes. I don't think I ever heard him raise his voice in anger at any of us, and he surely never lifted any of us from the carriage when we didn't do what he commanded."

Bray looked behind him again. "Well, whatever I said or however roughly I lifted her from the carriage and set her on her feet, it must have worked. Look—she's not crying."

"If I were her, I'd be afraid to cry in front of someone with such an authoritative manner as you."

Bray grinned confidently. "If only you were half so frightened of me as you seem to think Miss Lillian is, that would be wonderful."

It was then that Miss Prim smiled. "Well, you are a beast at times."

"And a monstrous beast at others."

"True, Your Grace," she said in a good-natured voice as she turned and waved to the girls once more. "Still, I'm not at all sure I'm comfortable leaving my sisters with strangers."

"They are fine, and Seaton is not a stranger. I've known him more than ten years. I wouldn't leave them if I had any fears for their well-being or safety. He will treat them as if they were his own grandchildren. A puppet show will be much better for them than riding cramped in this carriage for an hour with you and me."

"I think you were thinking of your own well-being and not theirs."

She was right. He liked the teasing light that shone brightly in her sparkling eyes. "Perhaps I was."

"Perhaps?"

"All right, hell yes, I was. And don't forget that 'hell' is a biblical word, Miss Prim. "

Again, she smiled at him. "How could I when you get such enjoyment out of reminding me."

Bray helped her back onto the chaise and then climbed up beside her. She moved over to the other side of the seat, leaving a respectable distance between them.

"Now, what did you say was the color of Miss Gwen's parasol?"

"You aren't going to let me worry about the girls, are you?"

The relaxed tone of their conversation was enjoyable. Louisa had seldom been so calm and easy with him. He admired her for taking the responsibility of caring for her sisters so seriously, even if she seemed to carry it to the extreme on occasions, when she did things such as putting her hands over her sister's ears.

"I'm willing for you to worry all that you want about the girls, but which ones do you want to worry about first this afternoon—the three with the grandfather and other children to play with, or the one with the rake?"

"All right, all right, you win." She smiled and then laughed lightly. "Let's go find Gwen and her green parasol."

Bray picked up the ribbons, released the brake, and they started riding through the bumpy park again.

Louisa was no longer sitting right up next to him, and
he couldn't feel her heat, but it was blissfully quiet.

"I suppose you have been patient today, Your Grace."

"Very patient," he said.

"It was nice of you to let the girls come with us."

"Very nice," he added, and threw a grin her way.

"I know they loved the ride, and they will enjoy the
puppet show, too."

She would never know how happy he had been to
see Seaton and with his grandchildren. "I didn't really
mind," he lied without really thinking about it.

"Are you sure?"

"No," he said, and clicked the ribbons on the horses'
rumps to pick up their pace. "But I'm trying to be as
nice today as you seem to think I've been."

"That will make your mother very proud of you."

"I doubt that, Louisa. I am her only child, but my
mother has never favored me."

"Did you just call me Louisa?"

"Yes, so what are you going to do about it, Miss Prim
and Proper?"

"I'm going to say that is a terrible thing for you to
say about your mother."

He laughed. "Terrible, sad, and true. She would agree
with me, I assure you. The duchess was an only child
and never quite knew what to do with a child of her
own, but the nurses, tutors, and governesses she hired
did. Her Grace's happiest day was when I was sent off
to Eton to live."

"I'm sure that's not true, either."

Bray looked over at Louisa's wide eyes and realized
how much he enjoyed being with her. "I'm sure it is,
but don't look so aghast. We get along well enough now
that I'm grown."

"What about your father? Was he the same way?"

Worse.

But he didn't like to talk about his father. He didn't even like to think about the man. "I saw very little of him when I was a child. My parents weren't fond of each other, Miss Prim. Their purpose for getting married was to give my father an heir. After I was born and declared a healthy child, my mother moved into her own house. She and my father never lived together again."

"Oh, I see," she said softly. "That must have been a challenge for you."

"Not really," he said, watching for Standish and Miss Prim. "Boarding schools were always in my future. I adapted."

"I suppose your life has been very different from mine."

"I'm sure. For some reason, I envision you growing up with the whole family sitting around a dinner table, enjoying your food and your chatter. In the evenings, all of you probably played chess and cards, or listened to your father read to you by the light of a roaring fire."

Her eyes brightened. "Yes, we did so often. Dinner and evenings were always family time. How did you know?"

I see it in all you say and do.

"My friend Harrison had family. He told me about his life."

Bray looked away from her and clicked the ribbons again. A sudden longing for that elusive thing called "family life" gripped him tightly. He felt a lump in his throat and heaviness in his chest. He quickly shook the unwanted feelings away. Bray knew what family time was, though he'd never experienced it.

When he was a young boy, his meals were taken on a tray in his room with his nurse or governess. At boarding school, their food was served in a large hall at a long table with all the other boys who were just as lonely as he was. And as an adult, he never ate at home in the evening. He ate at one of his clubs. Bray's father had invited him to dine with him one evening a couple of years before his death. Bray decided to be a good son that day and obliged him. The meal was so painfully long and quiet that repeating the occasion was never broached again by either of them. His mother was barely a little better, inviting him to dine with her only on Christmas day and Easter.

Family time was for vicars and the like, not for dukes, and it was best he not forget that.

"Look, Your Grace, to your right," Miss Prim said. "There they are. See them, sitting on a blanket under that tree?"

Thankful for the change in conversation, Bray pulled on the reins to slow the horses. He surveyed the terrain, which was lightly dotted with trees and tall shrubs. "We'll go past them and move around to the other side. We'll find a place that can shield you from your sister's view. If you can recognize her from this distance, she will know you, too."

"That's a good idea. They don't seem to be sitting too close together. What do you think?"

"I think they look as if they are talking and enjoying something to drink, which is what we wanted to see."

Bray maneuvered the horses and chaise around the park until he found a place near a patch of tall spindly shrubs that looked as if Mother Nature had forgotten to give them their spring coats. It was a good place to watch Miss Gwen and Mr. Standish and not be seen by them. There was no one else in the vicinity because the bushes were barren and offered no shade from the sun. They would have more privacy than if they tried to find the sunshade of a tree.

Bray set the brake, jumped down, and reached back to help Miss Prim descend the steps.

"I'm afraid I don't have a blanket or a basket filled with refreshments." Bray swung his cloak off his shoulders. "But I have this to sit on, and it will work as well."

"I don't want to ruin your cloak or for you to get cold, Your Grace. I don't mind sitting on the ground. I've done it many times with my sisters."

"Perhaps you have, Miss Prim, but you will not sit on the ground with me. And no, I will not get cold. I find that whenever I am in your company, I am usually hot."

"Hot with anger because I've usually said something that has riled you."

"I will not make a comment concerning that." He spread his cloak near the shrubs so that there was a barrier on that side of them. He then helped her to sit down and made himself comfortable beside her. She reopened her parasol and let it rest on her shoulder.

"Comfortable?" he asked.

She nodded. "Tell me, what made you decide we needed to follow Gwen and Mr. Standish today?"

I was aching to see you.

"You didn't seem so concerned last night," she added.

"Today I felt it was the right thing to do." Not that he had ever been noted for doing the right thing. "I know that Mr. Standish already has two fathers angry with him over wooing their daughters last fall during some house parties and then not offering for their hand. And for now, I am Miss Gwen's guardian, and it's my duty to look after her. Besides, I knew you would be worried about her, too."

She gave him a grateful smile. "Thank you for caring."

Did he care or was it just an excuse to spend some time with Louisa?

"Though, I have to say that Mr. Standish was the perfect gentleman when he had tea with us before they left for the park."

"As I would expect him to be."

Bray looked at Miss Prim's face and smiled warmly back at her. Without a doubt, she was the prettiest young lady he had ever seen. Her eyes were bluer than heaven. Her lips were a delicious shade of pink, and he was thinking he'd love to feel them beneath his once again. He wished she didn't have on the matronly brown bonnet. He loved looking at her golden blond tresses.

"Have you ever been on a carriage ride with a man, Miss Prim?"

"No, I can't say I have."

"Watch how quickly this can be done."

Bray looked from his left and then to his right. There were other people sitting on blankets scattered within sight of them but none very close. He grabbed hold of the handle of her parasol and slid it down her chest until the canopy touched her bonnet. He then lowered his head underneath it and placed his lips on hers. He meant only to give her a quick kiss, but the moment his lips brushed hers, desire soared through him and he lingered, letting his lips rove softly and for much longer than he had expected. It was difficult to leave her sweetness, but he finally raised his head and gave her two more quick kisses before he lifted the parasol back to its original height and moved away from her.

"Now, Miss Prim, you know why a gentleman wants to take a young lady for a ride in the park."

"Yes." She moistened her lips. "I also just learned another use for the parasol, Your Grace."

Bray gave her a satisfied expression. "I don't think parasols were ever intended for keeping the sun off a young lady's face. You have your bonnet for that, right?"

She cleared her throat. "Well, I'm happy to say that Gwen isn't using her parasol right now. They seem to be enjoying their refreshments."

He looked over at them. "She's probably drinking chocolate with a little brandy in it, and he is drinking brandy."

Miss Prim's brow furrowed. "Gwen has never had brandy. It's very strong."

"So you are familiar with it?"

"When my father was so ill, I would pour him a glass in the evenings, and I have to admit that my curiosity got the better of me one night, and I took a little sip."

"Ah, that does surprise me. But don't worry. I don't think Mr. Standish would put enough in her chocolate to cause her to forget herself. But like you, she must grow up."

"And have her first kiss."

"And hopefully she will enjoy it as much as you enjoyed your first kiss."

She looked at him and matched his smile. It pleased him that she didn't try to deny she'd enjoyed the kiss.

"But I'm twenty and will be twenty-one before the end of the year. Gwen is only eighteen."

"She's of age to have her first kiss, Miss Prim and Proper."

"But last night was her first dance, and Mr. Standish the first man she has ever been alone with. At least I had been to a few dances and enjoyed conversations with gentlemen before you kissed me that afternoon at my house."

Bray reached up, swept his hat off his head, and dropped it to the ground. "And while no one is near and Gwen is not in any danger from Mr. Standish at the moment, I am going to kiss you again."

Bray took the parasol from Miss Prim and once again pulled it down until their heads were covered by the pale yellow canopy. He dipped his head low and pressed his lips on hers, and moved unhurriedly over her mouth. He placed his free hand to the back of her neck, where he could feel her warm bare skin, and gently caressed her. She parted her lips, giving him permission to probe the depths of her mouth, feeding his arousal. He heard short, choppy gasps and long generous sighs as his lips glided across hers.

She lifted her hands and circled them behind his neck briefly before stretching her arms wide around his back and hugging him closer to her. Bray softly moaned his approval and, in response, dropped his hand from her nape to hug her to him as well.

His lips left hers and he kissed his way down her chin, over her jawline. He swept his tongue down the length of her neck to the base of her throat, where the ribbon of her bonnet lay. With his teeth, he grabbed the ribbon, and in three quick tugs, the pieces of satin were fluttering away from her skin. He planted a moist kiss in the hollow of her throat before finding her lips once more to share in a deep, satisfying kiss that had him aching to lay her back and rest his body on top of hers.

The ribbing of the parasol dug into the top of his head, but Bray paid it no mind. His hand slipped back up behind her neck, then down her shoulder, under her arm, on her breast. He slowly applied pressure to the soft mound, letting his palm stroke and massage her. He felt her tremble, and her reaction caused his lower body to swell beneath his trousers.

Her lips parted again. Bray knew it was madness to continue kissing, fueling the passion that was growing hot and demanding between them, but he didn't want to stop. His lips roved hungrily, greedily over hers, and she matched his fervor with such excitement, it heated him all the more. It pleased him to hear her swallow small gasps of pleasure as his tongue explored the warmth inside her mouth. She was feeling what he felt, and it elated him.

He loved the way her lips moved with his, the way she tentatively searched his mouth with her tongue, but somewhere in the back of his mind, Bray knew it was time to withdraw. He'd always had a sixth sense about when to step back, and he needed to stop right now.

Reluctantly, he let her go and leaned away from Louisa.

Calming his labored breathing, he inhaled deeply and smoothed down his hair with his palm. He lifted the parasol and returned it to her. He picked up his hat and gave a quick look around as he settled it back on his head. He adjusted his coat and trousers while she retied the ribbons under her chin. No words were necessary while they gained control of their feelings.

Moments later, an elderly couple walking arm in arm came from around the other side of the shrubs and wandered past them. Bray tipped his hat and they nodded.

"That was too close for comfort, Your Grace," she whispered.

Privately, Bray agreed, but he didn't want to alarm her. "I heard their footsteps and knew they were close."

"Do you still think I am Miss Prim and Proper, now that I let you kiss me under the umbrella?"

"Yes," he said truthfully. "I have no doubt that it would take more than a few kisses and caresses to change you." He looked over to where Miss Gwen and Mr. Standish were seated. "They are rising," he said.

"Already?" Miss Prim asked, and rose to her knees. She looked around him. "I'm surprised. They haven't been here very long."

"They're not taking the basket with them, so they're not leaving. They're just going for a stroll."

"Do you think Mr. Standish kissed her while we were—?"

"Kissing?" he finished for her.

"Yes."

"If he did, it was a short kiss and not at all like what we just shared, so do not worry. She has not had time to be ruined, and neither have you."

"Perhaps we should take a stroll, too."

"I do feel the need to cool off," Bray mumbled under his breath.

He got to his feet and then helped her to stand, and they started walking in the direction that Miss Gwen and Mr. Standish had headed. They remained silent for a time. Bray assumed that, like him, Miss Prim was thinking back over their passionate embrace.

"My goodness," she said, breaking the silence for the first time. "Look at all the carriages on that pathway in front of us. I've never seen so many bunched up together like that. Why is it so crowded?"

"Rotten Row is usually well traveled this time of the afternoon."

"Oh," she whispered, and stopped.

Bray halted, too, and looked over at her. She stood transfixed to the spot and stared at the road as if seeing something for the very first time. He couldn't imagine what had mesmerized her so suddenly. She didn't face him, but he could see that her eyes started glistening. His stomach knotted. His chest tightened.

His gaze scanned the area, looking for whatever had caused her to stop. He noticed that her shoulders shook for a few seconds, but she made no sound as she stared straight ahead.

Was she silently crying?

"Louisa, what is it?" he asked, wanting to touch her but knowing that there were too many people too close to them to risk it.

"Rotten Row," she whispered softly. "That's where my brother died, isn't it?"

Oh, hell!

Chapter 20

. . . when he shall die,
Take him and cut him out in little stars,
And he will make the face of heaven so fine
That all the world will be in love with night
And pay no worship to the garish sun.
—Romeo and Juliet, act 3, scene 2

An unexpected shiver shook Louisa. Tears clouded her vision, and her breathing slowed and became so shallow that she felt light-headed.

"I'm sorry," the duke whispered. "I should have remembered."

"No, it's all right," she assured him, unable to keep the quiver out of her voice and hating the overwhelming sorrow that had engulfed her. "No reason for you to remember," she said, trying to deny the pain she was feeling. "It's been over two years. I'm sure you've been to the park many times since that night."

"But it's the first time you've been here. I should have been more intuitive and considerate."

Louisa kept looking at the line of carriages and riders moving along the path, and willed the tears in her eyes to dissipate before rolling down her cheeks. She wanted to cry so badly, her throat ached and her chest heaved, she was determined not to show any outward emotion.

She didn't want to look at His Grace. She was afraid if she did, she might throw herself into his arms, bury her face into his waistcoat, and cry for the loss of her brother. And not just for Nathan but for her father and mother, too. She had such a strong urge to seek the comfort she'd never received from anyone when she heard of Nathan's death. She hadn't been able to cry, because she had to be strong for her sisters. They needed her support more than she needed a shoulder.

She swallowed past a tight throat. Her whole body hurt from holding back her tears and fighting the grief that threatened to consume her.

The duke must have known what she was going through, because he stayed quietly beside her until she found the strength to say, "I have to admit that with the distraction of the younger girls being with us in the carriage, and worrying about Gwen, I failed to realize it until you said Rotten Row. That's the lane you were racing down when the accident happened, isn't it?"

"Yes. You don't know how many times I've wished we hadn't raced that night."

"Probably fewer than the times I've wished it, Your Grace."

"That goes without saying."

"Did you know there was a young lady in our village waiting for him to settle down and marry her?"

"No, he never mentioned anyone. We didn't talk about families or our lives outside the club."

"Inheriting the title never changed my father. We moved into the Wayebury estate, of course, a much larger home with more servants, but Papa never went to London. His health was already failing by the time he assumed the title. Nathan was a quiet, educated young man. For a time, he considered following Papa's footsteps to become a clergyman, but then Papa became the viscount and he needed Nathan to help him with all there was to learn and oversee—and for a time, he did. But then Nathan went to London and joined the Heirs' Club, and he changed."

"London has many vices to offer a young man."

"Especially for one who has suddenly come into wealth and a title, and is eager to enjoy both."

"Don't blame him for that, Louisa," the duke said quietly.

"When Papa died and Nathan became the viscount, I think he tried all the debauchery London had to offer. The power, the lands, the money, the gaming, and women—all of it changed him. He told me he became a different person when he went to London."

"It might have changed what he did and how he did it, but I'm sure it didn't change who he was. He was always friendly, fair, and well liked among the other members and the ton."

"Thank you for telling me that. The lamps that I see lining the road, were they lit that night?"

"They are always lit at dusk and extinguished at dawn," he said.

"Do you still race with your friends?"

"It's a young man's sport," he said, not really answering her pointed question.

"I was told it was foggy that night."

"It was."

Feeling stronger, her eyes drier, her chest lighter, she turned and faced the duke. "Can you tell me about the accident?"

For a moment, he looked at her with such tenderness that she was once again tempted to throw herself into his arms and weep. Instead she set a steady gaze on his piercing green eyes.

"I could tell you, but I'm not sure I should."

She wasn't sure either, but she wanted to know something about that night and trusted the duke to tell her only what she needed to know. "Don't you think I have a right to know more about what happened?"

"You know what happened, Louisa. He died."

"But not instantly."

"No."

"He talked to you."

"For a short time."

"Did the carriage overturn, lose a wheel, hit a tree?"

"No one knows for sure. He was in the lead. It was dark, foggy, and misting rain, too. No one saw what happened."

Louisa could tell it troubled the duke greatly to talk about this, but she pressed forward. "Still you raced."

"Yes. We all did foolish things whenever we got together. We were way too far into our cups to think rationally, and no one tried to stop us, because they had been drinking all night, too. Hell, they had money wagered on the outcome. I'm not making excuses, just telling the truth."

"You must have some idea about how the accident happened."

"We think his wheel ran over a limb or a bottle and it flipped the curricle, throwing him off the seat and into the air."

She tried to hide it but knew there was a slight tremor in her voice as she asked, "Did he break his bones, his back, or his neck?"

"No, Louisa," he whispered in anguish. "The physician we took him to said it was internal injuries. He tried, but there was nothing he could do to save Prim."

Clearly His Grace was tormented to have to talk about this with her. And perhaps in some small way, she felt he deserved that bit of punishment.

"So you did try to get him help."

His eyes narrowed and his brows knitted together in a frown of disbelief. "Yes, yes, of course. Did you doubt that?"

She wasn't sure. There was so much uncertainty in her about the duke that she suddenly wanted to weep again. She fought the impulse by biting down on her bottom lip, then closed her eyes and summoned an inner strength.

She didn't answer his question but asked, "What did Nathan say to you?"

"Not much."

Louisa understood the duke's reluctance to revisit that night. He'd given evasive answers to her questions, but she wanted to know more. "How did he convince you to promise him you would marry me when you didn't want to?"

The duke swept his hat off his head and breathed a heavy sigh. "Damnation, Louisa, don't make me do this. What he said is not important now."

"It is to me." She stepped close to him. "I believe I have a right to know what he said to make you swear an oath."

"No—no, you don't."

She rose up on her toes and raised her voice as she leaned toward him and said, "I do!"

"It was between him and me, and he wouldn't want you to know. He was in pain and he needed peace. I gave it to him. His last thoughts were of you and your sisters. He wanted like hell to live and to go back to Wayebury so he could take care of you. His dying thoughts were of you and your sisters, and that's all I'm ever going to tell you about that night. That's all you need to know."

In that moment, she saw that he was filled with pain and guilt about that night, even though he'd told her very little about it. It seemed so unfair that life had moved on for her, for her sisters, and for the duke—but not for Nathan. Louisa had an overwhelming feeling of wanting to cry again, and she stiffened. In a busy park, standing with a duke was not the place to cry. She also knew it was time to put Nathan's death and the events surrounding it behind her, because life did go on.

Louisa looked up at the duke and whispered, "Thank you, you've told me enough."

Chapter 21

The quality of mercy is not strain'd;
It droppeth as the gentle rain from heaven
Upon the place beneath. It is twice blest;
It blesseth him that gives and him that takes.
—*The Merchant of Venice*, act 4, scene 1

Where was she?

Bray leaned against the back side of one of the massive columns in the ballroom of the Great Hall. It was the perfect place to watch the entrance and avoid the pushy mamas and nosy lords.

The night was growing long, and Bray was restless. He had fulfilled his duty to the ladies along the wall of the dance floor more than two hours ago, and he'd danced with at least half a dozen young ladies throughout the evening. It was almost midnight, and Miss Prim and her sister still hadn't arrived at the ball.

Bray knew there were several smaller parties happening around Mayfair tonight, but the Great Hall was always the most well attended. He'd assumed that Mrs. Colthrust would have the good sense to let the sisters make an appearance before they quit the night. Now he was beginning to doubt that faith. He should have known he couldn't trust their chaperone to do what was best for Louisa and Miss Gwen.

No doubt, Mr. Standish had the same thoughts as Bray. The man was already at the Great Hall when Bray arrived, and he hadn't left either. And, like Bray, the man had done his share of dancing and conversing. Bray was fairly certain Mr. Standish had no genuine interest in Miss Gwen. The blade was just looking for another young lady to enjoy for a time and then discard as he had all the others.

But Bray couldn't be too hard on the man. He had done the same thing at Standish's age.

He whispered a curse to himself as his thoughts once again crept back to when he and Louisa were near Rotten Row. She became quiet after they'd discussed the night her brother died. He knew she needed time to ponder what he'd said so he didn't press her to talk as they'd made their way back to the carriage. Once they picked up her sisters, the girls kept the chatter going about the puppet show all the way back to their house. And the reason for the hasty ride in the park seemed to end up all right, too. He never saw Mr. Standish make an improper move toward Miss Gwen the entire time they had watched them.

That surprised him. Maybe the man wasn't like him after all.

Bray wondered how Louisa was doing. What was she feeling? He didn't want her to hate him for what had happened to Prim but it was probably inevitable that she would. Bray had had great respect for her brother. The hell of it was Prim was the only man who had ever made Bray do something he didn't want to do. Bray had promised to marry Louisa.

When he saw tears collecting in her eyes, he'd felt

like the worst kind of blackguard and desperately wanted to hold her. He'd wanted to kiss her brow and run his hands up and down her back, soothing her, but he knew that at that moment, he was the last person she wanted touching her, comforting her.

He might have done it anyway, had they not been in the park at the time, surrounded by dozens of people. As for himself, he didn't care a blast in hell what anyone thought, but if he had held Louisa and someone had seen them, it would have caused her even more heartache and sparked unwelcome gossip.

She was already dealing with too much. Why did he care so much about how she felt? How had she touched him so deeply, he couldn't rip her out of his thoughts?

He'd had sorrow and regrets about the night of Prim's death, too, but he was sure she didn't want to hear that from him. Hellfire, he'd hated telling her anything about that night. There was no good explanation for the foolish antics of two drunken bucks. He would never tell her that her brother had died in excruciating pain, begging him to marry her.

In truth, Bray had known she'd get around to asking him about the events of the accident one day, but why did it have to be after such a pleasant afternoon of easy conversation and sweet kisses?

She said he'd told her enough, and he hoped that was true. He'd meant it when he said he could never tell her more. Why should she have to learn about the gaping wound, the pleas for help that wasn't available, and the demented cries of pain that Bray remembered so well? She shouldn't have to live with that. He could never tell her how frightened her brother had been when he saw his injury, or just how long it took Bray to make that promise in the end, when Wayebury knew there was no hope he'd live. Bray didn't want her to know that the

other gentlemen standing around that night had co-
erced him into promising to marry her.

None of that mattered now.

"My dear, my dear, my dear, please don't tell me
you are holding up that column so the building won't
fall down and kill us all."

Bray straightened. "Good evening, Your Grace," he
said to his mother. "You are looking young and lovely
tonight."

She opened her fan and gave him a doubtful look.
"And you are looking as if you are brooding. I don't think
you looked so intense even when your father died. Should
I venture a guess as to why you are wearing that deeply
troubled expression?"

"Am I?"

"Yes."

"Then it's up to you whether or not you tell me."

"Very well. I believe it was easy for you to ignore
Miss Prim and your debt to her brother before you met
her and got to know her. Now that you have, you find
that she is constantly on your mind, and you are trying
to figure out why that is the case."

Bray snorted a laugh at his mother's intuitive suggestion. "It's true Miss Prim is on my mind right now,
but I don't know that I would agree to the word 'constantly.'"

"That's because you don't want me to know all you
are thinking."

"May you never know all that I think about, Your
Grace."

She laughed herself and said, "Yes, please. I don't
want to know. When I met her, I found Miss Prim to be
pretty, clever, and strong-minded."

"And you conclude this after only five minutes in
her presence?"

The duchess lifted her brows. "It was more than five minutes, and over two different meetings with her. Her sister is lovely, by the way, too. And besides, you know it doesn't take me long to make up my mind about a person, Your Grace. They either catch my attention early or not at all. I seldom give anyone a second chance to impress me."

"I'm well aware of that."

"I think she will do nicely to have your child."

Bray couldn't help but notice that his mother said "child." Not "children" and not "son" or "daughter." There was no warmth or love in her voice, just the word "child." His mother expected him to have the same pretense of a marriage that she and his father had had. Bray recoiled from that thought.

"I think you should go ahead and make plans to marry her before someone else catches her fancy and steals her from underneath your nose."

"Do you?"

"Immediately."

It would make the Prince happy and likewise all the other gentlemen with winning bets placed on a marriage with Louisa before the end of the Season, but there was one small obstacle that none of them knew about. Louisa had to ask him to marry her, and he didn't see that happening. Though she'd never said the words, he knew she blamed him for her brother's death. Bray didn't know if she could ever bring herself to get over that, or the fact that the Duke of Drakestone was a known rake.

"Why did you never live with the duke after I was born?"

Her eyes widened a little at his question. His mother was almost as good as he was at hiding her feelings. "Why should I? We couldn't stand the sight of each other. Our parents arranged the marriage and we agreed. He had everything I wanted—a title, power, and wealth. I had what he wanted—heritage, beauty, and intelligence. It was a perfect match."

But never a family.

"Did you ever have love?"

"Between your father and me? Don't be ridiculous. Certainly not. We never wanted it or expected it." She paused. "Is that what has you waiting to marry Miss Prim? Are you waiting to see if you will fall in love with her?"

Was he? Wasn't he already half in love with her anyway? He didn't know, because love wasn't something he'd ever let himself feel.

Over his mother's shoulder, he saw Mrs. Colthrust coming through the door with Miss Gwen right behind her. His heart started beating a little faster at the thought of seeing Louisa. He watched the two ladies take off their wraps and hand them to an attendant. He studied the entrance. Where was Louisa?

His mother kept talking, and he mumbled some kind of answer, but his attention was still on the door. Mrs. Colthrust and Miss Gwen walked down into the ballroom. He kept staring at the entrance. Louisa wasn't with them. He had to find out why.

"Are you?" his mother asked.

"Am I what?"

"Waiting to fall in love with Miss Prim before you ask for her hand?"

"Surely you don't think there is such a thing as love, do you?"

The duchess laughed. "If there is, I never found it."

"Did you ever look for it?" he asked.

Her eyes narrowed for the briefest time. She seemed to shake off whatever his question had made her feel or remember and said, "If I ever did, it was so long ago that I have no memory of it, and that is probably just as well."

Bray thought of the Prince and his damned wager. "It would be nice if Miss Prim and I were left alone to make up our own minds about what we want to do about marrying."

"You can't, Your Grace," his mother said in a tone that left him no room for argument. "You lost that right when you accepted her brother's dying plea."

"Yes, the vow. How could I forget?"

"Keeping your word is not supposed to be easy. Integrity would have no value if there were no effort associated with it. Now, I'm headed home. Enjoy the rest of your evening, Your Grace."

Bray watched his mother walk away. There was never a greeting kiss on the cheek or a parting hug between them, because sadly, there was no love. Mutual respect was the strongest emotion they shared.

Watching his mother's regal, retreating back, Bray realized he'd never seen his mother cry. There must have been times in her life when she'd wept, but Bray knew nothing about them. He'd known Miss Prim for only a few weeks, and already he'd seen her eyes filled with tears twice. When she thought he'd deliberately kept Saint from them and today, when she looked at the area where her brother had died.

Both times, he'd been angry with himself for being the cause of her tears.

Without further thought, Bray knew what he had to do. He placed his glass on a nearby table and went to find Mrs. Colthrust. He was stopped three different times by people to make conversation, but he managed to keep the exchanges short, and by the time he reached the chaperone, she was talking to Harrison, and Miss Gwen was talking with a young Italian count who seemed pleased that she could converse in his language.

After appropriate greetings, Bray said, "You and Miss Gwen are looking lovely this evening, Mrs. Colthrust."

The woman gave him a dazzling smile and fanned herself. "Thank you, Your Grace. We're so glad you noticed."

"I couldn't help but see that Miss Prim isn't with you?"

"Oh, I know, and it is your fault, Your Grace."

"Mine?" he said, feeling a stab of alarm in his chest.

"Yes, she told me that you arrived shortly after Gwen left and insisted on taking her and the girls to the park for an afternoon outing to see a puppet show. Apparently you were not careful, and she spent too much time in the sun. Said she had a headache and felt quite dizzy and wasn't up to a night of dancing."

Relief washed over Bray. For a moment, he'd thought Mrs. Colthrust was going to tell him that Louisa was upset over visiting the place where her brother had died.

"I'm sorry to hear that. Please give her my apology and my regards when you return home."

"Shall do, Your Grace."

Bray looked at Harrison and said, "If you've had enough dancing for one evening, why don't we head over to White's for a game of cards?"

"I'm all for that."

Bray and Harrison said their good-byes to Mrs. Colthrust, Miss Gwen, and the count and headed for the entrance. While they waited for the attendant to get their cloaks, Bray said, "I'm afraid I used you as a decoy, Harrison."

Harrison frowned. "I suppose I'm not opposed to that, but how so?"

"I am not going to White's with you tonight, but I do need you to leave the party with me and go to the club or somewhere after we part."

"Because?"

"I didn't want to make Mrs. Colthrust suspicious by leaving alone immediately after finding out that Miss Prim is not here."

"Ah." Harrison nodded. "And Miss Prim is home alone, I gather."

"With sisters and servants, I suppose she is never alone, and before you ask, yes, that is where I'm headed. I hope you don't mind."

Bray had no way of knowing if Miss Prim herself or one of the servants would come to the door, but at this point, he didn't care. He hoped he was right in thinking that Louisa wouldn't go to bed until she knew Gwen was home from the parties.

He wanted to see Louisa and make sure she was all right.

"Well, I do feel used," Harrison said with a teasing smirk. "And take my word for it, it's not so easy to jump from a bedroom window now as it was when we were younger."

"I appreciate the concern, but I don't plan to be jumping from any windows."

But he wasn't sure Louisa didn't feel like pushing him out of one.

Chapter 22

We cannot fight for love, as men may do;
We should be wooed, and were not made to woo.
—*A Midsummer Night's Dream,* act 2, scene 1

Louisa lay curled on the settee in the drawing room, her head propped on a pillow and the lamp on the table beside her burning low.

Feeling wretched by the time she'd returned home from the park, Louisa quickly said good-bye to the duke with hardly a glance in his direction. She immediately shut herself in her bedroom but soon realized that if she were alone, she would end up crying her eyes out and everyone in the house would know it, so she hurried down the stairs and stayed busy with the younger girls until she put them to bed.

Later, when it was time to dress for the evening's parties, she had no choice but to plead a headache from too much sun. She simply wasn't up to going out and pretending to enjoy herself.

Louisa needed time to be alone and ponder not only all the emotions stirred inside her from talking with the duke about Nathan and the night he died, but also her womanly desires for the duke. She hadn't been able to shake them. Every time he kissed her, she wanted him to kiss her again. It seemed so unfair that he had ended up being the man of her dreams. He didn't love her and she doubted he was capable of loving any woman. But she knew now that she wanted him to love her.

She'd believed him when he said that if she asked him to, he would marry her and fulfill his vow to her brother. And when she was in his arms kissing him, she was thinking she would very much like to be his wife so she could love him with all the feelings she had inside her—but could she really do that to him?

And would it be fair to her sisters? She'd watched him cringe every time one of the girls screamed, and seen how annoyed he was when Sybil cried. He'd looked as if he were about ready to chew nails into powder from their incessant talking when they were in the park. She could allow him to continue being their guardian, but could she subject him to living with her sisters on a daily basis and making a home with them?

She would not live without them, no matter how much she loved the duke.

In time, she would forget about his stimulating kisses, caresses, and embraces. She would keep telling herself she didn't love him, couldn't love a man like the Duke of Drakestone.

But she did.

Louisa had changed into her nightrail earlier in the evening, thinking she would go to bed. And she had for a few minutes, before she was up and donning her robe again. She didn't know what was wrong with her. All afternoon, all she'd wanted to do was be by herself and cry, and yet when the house went quiet and she was alone in the safety of her room, the tears wouldn't flow.

Her body was tired and weary, but her mind was as

active as ever. She decided she wouldn't try to sleep again until after Gwen and Mrs. Colthrust returned home. Maybe then she would finally be able to rid herself of the miserable feelings. Thankfully, Mrs. Colthrust hadn't given her any trouble about wanting to stay home.

Only a little warmth emanated from the fireplace, but Louisa didn't care that the drawing room was chilled. She snuggled deeper into her robe and tucked her long hair around her neck. Louisa had insisted that Mrs. Woolwythe and the other maids go to bed so she could be alone, but they wouldn't until all the fires had been banked and all lamps but the one Louisa was using had been extinguished.

She lay in the semidarkness, wondering how different her life would have been had her parents lived, if Nathan were still alive. She would probably be married by now, maybe with a babe of her own. She wouldn't be responsible for her sisters. Tears of sorrow for the loss of her parents and Nathan as well as her own lot in life puddled in her eyes, and just as she was thinking they would spill down her cheeks so she could release her pent-up emotion and weep in earnest, she heard a noise that sounded like a light knock. She sat up and strained her ears to listen. It would be horrible if Bonnie, Sybil, or Lillian came running in and caught her crying like a baby.

The knocking came again.

Louisa wiped her eyes with the back of her hands and scoffed a rueful laugh as she swung her feet off the settee and rose. She should know better than to think she had time to cry. She picked up the lamp and walked into the vestibule to go abovestairs to check on the girls. Halfway up the stairs, she heard the knocking again and realized it was on the front door.

It couldn't be Gwen and Mrs. Colthrust back so

soon. And they wouldn't knock, unless someone had accidentally locked them out. Louisa set the lamp on a table and walked to the door, opening it only enough to peek out.

"Your Grace," she said, her heartbeat racing at the sight of him. He was handsomely dressed in his evening attire, and she was most inappropriately dressed in her nightclothes. She immediately grabbed the lapels of her robe in her hand and tightened the garment around her.

He pushed the door wide and walked inside, closing it behind him. He laid his hat and gloves on the table by the lamp and asked, "Where are the servants?"

"I sent them all to bed some time ago. You shouldn't be here this time of night, especially with me dressed as I am."

"This isn't the first time I've done something inappropriate, Louisa, and it won't be the last. Where are your sisters?"

"Asleep. Why? And what are you doing barging into my house?"

"I came for this." He gently pulled her to him, circling her back with his strong arms, and hugged her close to him. He laid his cheek on the side of her head and whispered, "I had to make sure you're all right."

Despite her intentions, Louisa's body betrayed her, and she melted against the warmth of the duke's hard chest.

"I'm fine," she whispered back, glad her face was hidden in his waistcoat when she fibbed. She wasn't fine, but oh how the comfort of his embrace made her feel better.

"I don't think you are, Louisa. I feel your body trembling."

"It's cold," she managed to say, knowing that was only half a fib.

He picked up the sides of his cloak and wrapped them around her, cocooning her into his embrace. She tried to pull away, but he held her to him. She had been at the point of crying all afternoon, and she feared receiving his kindness and concern now would push her over the edge.

He held her tighter and kissed the top of her head. "You might as well be still," he said softly. "I am not going to let you go."

She swallowed hard and stopped struggling.

After a few moments, he said, "I want you to know that I'm sorry your brother died."

"No, please don't tell me that," she said. She didn't want to talk about the accident. She didn't want to go through the pain of talking about Nathan again.

"I have to. I wanted to this afternoon. You must know, if I could go back and change that night, I would."

Louisa shook her head, choking back tears and trying to cry silently, as she had at the park, so he wouldn't know. His heartfelt sympathy was draining what little control she had of her emotions.

"I should have told you a long time ago." He kissed her temple and the edge of her eye while he ran his hands soothingly up and down her back. "I would take his place so he could be here with you and your sisters if I could."

"I don't want to hear that. Please, let me go, please," she begged, despair filling her. She struggled to get free again, knowing she couldn't deny herself the relief that comes from crying, but not wanting him to see her cry.

The duke held her tighter, cupping her head to his

chest, forcing her to accept the comfort of his arms and his words. "I'm not letting go, Louisa."

"You must," she said between choking breaths.

"You don't know how badly I wanted to hold you this afternoon and comfort you like this."

As if those were the magic words, the words she'd longed to hear for two years, the tears started flowing and her body started shaking. She knew she was being lifted into his arms and carried, but she no longer wanted to struggle. She snuggled deeper into his embrace, hiding her face in his waistcoat again, and wept as she had never wept before.

Louisa didn't know how long she cried before the sobs, shaking, and sniffling faded. Her throat hurt and her breathing was labored, but inside, she felt better than she had in a long time.

As she calmed, she noticed they were in the drawing room on the settee and she was sitting on his lap. And she had on her nightclothes! That was definitely not proper behavior for a young lady, but she didn't move. She wanted to stay forever with her cheek pressed to the duke's chest, hearing his heartbeat and feeling his arms wrapped tightly around her.

She took in a deep shuddering breath and lifted her head to look at him.

"You can use my handkerchief," he said, brushing her hair away from her damp face. There was a little light from the corridor shining into the room, but Louisa didn't have to see his face and eyes clearly to know he was smiling warmly at her. She heard it in his voice.

"Thank you." She took the handkerchief.

"Do you feel better now?"

She nodded. "How did you know I needed to cry?"

"It was more that I knew I wanted to hold you."

His words touched her heart. For all his bluster and

complaining, he realized what no one else seemed to know: She needed to be held. And she was glad it was the duke who'd figured that out.

"I've heard it said that a kiss can make something that's hurt feel better," he said.

"I've heard it, too. Have you ever tried it?"

"No. Do you want to?"

"Yes," she said softly.

He placed his hands on each side of her face and looked into her eyes as if to ask her if she was sure. She wound her arms around his neck. He bent his head, and his lips found hers and moved tenderly, sweetly, briefly over them before he raised his head and looked into her eyes once more. "Did it work?" he asked.

"I don't think the kiss was long enough. Perhaps we should try it again." She placed her lips on his, and the kiss started the same way as before—slow, soft, a lightly brushing of their lips together. The contact was delicate, feathery, and enticing.

The moments ticked by. The longer they kissed, the more kisses she wanted. She opened her mouth, and his tongue explored it with eager yet soothing strokes. His hands moved down her chest. He parted her robe, and his palm molded over the fullness of one breast, lightly squeezing and caressing. Her nipple stiffened beneath his gentle touch. Louisa moaned her approval and leaned into his hand, enjoying the exquisite feeling. Tremors and shivers tingled all the way down to her abdomen to gather and settle between her legs.

Louisa relaxed and let go of the tight control she'd always kept on the passion she felt for the duke. Without thinking, she shifted and adjusted her legs so that she straddled him. She heard his hissing intake of breath at her movements. He deepened their kiss as she settled her bottom on his lap.

The duke trembled, and she realized he was as affected by these wonderful cravings as she was. His arousal thrilled her almost as much as his touch.

While his mouth and tongue ravaged hers hungrily, her hands roved through his thick, luxurious hair. She pressed him closer, gaining confidence in what she was doing, reading the desire she knew he felt for her and she for him.

"Your nightdress is so thin, it's almost like touching your bare skin," he whispered into her mouth as he fondled her breast.

"I love the feel of your hands on me," she answered.

He chuckled as his fingers searched for and found her nipple again, hidden beneath her cotton gown. At his caressing, it puckered and rose once more. Ripples of desire tightened across her breasts and sent pleasure sweeping down her body again to resettle into her most womanly part.

Their tongues swirled in each other's mouths as he untied the ribbon at her throat and parted her gown. He shoved one side of her robe and gown off her shoulder and slid them down her arm. He lowered his head and caught her nipple in his warm mouth and sucked.

She gasped and her stomach tumbled with expectancy as the awareness sent chills of pleasure skipping along her spine. Her head fell back and her chest arched forward and she enjoyed the glorious sensations. His lips moved up to kiss her shoulder, the crook of her neck, and her chest before finally letting his mouth find and cover her breast again. His tongue circled her nipple, bathed it, and then gently drew it fully into his mouth. His lower body lifted and pressed into her with slow rhythmic movements.

Desire bloomed and blossomed inside her, and all her senses reeled in delight.

She gasped again with pleasure. "That feels so wonderful," she said softly while wave after wave of heat radiated through her. "I don't want you to stop."

He chuckled once more and brought his lips back to hers. Their uneven breaths melted together once again before he mumbled, "That's good because I don't want to stop. Passion can make you feel that way, Louisa, but what we are doing is dangerous."

"Then let me do something dangerous for once in my life."

"If you insist on shedding Miss Prim and Proper tonight, I'm glad you decided to do it with me," he said between kisses, "but I think you will hate me in the morning if we continue on the course we are heading."

"I think I already hate you for making me want you continue what I know we shouldn't be doing."

He chuckled yet again, and she savored every feeling, every tender caress. The gliding movements of his hands on her breasts thrilled her. He reached over and covered her mouth in a brief but passionate kiss.

"It does not bother me that you will hate me, Louisa." He kissed the hollow of her throat, teasing her skin with his tongue. "You already think me a beast. I don't want you to hate yourself, but I promise you will enjoy this."

"I will forgive myself in the morning and you, too, if you will continue to make me feel this way. I've never had these, these strange urges before."

"They are called primal urges."

"Yes, that's it, and if you will think me a wanton beast tomorrow morning for wanting these feelings, so be it."

"Louisa, you are sitting astraddle my lap, and my hands are on your breasts—I am aching for you. This is not the time to keep making me laugh with your clever words. You must know that there will be no going back if we finish what we have started here."

She kissed him before looking into his eyes. "I understand, Your Grace."

He brushed her hair to the back of her shoulder. "My name is Bray. From here on, you must call me by my name and not my title."

"I understand, Bray," she said, and slid the other side of her night rail and robe off her shoulder and down her arm, letting the garments pool around her waist.

His gaze feasted upon her for a few seconds. "I knew your breasts would be beautiful," he said in a husky voice. "Look how the light from the corridor is shining on them. Look how beautiful you are."

Louisa looked down and watched his fingertips glide from the swell of one breast to the other. The lace from the cuff of his sleeve tickled softly across her bare skin. He palmed both breasts and lightly squeezed them. He kissed one and then the other, filling her with a longing for something more.

He lowered his head and caught the rosy tip of one breast into his mouth again. With his tongue he sampled her heated skin over and over again, and she delighted in every touch and each new and building sensation.

"I want to feel your body, too, Bray." She reached under his waistcoat and started pulling the tail of his shirt from the waistband of his trousers. She wanted to know what his skin felt like.

He stilled her hands. "I wish we could, but there is no time for me to undress tonight. We must make do. Help me unbutton my trousers and slide them down my hips."

With frantic movements of hands working together, his trousers were unfastened and her gown was shoved up. Bray dragged his cloak underneath her as he gently laid her on top of it and stretched his warm body over her. A tremor of anticipation shivered through her. Bray rose on his elbows and looked into her eyes for a long moment before his gaze drifted down her face, lingered over her breasts, before sweeping back up to her eyes again.

"You need not worry," she whispered. "I have no hesitation."

"I have plenty for both of us, but I won't let it stop me. I will be gentle with you."

"I know."

He bent down and seared his lips to hers. His lips were moist, hot, and demanding as he kissed her deeply, roughly, crushing his body upon hers. His intensity should have frightened her, but instead it thrilled her. His hands tangled in her hair. Their lips and tongues clung together as passion flamed between them.

With his knees, he opened her legs and then pushed inside her. She gasped from the shock, but he swallowed her sounds. His kisses changed from desperate to slow and sensuous. With one hand he found the warm spot between her legs, and he stroked and fondled her as his body moved up and down.

He made love to her with gentleness that overwhelmed her. His movements were leisurely, sensual, and reverent. He kissed her, caressed her, and moved on top of her until she felt an indescribable pleasure rise up inside her. Louisa lifted her hips and moved with him until waves of explosive sensations tore through her. She cupped his body to her as those languid, heavenly ripples ebbed. She heard Bray's breath quicken, felt him tremble. His body shuddered, and he softly said her name.

She whispered his name, too, before collapsing back down onto the settee with no breath left in her lungs, no strength in her muscles. He lay still and heavy upon her with his face buried in the crook of her neck.

They stayed that way only for a few moments before

Bray lifted himself onto his elbows and asked, "Are you all right?"

She smiled and softly answered, "Yes. I didn't really know what to expect, but my imagination didn't do it justice. That was quite impressive."

He grinned and kissed her tenderly. "I'll take that as a compliment."

He rose and helped her to rise. He then turned his back and started adjusting his clothing, and Louisa did the same.

"Don't you have something you wanted to ask me?" he said when he turned back to face her.

Louisa was tying the ribbons of her gown, and her fingers stilled. Did she? Maybe she was supposed to ask him if she'd satisfied him. "Did I measure up to your expectations?"

He frowned. "Of course, Louisa, that goes without saying. Why would you ask me that?"

"You said I was supposed to have a question for you."

"Not that. Hellfire, couldn't you tell that you satisfied me greatly, completely?"

Annoyed that he was annoyed, she said, "I thought so, but I couldn't be sure, so it's nice to hear you say it."

"Fine, I'll remember that in the future and always tell you. Now, don't you have something else to ask me?"

Louisa thought and stared at him. "Am I supposed to ask if we can we do it again sometime?"

His eyes narrowed and his lips tightened. "What?" he asked in an exasperated voice.

Something told her that wasn't the correct question either. "I really don't know what I'm supposed to ask you after what we just did, Your Grace. Couldn't you tell this was my first time?"

"It's Bray, Louisa. My name is Bray, not Your Grace, and of course I knew it was your first time."

"Then why are you irritated that I don't know all the rules yet?"

"There are no certain rules." He stopped and ran his hand through his hair. "You will drive me to madness. You are supposed to ask me to marry you now that I've taken your virtue from you."

Confused, she asked, "You should have told me that before we—we did it."

"I did. We discussed this. Now, granted, we were in the throes of passion at the time, but you told me you understood. In fact, you told me twice that you understood the meaning of what we were doing."

"I did. I do. It meant I am no longer a virgin, but I never said I'd ask you to marry me."

"That's what I meant when I asked you if you understood."

"Well, you didn't make yourself clear."

"Could you at least act a little more worried about this?"

"There is nothing to be concerned about. It happened and it's over, and that's all there is to it."

"No, that isn't all there is to it, Louisa. There is always the possibility of a child from our coming together."

Merciful heavens!

That danger should have crossed her mind when he had his hands and lips all over her body but it hadn't. All reasonable thought had deserted her.

She summoned an inner strength and said, "I will not borrow that kind of trouble and make myself go mad with worry over something that may not happen."

"Then let's settle it here and now." He advanced on her and quietly said, "Ask me to marry you, Louisa."

He seemed so serious. This was her chance to marry the man she loved. But what would it mean for her sisters if she married a man who knew only about the things that made him happy and nothing about what a real family life was like? She could handle the wild duke, but could he accept her sisters? He would not love her or help her care for her sisters. He could hardly bear to be around them.

"No, I will not," she insisted, and pulled her robe together. "I don't want to marry you. I think it's time for you to go."

"What just happened between us leaves you no choice."

Louisa stood her ground. "I beg your pardon. I do have a choice, and my choice is no. I will not ask you to marry me, and I will not marry you if you should ask me again."

"That won't happen."

"Good," she said on a breathy sigh. "Now, please go before Gwen and Mrs. Colthrust return and find you here."

"Well, we wouldn't want that, would we? Mrs. Colthrust might try to insist that you marry me!" Bray jerked his cloak off the settee and slung it carelessly over his arm. Not even trying to be quiet, he stomped from the room and out the front door, shutting it soundly behind him.

Chapter 23

A heavy heart bears not a nimble tongue.
—*Love's Labour's Lost,* act 2, scene 2

Louisa and Mrs. Colthrust sat in uncomfortable chairs and waited in the vestibule of the Court of Chancery building. She had asked to see either the Master of the Rolls or the Lord Chancellor but was told she must talk to a Chancery solicitor first. He would evaluate her petition and decide if it should be considered further by anyone else.

It had taken three days and a basketful of persuasion, but Louisa finally wore down Mrs. Colthrust's reluctance and convinced the woman to go with her. Louisa had promised her that she wouldn't have to speak but simply act as her chaperone, as she had for all the parties, teas, and balls they attended. She also promised that she would never breathe a word to her uncle that his sister-in-law had gone with her to the court.

Louisa was not unhappy that she had given her innocence to Bray a few nights ago. She wished with all her heart that somehow they could be together again, and that was what had her sitting here, waiting to find out what she needed to do to have the duke removed as their guardian.

She had to deny her own loving feelings for Bray and focus on her sisters. She couldn't marry and give a husband and children of her own the attention they deserved until all her sisters were wed. She couldn't leave them as her parents and brother had, and if she kept up her association with Bray, she feared she might give in to his charms again.

Bray had no tolerance for her younger sisters. It was best that they cut all ties with him—and the sooner, the better.

After more than an hour of waiting and listening to Mrs. Colthrust grumble, they were finally ushered into a small office to meet Mr. George Thurgood.

"Come in, come in," said the short, heavyset man in a white curled wig jovially. "How are you lovely ladies doing today?"

"We are quite well, thank you, Mr. Thurgood," Louisa replied, thankful the man wasn't dour. He held out chairs for them and then walked around to his desk and eased his bulky frame into a squeaky leather chair.

He picked up his quill, readying it to dip in the ink and write on the vellum before him. His smiled and in a friendly voice said, "What can I do for you?"

"I had wanted to speak with the Master of the Rolls or the Lord Chancellor about having the guardianship of me and my sisters changed."

He smiled again. "They are much too busy to see everyone who comes to court wanting their attention. I'm sure you can understand that. I'll be happy to answer your questions if I can, and if not, I'll take your information and speak to them about your concerns at a later date."

She supposed that would have to do. "Thank you. My uncle, Lord Wayebury, signed the guardianship of me and my four sisters over to the Duke of Drakestone."

His eyes lit with recognition. "Yes, yes. I thought I recognized your name. I remember when that happened. Quite frankly, we were all surprised Lord Wayebury wanted to do that, until he explained he was going out of the country on an extended holiday. And we were even more surprised when the duke didn't protest his actions."

"No one more than I. That is why I'm here. I would like to petition the court to have the duke removed and someone else appointed as our guardian."

"What?" He laid the quill down and laced his chubby fingers together across his girth. "Surely you can't be serious."

"Of course I am."

Mr. Thurgood looked from Louisa to Mrs. Colthrust. He then leaned back in his chair and laughed. "I don't know what kind of trickery you are trying to come up with, Miss Prim, but I really don't have time for this today. My schedule is hectic, and there are people with real problems to solve. So unless you have something important to discuss with me, I'm very busy." He started to rise.

"Wait, Mr. Thurgood," Louisa said, moving to the edge of her seat. "I assure you, this is not a trick of any sort. I don't know how I could have given you that idea. The duke is not an acceptable guardian for us, and I have the right to ask the Lord Chancellor to remove him and appoint another in his place."

"Yes, you have the right, but there must be strong

reasons. What has the duke done? Has he harmed you or your sisters?" he asked, sitting back down again.

"No, of course not. Not in any physical way. I shouldn't have to tell you of the duke's reputation. You've probably been in London much longer than I have. He is not a good example for my sisters. Our father was a vicar, and my sisters are used to a kind and gentle man. The duke is not only known for his excessive gambling and debauchery, he is also impatient with my sisters, uses inappropriate language in front of them, and he even called them banshees."

The corners of his mouth twitched with a smile. "Banshees?"

Louisa cleared her throat. "Let's suffice it to say, we need a well-respected, kind, and older gentleman to be in charge of us. Not a young and careless duke."

The man looked baffled and turned his attention to Mrs. Colthrust. "You've been quiet thus far, madam. What do you have to say about this accusation against the duke?"

"Ha! As little as possible," Mrs. Colthrust said.

"Do you agree with her complaint?"

"Not at all."

"Mrs. Colthrust, how can you say that?"

"Because it's true and you know it. It's foolish to have a duke removed as your guardian. Mr. Thurgood, I am Lord Wayebury's sister-in-law, and I am here only because I am her chaperone. I have tried to tell her many times: No one tries to have their guardian dismissed if he is a duke—and a handsome one, at that."

"I'm afraid I have to agree with Mrs. Colthrust," he said.

Louisa lifted her shoulders and straightened her back, and remained calm. She smiled pleasantly and said, "Mr. Thurgood, I don't want to seem unfair about any of this, so would you please be so kind as to write down my information and ask the Lord Chancellor to speak with me about this?"

He rose. "I will be sure to speak to the Lord Chancellor about this for you, Miss Prim." Mr. Thurgood walked from around his desk and over to the door and opened it. "Now, if you'll excuse me, Miss Prim, I have others waiting for my time."

Louisa held her head high, though her heart was aching as she and Mrs. Colthrust walked out of his office.

"I do hope you can now forget this silly notion of having your guardianship changed, Louisa," Mrs. Colthrust said as they stepped out onto the pavement. "You are the only one unhappy with the duke. The other girls seem to tolerate mention of him with no problem whatsoever. In fact, they quite enjoyed their day in the park with him. I'm beginning to believe the reason you want to have him removed has nothing to do with your sisters but lies solely with you. And I don't think it has anything to do with his reputation. I think it has to do with your heart."

Louisa remained silent and kept walking.

Chapter 24

. . . my heart dances;
But not for joy; not joy.
—*The Winter's Tale,* act 1, scene 2

Bray's stomach was twisted into a knot. A feeling he didn't quite understand or know how to handle stirred inside him. He kept telling himself it couldn't be jealousy.

He refused to let it be jealousy. He could have any woman he wanted. Why did he only want Louisa?

This was the third night in a row he'd come to the Great Hall and watched Louisa dancing with Lord Bitterhaven, and it was at least the eighth night they'd danced in the past two weeks. There could have been other times—probably *were* other times—that Bray didn't know about. The thought of that man making inroads into her affections ate at Bray, making him want to walk over and yank the earl away from her.

Bray hadn't tried to speak to Louisa since the night they spent together. She hadn't tried to talk to him either. It had been almost three weeks since he went to her house and comforted her, held her, and made love to her. Many were the times he'd closed his eyes and remembered each whispered sigh, each caress. Thoughts of her beneath him again were killing him.

But his feelings were more than just being restless and missing Louisa. He missed the girls, too. He wanted to see if Bonnie's teeth had started coming down. He wanted to know what Sybil was up to and if Lillian was still playing the pianoforte. Blast it all, he wanted to hear them squeal in laughter again.

A server passed by with a tray, and he grabbed a glass of red wine. When he turned back around, he saw that Lord Sanburne had walked up beside him. Bray was in no mood for the man's idle prattle.

"Good evening, Your Grace."

"Lord Sanburne," Bray acknowledged dryly, and took a sip of the wine, but kept his gaze on the crowded ballroom below.

"We're more than halfway through the Season, and no one has seen you dance with Miss Prim yet."

"Is that right?"

"Yes, and quite frankly, we all find it extremely odd."

"Do you?" he said, still not bothering to look at the pompous earl.

"Don't you?"

"No. You've danced with her, haven't you?"

"Y—yes," Lord Sanburne said, stumbling over the word. "Many gentlemen have danced with her, as you well know. Someone needs to, given the fact that you haven't. The question is, why haven't you? No one has even seen you talk to her since the first night of the Season. And that was more than a month ago now."

Bray knew exactly how long it had been, and he didn't need reminders from this man. "Sanburne, your fascination with my life is beginning to worry me."

"What? What do you mean? I don't have fascination

with your life. That's an absurd accusation, and you know it."

Bray took another drink from his glass and remained silent. The man didn't know when to quit.

"Well, what do you have to say?" the earl asked pointedly.

"Hold this," Bray said, and shoved his wineglass into the earl's hands.

"Ah, ah—now, see here, Your Grace, I'm not your servant!"

Bray paid the man no mind. He strode down into the swirling throng of people in the ballroom. As was his custom, he headed to pay his respects to the widows, dowagers, and spinsters. He waded through the crowd, speaking to some, nodding to others, but as usual, not allowing anyone to detain him for long until he'd kissed the hands of all the ladies lining the dance floor. He knew that would be the one part of the evening he would enjoy. The ladies looked forward to the attention he gave them, and he looked forward to their smiles.

By the time he'd greeted them all, a new dance was starting, so he invited an elderly but still lovely viscountess to join him on the dance floor. Louisa had a new partner, too, a younger, more handsome man than Lord Bitterhaven, but for the life of him, Bray couldn't remember his name. Miss Gwen was on the dance floor, too, with Mr. Standish. Bray assumed that meant the rakish blade was behaving himself when he was with her. That surprised Bray and pleased him.

Bray kept the conversation going with the viscountess, but he couldn't keep his eyes from straying to Louisa every chance he got. Her light pink gown was cut far too low. He didn't know what Mrs. Colthrust was thinking in letting her wear it. Surely Louisa could see that the dandy she was waltzing with had his thoughts on her bosom and not on what she was saying. Thankfully, just as Bray was thinking he'd leave his partner stranded in the middle of the floor and go jerk the man's head off, the dance ended.

He smiled at the vicountess and escorted her back to her seat. His duty for the evening accomplished, he searched for Louisa once more. He didn't know why he came to the Great Hall when it was such torture to watch her dancing, talking, and laughing with other men.

But then, he couldn't fool himself. He did know why. Every once in a while, he would catch her staring at him with her gorgeous blue eyes, and the attention thrilled him. He'd bet his title that whenever she was watching him, she was remembering, like him, their few moments of stolen ecstasy on the settee in her drawing room.

He still couldn't believe she'd let him make love to her and then had the nerve to tell him she didn't want to marry him. For days, he felt as if she'd gotten what she sought from him and then sent him on his way as if he were an unwelcome suitor.

He knew he was a difficult man at times, but Louisa was a difficult lady at times, too. She was just too damn independent for her own good. Not only that, but he didn't have five—he stopped and swore under his breath—*four* sisters to bring into a marriage. Hearing those girls' screams, squeals, and crying had always made him want to bolt for the door—but Louisa made him want to run *to* her door.

For over two years, he'd thought he would be happy if she didn't want to marry him. But that was before he met her, got to know her, kissed her, and made her his. That was before she made him feel things he didn't want to even think about: jealousy, anger, hurt, and love.

Love?

Hell no. He knew how to make a woman feel loved,

but he didn't know how to love one. It wasn't in him to do so.

Could that be the reason she'd rejected his offer of marriage, could it be that she was waiting for him to declare his love for her?

Hell, what was he thinking? She didn't want to marry him, because she didn't need to marry him. He was her guardian. She knew that he would see to it she and her sisters had very comfortable lives. Still, it rankled that she was the one dismissing him.

He glanced around the room, hoping to see Seaton or Harrison, but all he saw was Louisa heading to the dance floor with yet another partner. Was she going to dance every dance and wear out her shoes? He looked for a young lady he might quickly sweep onto the dance floor himself when he caught sight of Mr. Hopscotch standing on the landing, searching the faces in the crowded room. No doubt the man was looking for him. In Bray's current mood, he'd probably smash the man's face in if he insisted one more time that he must marry Louisa to save the Prince from embarrassment. Bray was near the door to the courtyard, so he quickly opened it and dashed out onto the slate terrace.

The night air had a chill, and to add to his already foul mood, it was foggy as well. There were several couples close together in various parts of the lighted grounds. He didn't want to watch lovers whispering to each other in the dark.

Bray walked down past the cupid fountain that centered the courtyard and saw even more lovers taking advantage of the foggy evening. He grunted to himself. There was no peace for him at this place tonight and maybe not anywhere. He knew the only reason he was hanging around and didn't go to one of his clubs was because he didn't want to leave so long as Louisa was there. But worse than that, he was aching to hold her, to hear her contented sighs, to feel her beneath him moaning softly with sweet pleasure.

A sound of feminine distress reached him and disturbed his thoughts. He listened. He could barely make out the woman's words, but it sounded like she was saying, "No, let me go."

He looked around. The sounds hadn't seemed to disturb any of the couples who were dotting the landscape and the terrace. Some young buck had obviously had too much to drink and was trying to steal a few kisses and caresses from an unwilling female. It wasn't his problem.

When would young ladies learn that the reason a man took them for a walk in the garden was so he could kiss them and touch them? Men were born to try to dominate females, and it was up to the woman not to let that happen. He certainly hadn't been able to dominate Miss Prim. If anything, she had been dominating his thoughts ever since he met her.

Bray started to walk off when he heard running. He stopped and looked in the direction of the footsteps and saw Gwen hurrying up the pathway.

His breath stalled in his lungs. "What the bloody hell?" he mumbled as a fierce protectiveness rose up in him.

He hurried across the courtyard at an angle and caught up to her and said, "Miss Gwen, stop."

She glanced over at him and quickly looked away. "No, please, I want to be alone."

He grabbed her arm, stopping her. He took notice of the other couples nearby. It appeared only one had paused their conversation to look at them, so he let go of her.

"You can try to run away and make a scene so

everyone will know what's wrong with you, or you can stand here and quietly tell only me what's going on."

"Nothing," she said, keeping her head down.

"That is not the truth."

She faced him, and Bray saw wide-eyed fear. It was the same look her brother had when he'd realized how badly he was hurt. And just like her brother's that night, Gwen's expression registered disbelief and sadness, too. That protective feeling inside Bray grew stronger.

"Tell me what happened," he said in a deadly quiet tone so she would know he wouldn't let this rest until she complied.

"Nothing," she said again as if trying to sound more in control of herself.

"If nothing happened, why is your lip bleeding?"

"Oh," she said, and put her fingertips to her bottom lip. "I must have bitten it myself when he—"

He touched the small of her back and ushered her away from the path and closer to the courtyard wall, away from curious eyes. There was no blood, but saying so had given Bray the information he was looking for.

"Were you with Standish?" he asked, handing her his handkerchief.

The fear returned to her eyes. "No, no. I wasn't. I swear."

"Miss Gwen," was all he said.

"Please don't tell Louisa," she whispered earnestly. "She will be so angry with me. She told me not to walk with him. She told me not to assume he loved me until he told me so. I didn't listen to her, and she was right. It was all my fault."

"How was it your fault?"

"He—he wanted to kiss me, which I didn't mind. I wanted his kisses, but then he wanted to touch me, and I told him he couldn't unless he asked me to marry him." Tears filled her eyes. "He told me he doesn't love me and doesn't intend to make a match with me. I thought he loved me."

"Shhh," he said. "Don't say more. You've told me enough. And don't cry," he ordered. "You don't want to walk back into the ballroom with tears streaming down your face or your nose red, do you?"

She shook her head and sniffled while wiping her eyes with his handkerchief. "I don't want Louisa to know I was so foolish. I can't believe he doesn't love me. I was so certain he did."

"Men are ungrateful nodcocks when it comes to a lady's affections."

"You won't tell her I made a fool of myself, will you? Promise me you won't tell her."

"I won't tell her. This is your affair, Miss Gwen, not mine. You handle it with your sister however you wish."

And I'll handle this with Standish.

"Thank you."

From over her shoulder, Bray saw Standish sauntering up the pathway.

"Look," he said to Gwen. "Sit over there on that bench and compose yourself for a few moments and dry your eyes. Don't go inside until I come back to walk in with you. Do you understand?"

She nodded.

Bray strode quickly across the grounds to the other side of the lawn and caught up with Standish just as he was about to step onto the slate terrace. "Standish, there you are. I've been looking for you. Might I have a word with you?"

He turned and acknowledged Bray. "Of course, Your Grace."

"Let's go over here. This is a private conversation."

The young man followed him around to the side of

the building. When they rounded the corner, Bray grabbed him by the bow of his neckcloth and pulled it tight, twisting and wrapping the length of it around his fist, choking Standish as he slammed him against the stone.

"You don't deserve it, but I'm going to do you a favor and give you some advice my father gave me years ago, 'Stay away from the innocents for your urges. Have all the doxies, mistresses, and orgies you want, but keep your hands off innocent ladies.' Now, do you understand what I'm saying, Standish?"

The man's face was turning red. He tried to speak, but Bray held the bow so tight around his neck that all he could do was sputter and nod. Bray squeezed a little tighter, nearly lifting the man off his feet.

"Good. You would do well to heed my warning. If we have to meet about this subject again, I won't be so pleasant to you as I am right now." Bray let go of Standish.

The man slid down the building to the ground, pulling at his neckcloth and gasping for air. "You must be mad to attack me like that!" Standish ground out while he tried to loosen his neckcloth.

"I am mad," Bray answered. "Mad as hell. And one other thing: I suggest that Miss Gwen receive a note from you tomorrow explaining that she is the most beautiful young lady you have ever met, and if you were ready for marriage, she would be the one, but you are far too immature to think of marriage at this time."

"You can't expect me to— Ouch!" Standish yelped as Bray's foot came down on his knee.

"What were you saying?" Bray asked.

"I'll have the message delivered tomorrow," Standish said from between clenched teeth.

"Good. I think it might be better for you to spend the rest of the Season out of London, don't you? Otherwise, you and I might find ourselves having another talk. Do I make myself clear?"

"Perfectly, Your Grace," he said, his face twisted in pain.

Bray lifted his foot off the man and walked back to where Miss Gwen sat.

She stood and she rose to meet him.

"How are you feeling now?" he asked.

"Better, I think. Are my eyes and nose red?"

"Just a little. Go splash water on your face, and that should take care of it. If they are still red, tell anyone who asks it was the champagne you drank. It makes a lot of people look flushed."

She nodded. "Thank you for your help, Your Grace."

He smiled. "I'm your guardian, Miss Gwen. It's my duty to look after you. You may come to me with anything, and I will help you."

She reached up and gave him a quick kiss on the cheek.

Bray was so startled, he stepped away from her.

"I'm sorry," she said. "I shouldn't have done that. Please forgive me for being so forward, but tonight I feel about you the way I always felt about Nathan. As if you were my brother taking care of me."

She thought of him as a brother? That gave Bray the oddest feeling. Was he acting more like a brother than like a guardian? Was that feeling he'd had when he saw that she'd been hurt by Standish something like brotherly love? Did she feel like a sister to him?

Bray had that now-familiar tightness in his throat, and he didn't know what to say except, "I don't need gratitude for doing the right thing. Let's go back inside."

Somehow whenever he was around Louisa and her sisters, all the training that went into hiding his emotions left him. He didn't know what to make of what was happening to him.

Chapter 25

Smooth runs the water where the brook is deep.
—Henry VI, part 2, act 3, scene 1

Louisa didn't know how much longer she could pretend she was having fun. She wasn't. The music was loud, the room crowded, and the constant roar from chatter and laughter had her wanting to look for Mrs. Colthrust and Gwen and tell them she was ready to go home. That this madness of parties would go on for another two weeks was almost more than she could bear to think about. As far as she was concerned, the Season was much too long. Surely a month of parties and balls night after night should be the most anyone had to endure.

She enjoyed dancing, conversing with people, and the glass of champagne she had each evening, but she was ready to return to her life of spending the evenings at home with her sisters, playing games, working on her stitchery, or reading. And she knew that Bonnie, Sybil, and Lillian were missing her and Gwen, too.

She thanked the young man she'd danced with and

bade him good-bye on the dance floor, having to insist she didn't need him to help her find Mrs. Colthrust.

"Miss Prim?"

Louisa turned to see a tall, portly gentleman she didn't recognize standing beside her.

"Good evening," he said. "I don't know if you remember me, but we met at the first ball of the Season. I'm Mr. Alfred Hopscotch."

"I met many people that first evening," she said, knowing she had no memory of being introduced to him. "Thank you for reminding me of your name."

"We didn't have the opportunity to talk. The party was a crush, and everyone wanted to meet you for obvious reasons." He ran his hand down the ends of his neckcloth and said, "I wonder if it might be possible for me to have a few moments of your time tonight?"

She looked around the room, hoping to spot Gwen or Mrs. Colthrust. "I was just trying to find my sister and chaperone."

"I promise I won't take much of your time," he said. "I am a personal attendant to the Prince, and he has asked me to discuss something with you privately."

"Are you sure it's me?" she asked, thinking if the man attended the Prince, then he must have mistaken her for someone else.

"Quite sure. Do you mind if we step over to the side of the room and away from the dance floor?"

"All right," she said, curious as to what the man wanted to discuss with her.

He led her over to a corner near a large urn. He looked around as if to make certain that no one was close enough to hear him and said, "What I have to say is of a most private nature to the Prince. At his request, I must ask that you keep anything I say to you in the strictest confidence. He wants assurances that what I say to you will go no further."

Louisa looked suspiciously at the man, still not convinced he had the right person. "All right," she said, and continued to stare at him. "But pardon me if I find it improbable that the Prince has sent you to a ball to talk to me."

He smiled reassuringly. "When the Prince told me this afternoon to approach you, I suppose I could have waited and visited with you at your home tomorrow. But when the Prince asks me to do something, I don't usually tarry."

"Perhaps you should tell me what it is, then."

"The Prince knows the Duke of Drakestone vowed to your brother that he would marry you and that His Grace has not made good on that promise."

"I believe everyone in London knows that, Mr. Hopscotch."

"The Prince has tried to impress upon the duke how critical it is that he keep his word and marry you, but the Prince has seen no progress in that direction."

"I had no idea this matter would even cross the Prince's mind. Surely he has more important things to concern himself with than a personal matter between me and the duke."

"What the dukes do and say is always important to the Prince. He feels strongly that the Duke of Drakestone should uphold the long-standing honor of the dukes before him and live up to his word and marry you."

The man paused and waited as if he expected her to say something, but she remained silent. She had stopped answering questions about the duke after the first week of the Season.

"Have you asked the duke to fulfill his vow and marry you?"

"Certainly not," she said.

"The Prince would like for you to."

Louisa's eyebrows rose, and so did her ire. "Sir, I don't know what to say to you or to the Prince other than it is by mutual consent that the duke and I do not wish to marry."

"The Prince must ask you to reconsider. I am not at liberty to give you the particulars of why it's necessary—the duke knows them, of course—but it is in the Prince's and England's best interests for your wedding to the duke to take place by the first day of June."

This conversation was getting more bizarre by the moment. "I find it difficult to believe that whether or not the duke and I marry would have anything to do with England or the Prince, Mr. Hopscotch."

"It is of great importance to the Prince and to England. I am not here talking to you about this as a lark, Miss Prim. The consequences of not marrying the duke by the stated date will create a very serious matter in England."

Very serious?

A flicker of unease prickled over her. "And you've talked to the duke about this?" she asked. "And stressed to him that he needs to marry me?"

"A number of times. I can't impress upon you enough that this is a matter of great concern to the Prince. If you do not marry the duke by the first day of June, there will be great embarrassment and scandal to England and the Prince."

She knew dukes were powerful and that many things went on behind closed doors concerning political matters, but she whispered, "I don't see how that could be."

She could understand how it might embarrass the Prince if he had made some kind of wager about the outcome of their marriage, as many gentlemen in London had, but how could it possibly affect England?

Suddenly something more pressing entered Louisa's mind. Now she knew why the duke had come to see her that night after their afternoon in the park. He didn't want to comfort her. He wanted to seduce her. He knew she desired him. He may even know she loved him. And Bray assumed once he had taken her innocence, she would feel obligated to marry him.

A pain gripped her stomach. He was trying to force her to marry him because the Prince wanted him to marry her. Heartache filled her. She had hoped that just maybe he wanted to marry her because he had some tender feelings for her, but now she knew that wasn't true.

"So Miss Prim, can the Prince depend on you to do what is right and ask the duke to fulfill his obligation to your brother and marry you with all haste?"

"As you know, Mr. Hopscotch," Louisa said stiffly, "it is difficult to force the duke to do anything he doesn't want to do, but you can depend on me to talk to him about this and get the matter settled as quickly as possible."

This time, the man smiled as if quite pleased with himself, and he ran his hand down the ends of his neckcloth again. "The Prince will not forget your consideration, Miss Prim," he said, nodded, and then walked away as quietly as he'd come upon her.

"Who was that?" Mrs. Colthrust asked, coming up to Louisa.

"He said his name was Mr. Alfred Hopscotch."

"Why were you over here in the corner with him?"

"We were just talking about the Prince," she said as anger at Bray grew inside her.

"I've never heard of Mr. Hopscotch. Is he related to a title?"

"He didn't say, and I didn't ask."

"Hmm, well, if you are interested, I can find out for you."

"No, Mrs. Colthrust, I am most certainly not interested in Mr. Hopscotch."

"Well, I might be," she said, watching him walk away. "He's not so dashing as some gentlemen, but he doesn't have a bad look about him either. Did he happen to say whether or not he was married?"

"Of course not, and that was the furthest thing from my mind while we were talking," Louisa said.

"Well, doesn't matter right now anyway. I see he is already leaving. I'll have to meet him another time, but I will make some inquiries about him. I've been looking for Gwen. Have you seen her recently?"

Louisa started scanning the ballroom. "No. The last time I saw her, she was dancing with Mr. Standish. That was several minutes ago."

"Maybe she's in the retiring room. I'll check there and you look on the other side of the dance floor. Perhaps she's standing in a corner by a large urn like you are."

"Could we meet at the front door? I think I'm ready to go home."

"I suppose we have been here long enough, but I don't know how you and Gwen will ever find a husband if we continue to leave early each evening. Go, go. I'll meet you at the front door."

As soon as Louisa located Gwen, she was going to find Bray and let him know she now knew the truth of why he'd finally decided to comfort her.

A movement out of the corner of her eye caught her attention. It was the door to the courtyard opening.

Gwen walked inside. Louisa expected to see Mr. Standish come in right behind her, but Louisa's feet halted and her stomach felt as if it fell to the floor. It was Bray who walked in after Gwen.

A soul-shattering pain ripped through Louisa.

Bray had been in the courtyard with her sister? A feeling of betrayal washed over her. Her hands curled into fists. Gwen turned back to Bray, and they spoke quietly before she hurried away. Louisa didn't know which emotion she felt strongest—anger, jealousy, or hurt that Bray would dare try to woo her sister. She could forgive him for ignoring her for two years, for having no patience with the girls, even for keeping the Prince's intentions from her, but she would not forgive him for pursuing her sister.

With single-minded purpose, she strode over to him, pinioned him with a glare, and in a frosty tone said, "How dare you take my sister out to the courtyard for a romantic interlude!"

Bray's eyes narrowed and he folded his arms across his chest. "I thought we had established long ago that I will dare anything, Louisa."

"But my sister!" she whispered earnestly. "I knew you were a scoundrel of the highest order, and you keep proving it to me day after day. I can understand you seducing me, thinking you would then be able to force me to marry you so you can do the Prince's bidding. I was a more-than-willing victim, but seducing my sister is unforgivable."

The courtyard door opened again, and they had to move out of the way to let the couple come inside.

"What did you say about the Prince?" he asked.

She knew they were attracting attention and noticed a couple of ladies were looking at them, but at this point she didn't care who knew she was angry with the duke.

Keeping her voice low, she said, "Yes, I know there is a dirty little secret between you and the Prince. Mr. Hopscotch told me that you are trying to force me to marry you in order to save the Prince, or England, or both from some kind of scandal. I don't care if Napoléon miraculously raises another army and threatens England once again. I will not marry you."

"Good."

She blinked. "Good?"

"Very good. Did he tell you why he is desperate for us to marry?"

"Only that it would cause a huge scandal for the Prince and England if we didn't."

"It will. Our Prince has wagered the Elgin Marbles."

"What?"

"Yes, the dirty little secret is that the Prince wagered the Elgin Marbles to the Austrian archduke that we would marry by June one. Mr. Hopscotch came to see me within a week of you coming to London, Louisa. He has been to see me several times, always impressing upon me the need for us to marry."

"I didn't know what it was. He didn't tell me."

"Oh, that's right, the Prince's minion told me not to tell, but when have I ever done what I was told to do? When I suggested that you should ask me to marry you that night in your house, the Prince's wager and what he'd asked me to do never crossed my mind! A man pays his own gambling debts. I have told this to Hopscotch repeatedly. As far as I am concerned, those damned stones will be just as well taken care of in a museum in Austria as in England. If the Prince loses them, maybe that will teach our glutton of a prince a lesson that he shouldn't raid England's treasury and antiquities on foolish wagers."

Louisa was trying to make sense of his words about

the Elgin Marbles, but Bray didn't give her time to think. He kept talking.

"And as far as Gwen, Louisa, do you really think I would try to seduce your sister after I have made love to you?"

He looked so stricken that she said, "No, no." And then, "I don't know. What else am I to think except that you asked her to take a walk with you in the court-yard?"

"Maybe you could think that we were talking." He stopped and let out a loud sigh. "If you want to know more, you will have to ask Gwen because quite frankly, Louisa, I find this accusation beneath you and I find it tiresome."

Beneath me? Tiresome?

"Let me tell you what is beneath me and tiresome, Your Grace. It's waiting for two years to hear from a scoundrel and then when I finally do, it's not an appropriate marriage proposal, it's an order, a command that we will be married. So here is my answer: No, thank you!"

Her breath leaped in her throat, and before she knew what she was doing, she drew back her hand and struck him across the face with her open palm. The sound of the slap reverberated around the room.

His head snapped back and he blinked. "I bet that stung your hand," he said dryly.

"No," she said honestly. "It felt good."

She turned to walk away and saw that everyone in the room had stopped what they were doing and was watching her and the duke. Even the music had stopped. No doubt those nearby had heard every word she said.

Louisa lifted her chin and her shoulders. *Let them gawk,* she thought. Let them banish her from the ton, write about her in the scandal sheets, or whatever they might do. She did not care and she was not sorry. The duke had had that slap coming for a long time.

Louisa realized that she actually felt better. In fact, she felt wonderful.

Without looking back at Bray, she started walking directly toward the crowd. To her surprise, clapping and cheering erupted from everyone. The people parted and allowed her to walk through. She heard shouts of "Well done, Miss Prim, and it's about time you showed him what you're made of!" and "You got what you deserved, Your Grace!"

Louisa paid them no mind. She kept walking and met no one's eyes. She would wait outside for Mrs. Colthrust and Gwen.

Bray worked his jaw. She had strength in her lovely arms and a sting in her soft hands. She had caught him by surprise, but she was right and he knew it. He'd deserved the slap a long time ago. He just never thought she'd do it.

"I think the crowd is thinking it's about time she let you have it square in the face," Harrison said as he walked up beside Bray.

"And they are right," Seaton added, walking around to the other side of Bray.

"Do you know what else they're thinking?" Harrison asked.

Bray nodded as the crowd swallowed Louisa from his view. "That I should stalk after her, force her into my arms, and kiss her right here in front of everyone in the ton, and horrify all the dowagers, spinsters, and innocents, and stake my claim on her once and for all."

"Well, it wouldn't be the first time you kissed a lady in public," Harrison offered.

Seaton said, "Please, Harrison, you can't equate Miss

Prim with Bray's mistresses when he was a mere boy of twenty-one. That was years ago, when he was still trying to shock his father. Besides, it was on a street where only two gentlemen saw it and then told about it. There are over a hundred people here tonight."

Harrison looked at Bray. "A kiss right now would surely please a gossip-hungry crowd who's begging for a better ending to the night than a well-deserved slap."

"But you're not going after her, are you?" Seaton added.

"No," Bray said. "Let's go get a drink."

Chapter 26

There is no fettering of authority.
—*All's Well that Ends Well,* act 2, scene 3

Bray never expected to find himself waiting for Louisa in her drawing room the day after she slapped him, but she'd given him no choice. She might be right in thinking she was too prim and proper for his rakish ways, but if she thought she could best him in any tug-of-war, she was in for a huge disappointment.

And he was just itching to give it to her.

"Your Grace," Louisa said, walking slowly into the room and clearly staying on the other side of the settee.

He didn't know why, but it angered him that she didn't come fully into the room to confront him but was keeping her distance as if she feared getting too close to him. Or maybe she thought she should stay near the doorway in case she had to quickly escape from him. "This is a surprise," she said.

Why did she have to look so damn fetching? Why did she have to have her hair falling across her shoulders just the way he liked it? And why did she have to look so frightened? Did she think he might seek retribution for the slap?

He cleared his head of those troubling thoughts and tried to remember the reason he was there. "I bet it is."

"Well, you are an admitted gambler so I'm sure 'bet' is an appropriate word for you to use. I suppose today you came to give me a lesson in sarcasm."

He noticed that she didn't meet his eyes when she talked. "Not sarcasm—but, yes, I think a lesson is in order."

"Well, you will be happy to know I need no further lessons from you. You have shown me all you have to offer. And if you came to see Gwen, I'm afraid you've missed her. She and Mrs. Colthrust are at Mrs. Roland's card party this afternoon and unavailable."

If she wouldn't come to him, he would go to her. He walked menacingly around the settee and stood in front of her, near the entrance to the room. His admiration inched up a notch when she stood firm and let him approach without fleeing.

"You know I didn't come to see Gwen. And I'm not even close to having shown you all I have up my sleeves, but I will. I heard a few minutes ago that you have been to the Court of Chancery to see if you could have me removed as your and your sisters' guardian."

"You only heard today?" she asked. "I did that a couple of weeks ago. I can't believe it took so long for you to find out."

"Your petition finally made its way up to the Lord Chancellor, and he told me as soon as it was made known to him."

"You look unsettled by this."

"Maybe that's because I am," he said tightly, thinking what he really wanted to do was wrap her in his arms and kiss her, tell she would never be free of him, and not let her go until she begged him to marry her.

"Why? I told you the first day we met that I was going to Chancery Court to see about having our guardian changed to someone more appropriate for us."

"You said a lot of things that first afternoon we met, Miss Prim, but I thought you were more intelligent than to actually go through with something like this."

He watched her bristle. "I have to think about my sisters' welfare. I needed to know what all my options are so I could make informed decisions as to what is best for them."

"Options?" He ran his hand through his hair. "I don't understand your relentless sense that you are responsible for your sisters' well-being. You are not. I am."

She stepped toward him. "I beg your pardon. In the past seven years, they have lost their parents and their brother. I'm all they have, and I will take care of them the best I can, and if that includes changing to a new guardian, I will see that it is done."

"Are you implying I have not been taking adequate care of you and your sisters?"

"Not so far as the things they need."

"Have any of my wild and reckless ways that you're always so concerned about ever hurt or damaged any of you? Have I ever hurt them or frightened them?"

"Not yet."

"Then why in the hell did you go?"

"Because I've known from the start you were not capable of being our guardian. You cringe every time you are around Bonnie and Sybil. You roughly handled Lillian when you took her out of the carriage. You seduced me one week, and the next week you are in the courtyard with Gwen, proving to me that I was not wrong to seek help to get away from you."

"I admit I cringe at those high-pitched sounds, and I did forcibly take Lillian from the carriage, but I never hurt her. I would not hurt any of your sisters. I am not pursuing Gwen, and she is not interested in me."

"So now you call her Gwen. Not Miss Gwen."

"A brother doesn't call his sister Miss."

A ripple of surprise threaded through Louisa.

"Are you two arguing?"

Bray and Louisa jerked around and saw Bonnie standing in the doorway.

"No," Bray said. "It probably sounded that way, but no, we were just having a discussion, isn't that right, Miss Prim?"

She hesitated, and he knew Miss Prim and Proper was debating whether she ought to lie to her little sister and agree that they weren't arguing.

She passed on the lie by saying, "Tell me what you want?"

Bonnie walked into the room and past Louisa without answering. She looked up at Bray and said, "I have something for you."

"You have something?" He looked at her hands. They were empty. He looked at Louisa, and she lightly shook her head.

Bonnie gave Bray a big toothless grin. "I've been waiting for you to come back, Your Grace, so I could give it to you. I made it for you all by myself."

She walked over to the secretary and opened a drawer. She pulled out a small piece of canvas and walked over and handed it to him. He took it from her and looked down at it. It was a child's painting. There were trees, flowers, and a big yellow sun in a blue sky. There was a carriage overcrowded with people in the center, and off to the side was a booth with puppets hanging in it. It took him a moment to realize she had painted a picture of their day in the park for him. His chest and throat constricted.

"It was the best day I've ever had," Bonnie told him.

He looked down at Bonnie's smiling face, and it dawned on him that he'd never been given a gift. He didn't know what to do. All his life, his father had given him anything he wanted. His mother, too, but neither of them had ever given him a gift. He had showered gifts of jewelry on his mistresses, gifts of money on doxies, and gifts of flowers and sweets on proper young ladies for years, but no one had ever given anything to him. He was a marquis the day he was born. Who needed to give him a gift?

"I don't know what to say."

"How about thank you," Louisa said from between clenched teeth.

Bray looked from Bonnie's disappointed features to Louisa's angry expression. How could he explain to them what he was feeling? How could he tell them how much this simple act of unselfish kindness meant to him? He had no words for this child's gift. He felt so undeserving.

"You don't have to keep it if you don't want it," Bonnie said. "It's all right. It's not very good anyway."

"No, no," he said earnestly. "Of course I want it." Bray dropped to one knee, held out his arms, and said, "Come here and let me give you a hug."

The little girl flew into his embrace.

Bray closed his arms around her slight frame. He wanted to hug her tightly, but she was so small in his arms, he was afraid of hurting her if he squeezed too hard. Her spindly arms went around his neck and pulled him close. She was warm and smelled like soap and sweetness.

Is this what a sister feels like?

The same feelings of protectiveness that he'd felt when he saw Gwen in the courtyard stirred inside him now. At one time or another, he'd held a woman of just about every size, shape, and age, but he'd never held a child in his arms. That strong protective instinct swelled to overflowing again, and his resolve strengthened. Bonnie had been given to him to care for. This little girl had given him his first gift, and she had made it for him. No one was taking her from him.

"Thank you, Bonnie," he said. "Thank you. It's the most beautiful painting I've ever seen. I'll always treasure it."

From over Bonnie's shoulder, he looked up at Louisa. For the fourth time since he'd known her, she had tears in her eyes. Tears that once again he had caused. He didn't blame her for being angry with him. There was a lot he didn't know about doing the right thing, about being part of a happy, loving family.

But there was one thing he did know.

"I am her guardian, Louisa." He turned Bonnie loose and rose to his feet. "You don't have to like it and you don't have to like me, but I will be your sisters' guardian. I will be responsible for them. You will not change that."

Gwen's words about love invaded his thoughts. Is that why Louisa had refused to marry him? Was she waiting for him to confess that he loved her? Maybe he did love her. He didn't know.

"I'm not going to lie to you, Louisa, and tell you I love you. All I know is that I feel differently about you than any other woman. I think about you, I want you, I want to be with you, but I don't know that it's love." He took a step closer to her. "I know I told you that you would have to ask me to marry you, but now this time I am asking you properly to marry me."

Her eyes searched his face. He knew she had feelings for him, too, but did she like him enough to marry him?

"How can I marry you when my sisters make you flinch and swear when they laugh, or cry, or play? Bray, you don't even know how to say thank you to a little girl."

She was right—he didn't—but he was capable of learning.

"I can't subject them to you or you to them," she continued. "I'm afraid all of you will end up hating me. You don't have the patience to live with them day after day, and I refuse to live without them."

"I have had the patience of Job concerning the girls and this household," he ground out fiercely.

He couldn't believe she'd refused him again. Didn't she know what it cost him to ask her to marry him after he'd told her that it was she who would have to ask him the next time? He had never allowed himself to be that vulnerable to anyone. Didn't his capitulation on that tell her anything about the way he felt about her?

"I'll marry you," Bonnie said. The small voice penetrated Bray's thoughts.

He looked down at Bonnie, and his throat tightened again when he saw how sincere she was. His feelings for her overwhelmed him, and he smiled at her. "I would take you up on that, missy, if you were a little older."

"I'm older," Sybil said, appearing from around the doorway. "I'll marry you."

He smiled at Sybil, too. "You aren't old enough to marry, either, young lady, but when you and Bonnie are, I'll be around to help you pick the perfect gentleman to make you happy."

"I want him to be just like you," Bonnie said, smiling back at him with her missing teeth.

"Bray, I—"

"You've said enough, Louisa," he said, knowing that trying to learn how to love her had been his greatest challenge and it looked like he had failed miserably at it. "You've said all I need to hear."

Bray rolled the painting and stuck it in his pocket. He reached out both his hands and said, "Sybil, Bonnie, come walk with me to the door."

They took hold of his hands, and the three of them walked out.

Chapter 27

Every why hath a wherefore.
—*The Comedy of Errors,* act 2, scene 2

As soon as Bray had left, Louisa sent Sybil and Bonnie up to Miss Kindred. She put on her bonnet, grabbed a shawl, and headed to the back garden.

Gray skies threatened rain and matched her mood. Louisa walked along the edge of the shrubbery, letting her hand gently skim along the scratchy leaves. What was she thinking? She knew Bray didn't have designs on Gwen. She should never have accused him of such a thing, but at the time, she was angry about him for not telling her that the Prince wanted them to marry. She was shocked when she saw Bray walk in from the courtyard behind Gwen.

Did he really feel like Gwen was his sister? Even though it took him a few seconds, he did finally figure out how to properly thank Bonnie for her gift. But had Bonnie and Sybil really said they would marry him? Maybe her sisters could live peacefully with Bray and he with them. The thought of that made her love for him soar. Oh, how could she have been so wrong?

Louisa didn't know what she could say or do to redeem herself. She had acted like a shrew to Bray and then let him walk out the door without apologizing.

She heard the back door open, and she saw Gwen standing on the top step. All of a sudden, Gwen flew down the steps and threw herself in Louisa's arms and started crying.

"Gwen, please tell me what's wrong! Did something happen at Mrs. Roland's card party?"

No amount of talking and soothing was going to calm Gwen until she finished crying, so Louisa just held her and let her weep.

When the sniffling faded, Gwen raised her head and said, "Read this. It was waiting for me when I got home."

Louisa took the note and opened it. Her gaze immediately dropped to the bottom of the letter, where she saw Mr. Standish's signature. Her heart squeezed. She scanned the note and then said, "He's leaving Town for the rest of the Season."

"And he doesn't love me, Louisa. I had thought he felt for me the same way I felt about him." More tears ran down Gwen's cheeks.

Louisa took the end of her shawl and wiped her sister's damp cheeks. "I'm so sorry, Gwen. But here, read it again. Mr. Standish doesn't actually say he doesn't love you."

"He didn't have to. He told me so last night."

"When?"

"I took a walk with him in the courtyard. I know you and Mrs. Colthrust told me not to, and even the duke told me I shouldn't have walked with Mr. Standish, but I thought he was going to propose to me. That's when he told me he didn't love me."

Now, Louisa knew why Bray was coming in from the courtyard with Gwen. Oh, how could she ever have accused him of pursuing her sister? Would he ever forgive her for declining his proposal of marriage?

"What am I going to do?" Gwen asked. "Mr. Standish doesn't love me."

"Well, the first thing you can do is understand that you can't make someone love you. They either do or don't. And it sounds like Mr. Standish just isn't sure yet."

Much like the duke wasn't sure he loved her.

"Now, you can be miserable and cry every day while you wait for Mr. Standish to return so that you can continue to enjoy the gentlemen you are dancing with, and conversing with, and playing cards with, and enjoy the rest of the Season while you wait for him to come back. It's your choice how you spend your time."

"Do you think I'll have another chance to win his love?"

"I don't see why not. He admits that he's too young to think of marriage but that if he were going to, it would be with you. That should lift your spirits and make you feel better."

She sniffled again. "Yes—yes, it does."

"Good. Now, why don't you go send him a note thanking him for his lovely letter and that you'll look forward to renewing your acquaintance with him when he returns?"

Gwen's eyes brightened and a smile spread across her face. "Thank you, Louisa—you are the best sister in the world. I'll do that right now." She spun away.

"Gwen?"

Gwen stopped and turned back to her.

"I'm glad the duke was there for you to talk to last night."

"So was I, Louisa. It was almost like having Nathan back."

So Bray and Gwen really did feel like brother and sister.

Louisa shivered and her eyes closed as understanding flooded her. She wrapped her shawl tighter around her and wondered how she could have let Bray walk out the door without explaining her feelings of hurt and anger?

Bray hadn't done everything right, but neither had she. He'd admitted he didn't have the kind of childhood she'd had, that he'd never been around girls. Maybe he had been patient with the girls—for him. She once thought he could never learn to accept her sisters, but just maybe he already had. And she'd been too blind to see it, but Bonnie, Sybil, and Gwen hadn't.

She had always thought she'd marry a gentle soul like her father, a man who didn't argue, demand, or raise his voice no matter the situation. But she now knew she would never be happy with a man like that. She wanted there to be laughter and sparks of excitement between her and her husband. She wanted the passion she'd experienced when she was in Bray's arms.

Louisa had to go to Bray and ask him to forgive her. She knew it wasn't proper for a young lady to go to a gentleman's house, but she had been improper with him before. She hoped she wasn't too late and that he hadn't already decided to completely wash his hands of her.

Hearing the back door open, she turned to see her uncle step out on the landing. Louisa's mouth dropped open.

"There you are, Louisa."

"Uncle, you're back."

"Yes. Mrs. Woolwythe said she thought you were in the garden. She's seems a nice woman, but we'll have to let her go now that I'm back with my staff. Well, don't look so shocked. I can't have two housekeepers."

"I'm shocked that you're back, Uncle. We never heard a word from you while you were away."

Her uncle walked down the steps. "You knew I would return one day," he said.

"Yes, of course. How is your wife? How was your journey?"

"My wife is blessed to be with child. We discovered she was not long after we arrived in Portugal, so we immediately started making plans to come back to England. We didn't want there to be any chance that my son would be born abroad."

"I'm very pleased for you, Uncle."

"Have things been well here? Has Ramona behaved herself and done what a proper chaperone should?"

"Yes."

"Good. I didn't speak to her. Mrs. Woolwythe said she naps every afternoon before readying herself for the evening's parties."

"She has done an outstanding job, Uncle," Louisa said, knowing she was fibbing a little on the word "outstanding."

"Excellent. I'm glad the Season is almost over. Are there any offers of marriage on the table?"

She hesitated, and finally said, "No."

"Well, of course, you and Gwen can remain here until the Season is finished, but I'll have to send the younger girls back to Wayebury immediately."

Louisa recoiled from that thought. "Why would you want to do that?"

"First, there's no room for us here with all of you, and my wife can't be subject to that many people in the house, anyway. She's delicate, you understand. We've checked into an inn until I can send the other girls back to Wayebury. She wants to get settled back into her home as soon as possible. Of course, you and Gwen will be able to stay and finish your Season—and hopefully she will make a match. If she doesn't, I should be able to find someone to offer for her."

Over my dead body, Louisa thought, but remained silently seething.

"I'll go to the Court of Chancery tomorrow and apply to have my guardianship of you and the girls reinstated."

Louisa's heart started pumping faster. "Can you do that after tossing us aside?"

"Of course, so long as the duke doesn't fight it. And, I mean, why would he? You don't think he wants to take care of half a dozen girls one day longer than he has to, do you?"

"Five, Uncle," she ground out. "There are five of us, and being that we are your brother's children, you should know that."

"Don't get huffy with me, young lady." He rolled his shoulders and pulled on the tail of his coat. "The details of this really don't concern you. Don't give it another thought. I'll take care of everything tomorrow. Now I should go. I won't bother Ramona today. I'll wait and speak to her tomorrow."

"Thank you, Uncle," she said, knowing exactly what she was going to do.

Louisa followed her uncle into the house. She found Mrs. Woolwythe and asked her to see that the footman had their carriage brought to the front of the house. She then went up to the schoolroom and asked Miss Kindred to help Bonnie, Sybil, and Lillian get their bonnets and coats for an outing and to meet her belowstairs. She found Gwen and told her the same.

She went into her bedroom, and from her wardrobe she grabbed her coin purse and put it inside her reticule. The girls and Saint met her at the front door.

"Where are we going?" Gwen asked.

"I don't care where we're going," Sybil said. "I'm just glad we're getting to go somewhere."

Louisa smiled. "Girls, we are going to the duke's house."

"Yippee!" Sybil and Bonnie squealed.

"But no screaming," Louisa said good-naturedly. "You must talk softly at all times. And Sybil, why don't you get your button collection to look at or something to keep your hands busy, so you won't be tempted to touch anything."

"All right," she said, and started running up the stairs.

"Can I take my doll?" Bonnie asked. "I don't want to touch anything and get in trouble either."

"Of course, but hurry." Louisa looked at Gwen and Lillian. "If you want to take anything with you, now is the time to go get it."

"If we can take Saint," Lillian said, "I'll get his leash."

Louisa thought about that and then said, "Yes, let's take him." The duke needed to know exactly what he was in for.

A few minutes later, they were all standing outside the duke's door, staring at the rather stern-looking Mr. Tidmore, who gave them the once-over as he said, "Have you brought the dog back?"

"No," Bonnie said, loud enough for every neighbor on the street to hear, and Saint barked several times, too. "He's ours."

"Bonnie, remember what I said about talking softly," Louisa said, and then looked back at the butler. "May we see the duke?"

"I'm afraid he's not in, miss."

Louisa moistened her lips and said, "May we wait inside for him?"

"I'm afraid I can't allow that, miss. I have no idea what time he will be returning. It could be rather late, and he may not want visitors."

"I won't touch anything this time, if you let us stay," Sybil said. "I learned my lesson about that."

"I didn't have a lesson to learn," Bonnie said, "but I won't touch anything, either."

Mr. Tidmore stared blankly at the girls but said nothing.

"Girls," Louisa said. "I'll handle this. Mr. Tidmore, the duke is our guardian, and it's most urgent I speak to him when he returns. We will either wait for him in the warmth of the drawing room or we will wait for him in the chill on the front steps."

"Very well," Mr. Tidmore said, sounding a bit annoyed. "Come in and sit in the drawing room and wait, and see that you don't touch anything. I'll send someone to see if we can locate the duke and tell him you are here."

"Thank you," Louisa said.

They settled themselves in the drawing room and waited and waited. Louisa was happy that the girls didn't seem to mind sitting so quietly for so long. When it grew dark, Bonnie and Sybil became restless. A servant came in and lit a fire and the lamps. Mr. Tidmore came in and asked to speak to Louisa alone, so she joined him in the corridor.

"The dinner hour will be approaching soon, Miss Prim. Would you like for me to have our cook prepare something for you and your sisters, or will you be leaving to dine in your own home?"

Louisa's stomach jumped nervously. Should they

leave and return another time? She had no idea what Bray might say or do when he came in and saw them waiting for him. "We'll be staying, Mr. Tidmore. Dinner would be lovely, if it's not too much trouble for the cook."

An hour later, Mr. Tidmore showed them into the dining room. Louisa and Gwen sat on one side of the table, and Lillian sat between Sybil and Bonnie on the other side. The first course was a bowl of chicken and vegetable soup. To begin with, the girls were quiet in the elaborately decorated room, but by the time the servant had picked up the bowls, they were chatting as if they were in their own home.

Suddenly from the front room, Louisa heard Saint barking. Her back stiffened.

The duke was home. Had she made a mistake coming to his house?

Moments later, she heard boots stomping down the corridor. She thought about jumping up, gathering the girls to her, and running from the house. But she sat there with her gaze fixed on the doorway.

If Bray didn't want them there, he would have to throw them out.

Chapter 28

Love sought is good, but given unsought is better.
—*Twelfth Night,* act 3, scene 1

Bray strode through the front door, taking off his gloves. He threw them and his hat onto a side table. He heard barking and looked up to see Saint heading toward him. The dog jumped into his arms. Bray rubbed the top of his head and was happy to see Saint for about three seconds. Then it dawned on him, *What is the spaniel doing here?*

Was Louisa so outraged with him that she took Saint away from the girls and brought him back?

Did she hate him so much that she would punish her sisters and not let them keep the dog? This went beyond the pale, even for Louisa. He would not have it. He kept Saint in his arms and picked up his hat and gloves. He would show her who was in charge. He was taking the dog back to the girls, whether she wanted him to or not. Saint was their pet, and she might as well like it—because the spaniel stayed with the girls.

"Your Grace," Mr. Tidmore said, rushing into the vestibule. "I'm so glad you are home."

"Not anymore, I'm not. I'm heading right back out."

"But, Your Grace, didn't you get my message?"

Bray opened the door. "No, but whatever it was, it can wait. I'm taking Saint back to the Prim sisters."

"But the sisters are here."

Bray quickly turned back to his butler. "What did you say?"

"The Prim girls are here—all five of them. They are in the dining room, having dinner. They arrived about midafternoon, and when it neared dinnertime and they made no attempt to leave, I didn't know what to do except prepare for them."

"Here? In my dining room?" Bray asked again, just to be sure.

"Yes, Your Grace."

Bray stuffed the dog, his hat, and his gloves into the butler's arms. His mind was swirling with different possibilities as to why Louisa and her sisters might be at his house, but he was too stunned at the moment to make sense of any of them.

He walked into the dining room, and the most inviting and welcoming feeling he'd ever felt flowed gently over him like a pail of warm water, covering him from head to toe.

The girls immediately rose from their chairs and stood silently beside them. Flames crackled in the fireplace. A white cloth, lighted candles, and beautiful china, silver, and crystal sparkled on the table. Bray had never seen his dining room set for dinner.

His gaze lighted on Louisa's face. She looked beautiful and wary, almost frightened, as if she thought he might throw them all out.

"Please, sit down," he said. "Finish your dinner."

"I'm sure they won't be much longer, Your Grace," Mr. Tidmore said behind Bray.

"We've just started," Louisa said softly. "Would you like to join us?"

Would I?

Bray didn't speak but went to the head of the table and pulled out his chair. They all sat down.

Mr. Tidmore said, "I'll have your place set at once, Your Grace."

One maid served the girls while another laid a plate, silver, and a glass in front of him. He kept looking at Louisa. He didn't want to make any more mistakes. He didn't know what had brought her and her sisters to his house, but now that they were here, he didn't want them to leave.

He'd been at countless dinner parties with the finest china and silver, and the best wines money could buy, but he'd never sat down at his own table. He really didn't know what to do, so he picked up his wine and sipped it.

After everyone had been served beef, potatoes, and something green, Bray noticed that no one picked up her fork.

"Aren't you going to eat?" he asked, looking from one sister to the next.

"You are at the head of the table, Your Grace," Gwen said. "We are waiting for you to pick up your fork."

"Oh, yes." He knew that but had forgotten. Bray reached for his fork.

"Do I have to eat that green mash on my plate?" Sybil asked.

"You know you do," Louisa admonished, and picked up her fork.

"I don't want to eat it either," Bonnie said.

"It looks like—"

"Sybil," Louisa said, quickly cutting her off. "Mind your manners."

Bray didn't like the looks of the green food either. "Would you girls like to know what we used to do with food we didn't want to eat when I was at Eton?" he asked, setting down his fork.

"Yes," came the loud and collective answer.

"The rolls were always hard." He picked up his roll and hit it twice on the table. "Much harder than these, as I remember." He took his knife and cut a hole about the size of a penny in one end of it and laid the piece of crust aside. "After you've cut the hole, take your knife like this and scrape out the entire soft center. Be careful you don't break the crust."

The girls watched him with rapt attention, and so did Louisa. He kept returning his attention to her. He couldn't believe she was actually sitting at his table.

"Once you have the bread out of the middle, take your spoon and carefully poke the green mash into the hole like this. You may not get it all in there, but you'll get most of it. Then shove the little piece of crust back into the hole like this to cover up the evidence. See." He turned the bread around and showed them there was no sign of green mash inside the roll.

They clapped and laughed.

"I'm going to do it," Sybil said.

"Me, too," Bonnie agreed.

"Do you know what you are teaching my sisters, Your Grace?" Louisa asked.

He looked at her. There was no reprimand in her tone or her expression. "Yes, Miss Prim, I do," he said, and picked up his fork again.

The girls laughed and chatted as they worked on their rolls.

"May I speak, Your Grace?" Lillian asked.

"You can always speak in this house, Lillian."

"I learned the score that plays on your music box. I can play it on the pianoforte for you after dinner if you would like."

"Lillian, you shouldn't—"

"No, wait, Louisa," he said. She looked tentatively at him. He gave his attention back to Lillian. "You learned to play it after hearing it only a few times that afternoon?"

She nodded. "It was a simple tune."

"Then yes, I'd love to hear you play it after dinner."

"I can show you my button collection," Sybil said while stuffing her green mash into her roll. "Louisa let me bring it with me so I would keep my hands to myself and not touch anything."

He looked over at Louisa, and she smiled shyly at him. He smiled, too.

"I have some real old ones and some military ones you might like to look at," Sybil continued. "And if you have a collection, you can show me yours if you want to."

Bray laughed softly. "I don't have a button collection, Sybil. I've never seen one, but I would love to see yours."

"I have a doll," Bonnie said. "You can hold my doll if you want to. Her name is Caroline. She's a girl, but she won't mind if you hold her. I've told her you're a nice gentleman."

"Thank you, Bonnie," he said, and looked at Louisa. "I'm glad there is at least one young lady at the table who thinks I'm a gentleman."

"You'll like Caroline. She's soft."

"I've never held a doll, but I suppose I could learn how to do that, too."

Bray sat back in his chair and thought, *So this is what family dinner was all about: sharing.*

"Gwen, do you have something you would like to show me tonight?" he asked.

She looked down at her plate, hesitating. "The only thing I brought with me is a letter from Mr. Standish. I think it will be all right if you read it."

Good. The rake had listened to him. "Only if you want me to."

"And what about you, Louisa? Do you have anything to say tonight?" he asked.

"I have a question for you, Your Grace," Louisa said.

He looked at her and wanted to kiss her so bad, his hand tightened on his fork.

"Will you marry me?"

Gasps sounded all over the room, and the loudest came from Bray. He rose, almost knocking over his chair. "Hell yes." He stopped and looked down the table at the girls and added, "That's a biblical word, girls, and you might as well get used to hearing it."

Louisa rose as well, and he wrapped her in his arms and hugged her to him as closely as he could. Damn, she felt good. He looked down into her sparkling blue eyes, thinking it would upset her, but he was going to have to kiss her right in front of all her sisters.

"I love you, Bray," she whispered earnestly, softly. "I want to be your wife. I can accept that you only want me and don't love me."

He placed his fingertip to her lips and hushed her. "I do love you, Louisa. It must be love, and I love this big noisy family you have given me. I accept."

"Does the hug mean you'll marry Louisa?" Bonnie asked.

"Yes," Bray said. "Now, all of you close your eyes because I'm about to kiss your sister."

Bonnie, Sybil, Lillian, and Gwen jumped up and started screaming.

Bray kissed Louisa with all the love he was feeling for her. Suddenly, he felt a set of small arms go around his waist, squeezing him, but he kept kissing Louisa. Another pair of small arms went around him and then another. He broke the kiss and looked down to see that all four girls were hugging him.

"Does this mean we will live here with you?" Sybil asked.

Bray reached out his arms and hugged all the girls to him. "Yes, all of you will live with us until you marry, but don't scream," he said, but it was too late—they were already squealing and jumping for joy.

Bray tuned them out and claimed Louisa's sweet lips once again.

Epilogue

And ruin'd love, when it is built anew,
Grows fairer than at first, more strong, far greater.
—Sonnet 119

"Your Grace."

A soft voice stirred Bray's slumber, but he mentally batted it away like a pesky fly.

"Your Grace?"

Bray's lids fluttered open, and he was looking at a pair of six-year-old blue eyes leaning right over his face. Startled, he jumped up. Bonnie jumped back, too. He quickly pulled the sheet up to his neck to cover his bare chest.

"Bonnie, what are you doing? How did you get in here?"

She pointed behind her. "I walked through the doorway."

He looked. Sure enough, the bedroom door was open. *Damn!* He must have forgotten to lock it last night when he and Louisa came to bed. That was a lesson for him to be more careful, no matter how eager he was to get his beautiful wife under the sheets.

He glanced over at Louisa. She was still sleeping soundly beside him. Her beautiful hair was spread across the pillow. Her softly rounded shoulders were bare, so he eased the sheet over her skin.

"Bonnie, what's wrong? Why are you in here?"

"Louisa doesn't usually sleep this late, so I came to wake her up."

He cleared his throat and thought on that a moment. "Ladies sleep later once they are married. So you won't need to check on her anymore in the mornings. You wait until she comes looking for you, all right?"

Bonnie nodded.

"Good. Go back belowstairs now and close the door on your way out."

She nodded again and turned away and stumbled and fell. Her feet had gotten tangled in his trousers. *Damn!* His and Louisa's clothing were scattered from the doorway to the bed. They had not been careful in their haste to undress last night.

Bonnie untangled her feet, picked herself up, and laid his trousers on the bed. She smiled sweetly at him. And he thought, for the first time in his life, that he blushed. She quietly walked out and closed the door behind her.

That should not have happened, he thought.

Bray rose and stepped into his trousers and then threw his shirt over his head just as the bedroom door burst open. Sybil and Bonnie came skipping inside.

"Damnation," Bray mumbled under his breath. He'd barely gotten his trousers buttoned.

"Louisa, look what just came for you and the duke."

Louisa woke with a start and she jerked the sheet up to cover her nakedness as she sat up in bed. "What's going on?" she asked, brushing her long tangled curls away from her sleepy eyes. "Sybil, Bonnie, why are you here in our bedchamber?"

"I came to give you this," Sybil said, and tried to hand the envelope to Louisa. "A man at the door gave it to me and said it was from the Prince and very important. He said I should give it to the Duke and Duchess of Drakestone right away."

"Sybil, you know you are not to answer the door," Louisa admonished.

The little girl gave her sister an annoyed look and continued to hold the envelope out to her.

"You take it, Bray," Louisa said, since she couldn't let go of the sheet covering her to open the envelope.

Bray grinned at her, a bit amused that she was caught in the same situation he was in just moments ago. He reached over, took the envelope from Sybil, and opened it.

"What does it say?" Bonnie asked.

"It says that the Prince is inviting us to attend a private showing of the Elgin Marbles with him next week." Bray looked at Louisa.

"Can I go see the marbles?" Bonnie asked.

"I want to go, too," Sybil said. "I have some marbles. Do you think the Prince would want to see my marbles, too?"

"We'll take all of you with us," Bray said, "but for now, out. And girls, from now on, when that door is shut, knock and do not open it to come inside until you have received an invitation. Understood?"

They both looked up at him with big blue mischievous eyes and nodded.

"All right. Now, get out of here and wait for us belowstairs."

Bray locked the door behind the girls. With those two, he might be safer putting two locks on the door, just to be sure. He had a lot to get used to about family life, and he was going to enjoy every moment of it.

He sat down on the bed and pulled Louisa into his arms and kissed her warm lips.

"Thank you for not getting angry with the girls for coming into our room without knocking."

He laughed and squeezed her. "I did get angry. But I can handle it."

"I love you for that."

"I love you, too." He kissed her again and then laughed. "I really can't blame them. It's my fault. I should have locked the door last night, but I was in too big a hurry."

She laughed. "I believe I was in a hurry, too," she said, laying her head against his shoulder and snuggling into the crook of his arms. "I guess that the invitation means we were married in time to save the Prince and England from certain embarrassment."

"Yes, and we didn't even try. I married you so fast because I didn't want to spend one more night without you in my bed."

"But the Prince doesn't have to know that, does he?"

Bray shook his head. "No, and he never will. We can let him think he was the mastermind behind me finally living up to my vow."

Louisa looked up at him. "But we know it was love."

He looked back at her with all the love he was feeling for her. "Yes, it was the love of a woman and the love of family."

Louisa pushed Bray down on the bed and rose up over him. "Perhaps I should show you just how much I love you."

"Perhaps you should."

Louisa settled her body on his.

Bray thrilled to her touch.

Author's Notes

I hope you have enjoyed the first book in my new trilogy, The Heirs' Club of Scoundrels. I've had immense fun writing this book. I grew up with four sisters and two brothers, so I put a lot of my knowledge of a large family to good use in this story.

My plot in this book depicting the Prince Regent was all in fun and jest and merely to add entertainment to the story. I don't know of any recorded history where the Prince wagered any of England's treasury or antiquities. All that I wrote about the Elgin Marbles and the controversy concerning them was true, except, of course, for the Prince using them in a wager. However, it is well documented in history that the Prince was known for his spirited, high-stakes gambling. Also widely written about is his love for and his uncontrollable spending on art, antiquities, gardens, and grand buildings such as Brighton Pavilion.

I first heard the statement, "Wouldn't it be wonderful if" from the late editor Jackie Bianca, who was with Harlequin Books at the time. It is my goal with every book always to leave the reader with the feeling of "wouldn't it be wonderful if this happened to me." Sometimes that means as an author I stretch the boundaries of the imagination and skewer and blur the historical facts for the sake of writing a fantastic work of fiction.

I love to hear from readers. Please e-mail me at ameliagrey@comcast.net, visit my Web site at amelia grey.com, or follow me at Facebook/AmeliaGreybooks.

Happy reading,
Amelia Grey

Read on for an excerpt from Amelia Grey's next book

The Earl Claims a Bride

—coming soon from St. Martin's Paperbacks!

A soft smile lifted just one corner of her lips and Harrison felt warmth and tightness surge through his loins. She was more than fetching. She was downright desirable.

He watched as she untied the ribbon under her chin and swept off her hat. He reached for it and she handed it to him. She was naturally sensual and she didn't even know it. Another twinge of desire shuddered through him. He had undressed many ladies over the past few years, but he was certain he'd never acted the servant's role for a young lady before. He didn't realize how stimulating it could be. He found her every move tremendously seductive.

She pulled the apron over her head. She wore a simple pale gray dress with a round neckline that laced up the front of the bodice. The thought of untying those laces gave him ideas he didn't need to explore when he was alone with her in a garden. It would be too easy to pull her to him and see if her lips were as soft and tasty as they looked.

"Excuse me," she said, looking behind her. "I forgot to cover my work."

Harrison followed her over to a table where her painting supplies were scattered. "What did I interrupt?" he asked, catching a glimpse of a fan with columns painted on it before she covered it with a tin dome.

"Nothing important," she said, averting her eyes from his and laying her apron on top of the dome. "I don't like to leave my paints unprotected. Insects have been known to land in them and create quite a mess."

It surprised him that she hid her work so quickly. Most young ladies were always eager to show him their stitchery or paintings, or read him their poetry. Miss Rule shielded hers as if it wasn't very good, or she didn't want him to see it for some reason. That was refreshing.

"What were you painting?" he asked.

"I paint many things," she said, rubbing some of the paint from her hand with her thumb. "Lids to snuffboxes, mourning boxes, and miniatures. The usual things." Then, as if realizing the paint wasn't going to come off, she reached for her hat and he gave it to her.

While Harrison was thinking it was a sin to cover her glorious long curls with that brown straw, he felt something wet and cold on the tips of his fingers and realized that Sam had decided it was time to walk over to sniff him. It took all his willpower but Harrison forced himself to let his arm remain hanging still at his side and let the animal sniff him wherever he wished so the dog would become comfortable with him.

"Your father obviously likes dogs," he said to Miss Rule.

She laughed lightly as she loosely tied the ribbon under her chin.

"Why does that amuse you?" Harrison asked.

"Sam, leave Lord Thornwick alone and go lie down. Now," she ordered, giving him a firm stare. The dog obeyed and she continued. "My father doesn't like dogs or animals of any kind. He indulges me from time to time and allows me to keep a stray that happens by our house, but not often."

"Sam was a stray?"

"Yes, he was wounded and starving when I found him. I nursed him back to health."

"No wonder he is so protective of you."

"I think it's natural of his breed to be that way. He has some bull terrier in him, I'm sure, though what the other breeds might be I have no idea. He gets along well with the other dogs and that's what matters."

"How many do you have?"

"Three."

"All strays?"

"Yes. Rascal was the first and is the oldest and part hound. The newest addition is Mr. Pete. He's a puppy and I think he might be part beagle." She paused. "Well, we really have four dogs as my father often reminds me. My grandmother has a Maltese, but she is so small she hardly counts. And she wasn't a stray. It's always important to my grandmother that people know Molly is the only purebred dog in the house."

His gaze swept easily down her face and then back up to her eyes. So Miss Rule was not only very loyal to a father who would force her to marry a man she didn't love in order to save his hide, she had a love for wounded animals. Somehow that didn't surprise him. He didn't need one more thing to like about her, but how could he not be impressed and drawn to the fact that she took in strays and cared for them?

"The wind is picking up. You should put this back

on," he said, holding out her shawl. She reached for it and he said, "Allow me."

She hesitated only a moment before turning her back to him. He placed it on her shoulders, and before she had time to turn back around, he lifted her long hair from beneath the shawl. It was warm and soft in his hands and smelled heavenly. He was tempted to lift its weight and bury his face in it.

Everything about her was intoxicating. There was something exciting about her, and something elusive, too. He couldn't fool himself. He knew what it was. She said her heart belonged to another, and as much as he didn't want it to be so, the fact was it presented a challenge for him to woo her and to win her.

Damnation, he didn't want to pick up that gauntlet. There were too many ladies willing to share his bed, and his life for that matter, to worry with fighting for one who had already made it clear her heart belonged to another.

But Miss Rule was different from all the others. That was as clear and simple as night and day. And even though she claimed to love someone else, she wasn't completely uninterested in him, either. He'd watched her look him over with a discerning eye, and she'd appreciated what she saw. He was sure of that.

So how hard would it be to win her away from a soldier if he decided he wanted to?

He liked that she was passionate about trying to help her father. Loyalty was an admirable quality in anyone. She was obviously passionate about helping others or she wouldn't take in the wounded strays. Something told him she'd bring that same spirited passion to her bed.

When she faced him, she looked directly into his

eyes and said, "So tell me, my lord, have you decided whether you will help me save my father or are you still thinking?"

That was the furthest thing from his mind presently. "I am thinking, Miss Rule, but not about that."

Her brow wrinkled. "Then what?"

He stepped closer, deliberately towering over her so she would know he was the one in control, and said, "I'm thinking about kissing you."

She went very still. He watched a flush creep up her pretty neck and onto her lovely face. He wanted to kiss her. He wanted her, and he no longer wanted to ignore what she was making him feel.

"That wouldn't be wise, my lord," she said.

True.

"Probably not, but I have done many unwise things in my lifetime. What will it hurt to do one more?"

He lifted his hand and skimmed the backs of his fingers down her soft cheek and brushed aside a wispy strand of hair that hadn't been caught back by her hat. She didn't flinch from his touch. He took that as a good sign, but asked, "Will you slap me if I kiss you?"

A flicker of astonishment flooded her eyes, but there was no panic. Another good sign that there was a possibility this conversation would end in a kiss.

"What? No. I mean, I don't know. I've never thought about it."

"You've never thought about being kissed?" he asked, deliberately misunderstanding her.

She hesitated, seeming to study over what to say. "No, of course, I have," she conceded. "I meant I've never thought about the possibility of slapping a gentleman for kissing me."

"So you've been kissed?"

"Definitely not," she assured him and wrapped her shawl tighter about her arms as if the woolen garment would protect her from his probing words.

It was another good sign that she hadn't moved away from him. If she hadn't been considering letting him kiss her, she would have already been backing up, showing him the door, or calling Sam over to intimidate him.

"Not even by the captain?" Harrison asked.

She looked aghast. "He is a gentleman, my lord. I haven't even seen him in over a year. I wasn't old enough to be kissed last I saw him."

Never been kissed.

That pleased Harrison.

He wanted to be the first to kiss her. He would be. Why should the captain have that right just because she'd given her heart to him? She wouldn't be the first young miss to receive her first kiss from Harrison, but he couldn't remember ever wanting to kiss one more than he wanted to kiss Miss Rule right now.

The sun was warm, the breeze was cool, and the garden was empty of chaperones, save Sam, and he couldn't talk. The timing was perfect. Yes, the more he thought about it, the more he wanted to do it. He wanted to feel her in his arms. He wanted to know how those pink-tinted lips would feel beneath his.

"You are of age now," he said in a low tone as he inched even closer to her.

"Yes, I'll be nineteen by early summer."

Oh, yes, plenty old enough for a first kiss.

He noticed the words in her last sentence were softer, and she sounded breathless. She was already contemplating his kiss. That made his breathing a little ragged, too.

"Kissing is against the rules of Society for young ladies," she warned him.

He moved closer to her. Again she didn't flinch. Did she know that was as good as an invitation for him to continue? "But surely you know that some rules are made to be broken."

She remained quiet. Pensive.

"And this is one of them," he added. "So don't blink."

"Don't blink," she questioned him with an uncertain expression on her face. "Why?"

I want you to see me and no one else.

"Because I'm going to kiss you and you'll want to witness your first kiss."

"Telling me not to blink makes me want to."

"Then it will be your fault if you miss this."

He lowered his head and let his lips graze across hers with the merest amount of pressure. The contact was sweet, enticing, and undemanding. It sent a quick, hard throb of pulsating heat sizzling directly to his manhood, causing an unexpected rush of intense desire to shudder through him.

Harrison only meant to give her a proper, innocent first kiss, but his body was insisting on much more. He hesitated before deepening the kiss further, slanting his lips seductively over hers, seeking more of a response from her until he realized she was too in awe of the kiss to answer the instant passion that had erupted in him.

He hadn't expected the kiss to be so powerful or to feel such satisfaction that she'd obeyed. To her credit, her wide-eyed blue gaze stayed open for the entire kiss. He wanted to abandon his reserve and show her just how quickly she'd made him want her, but not wanting to frighten her, he refrained.

When he heard a soft sigh from her, he lifted his mouth an inch or two and whispered, "You just witnessed your first kiss."

GREY   Romance